THE
FOREIGN
EXCHANGE

ALSO BY
VERONICA G. HENRY

Bacchanal

The Mambo Reina Series

The Quarter Storm

THE
FOREIGN
EXCHANGE

A NOVEL

VERONICA G. HENRY

Published by 47North, Seattle

www.apub.com

Amazon, the Amazon logo, and 47North are trademarks of Amazon.com, Inc., or its affiliates.

ISBN-13: 9781662503788 (paperback)
ISBN-13: 9781662503771 (digital)

Cover design by Faceout Studio, Amanda Hudson
Cover image: © khr128 / Getty; © Cozine / Shutterstock;
© Cara-Foto / Shutterstock; © BLAGORODEZ / Shutterstock;
© GJGK Photography / Alamy; © Katarzyna Mierzwinska / ArcAngel;
© Xinzheng / Getty

Printed in the United States of America

This one, dear reader . . . this one's for you.

CHAPTER ONE

It was nearly pitch black out, thanks to the busted streetlights and a chickenshit moon quivering behind the clouds, the encroaching darkness grim and tense. The street was thick with an impenetrable quiet, as if poised and waiting for something to finally release it from its crumbling chains. The man craned his neck and squinted through the darkened windshield. He circled the block three times before he found a parking space in front of the puke-colored house at the corner of Laharpe and North Dorgenois.

A mangy mutt trotted by, something limp dangling from its mouth. Down the street, someone hauled a trash can out to the curb. A flash of headlights up ahead. The man slid down in his seat as the car rolled past, a deep bass rattling his windows. And when all was quiet again, he fixed his attention back on the house.

The driveway had been swallowed whole by a rusted metal dumpster, overflowing with construction debris. Tree branches crisscrossed overhead like a skeletal, protective shell. Windows barred. A filigreed security door with a heavy lock.

Inside the car, the man reached into the inside pocket of his jacket. When his hand emerged, it held a glass vial and a syringe.

The vial was no more than a couple inches in height, scraps of the hastily removed label clinging to the exterior.

The syringe was still wrapped in its plastic packaging.

It was by accident that he'd discovered the drug boosted him. He was getting older and had only sought to enhance his workouts, help himself recover faster. But he found it also aided in his other training—the special training.

His playing days were long over, but the nickname he loved, "Top Dog," had stuck.

Top Dog flipped down the vanity mirror and checked his reflection. A small, satisfied smile lifted a corner of his mouth. He liked what he saw. He ran a thick fingertip over a spot of marred skin above his right eyebrow. He thought of it as a medal earned in a just and necessary battle. An accident from before, when he hadn't known how to control the flame. He had read the books and tried a few things at home. But tonight, he would practice on a real live human being.

He stepped out of his car and turned in a circle, surveying the area. It was humid. Armpit-after-double-overtime humid. A cold drizzle needled his exposed hands and face. He hated this city's weather almost as much as he hated coming to this part of town. It angered him to see how some people chose to live.

Cheap real estate was the draw. Locally, the Seventh Ward was a saga. A soap opera of good times gone bad and everything in between. A labyrinth of curiously named streets in the shape of a broken-off rock shard. And for kicks, some genius had sliced the neighborhood in half with an overhead interstate.

Lights spilled from a few windows. Aside from being able to thwart the mutiny he sensed was building, he was also glad of the chance to check on the construction progress. If his operation grew the way he planned, the three houses he'd purchased would be joined by many more.

The contractors had been paid to do a lipstick job, nothing too fancy. Just enough to keep the place from being condemned. The first thing he spotted was the two windows that should have been replaced a week ago. Shutters were barely hanging on, but some idiot had painted them a bright white. He shook his head. He was right to come and check on his incompetent worker bees.

With one last look around, Top Dog jogged up to the house. He paused at the door, anticipation building.

Loud music was coming from inside.

He didn't knock but instead took the key from his pocket and thrust it into the lock. He turned the doorknob and stepped inside. Something hard crunched beneath his feet. Broken glass? Nails?

The front room was dark, but light from the rear room told him where his number two was.

His rules were simple: get the job done, no small talk with nosy neighbors, and to lessen the chance that rules one and two were broken, no drinking on the job. Yet the unmistakable skunky smell of beer rolled out and greeted him as if on a welcome mat.

You couldn't trust anybody to follow directions if you didn't sit and watch them every damn minute.

He stepped into the light.

"What are you doing here, Top Dog?" His sometimes friend and forever subordinate Beau Winters was hunched over, using a small mallet to seal the lids on paint cans stacked in a corner.

Old Beau hadn't so much as dribbled a basketball in a couple of decades, but the days where you caught him without one of his signature jerseys were rare. It was too cold outside to go without a jacket, but Beau clutched his lost youth like a man possessed. He liked to show off the biceps that Top Dog hated to admit were still impressive.

"Exactly what you think, Snowman." Top Dog knew Beau hated the nickname. But Beau had once had an affinity for the powder, which, along with a bum shoulder, had ended his career. "Making sure you're on the job."

The pair had met at the university where they'd worked, both former athletes. Top Dog had served as president of athletics for a brief, scandal-ridden three years before being bumped up to an NCAA gig. Beau had been the only slightly less controversial strength and conditioning coach.

"I've run this construction company for years. By myself. That's why you came to me. Best you don't forget that."

Beau had abandoned the paint and was now hyperfocused on picking up smashed beer cans and stuffing them in a black garbage bag.

Top Dog pulled one of the chairs that the contractors likely used for overlong breaks closer to the low workbench and took a seat. He crossed his legs and let the silence stretch out until it was as tight and uncomfortable as Beau's juvenile skinny jeans.

The Snowman didn't fidget, though, earning him an uptick in respect.

Top Dog said, "Earlier today, when you were at my house, you saw something you shouldn't have."

Beau stiffened at that. He picked up and then dropped a fast-food container. He set the trash bag aside, then pulled up another chair opposite the man. "Yeah, I saw it. Look like this here thing you got going is making you way more than you paying me. You stand to make a shit ton of cash off this deal. It was right there in that contract. Way I see it, it's time for a little renegotiation." He threw up his hands and folded his arms across his chest, flashing the biceps again.

Top Dog regarded Beau for a moment, then another. The slow grin made another appearance.

"I mean," the Snowman put in, "I'm willing to work with you. I know this is your thing, so I'm not talking half." The Snowman was bold and defiant as a glacier.

Top Dog removed his jacket, then took out the vial and syringe and set them on the workbench.

"Maybe a seventy-thirty split? Does that sound fair?" The Snowman was melting.

Top Dog pushed up the sleeve on his right arm. Beau's eyes followed him as he grabbed the syringe and vial. He poked the needle into the bottle and drew down on the liquid. He squirted a bit in the air.

There was fear and excitement in the Snowman's eyes. Fear, Top Dog suspected, because he'd never seen the man use anything, excitement because the former junkie in him wanted a taste.

"Yeah, Top Dog," the Snowman rambled, unable to tear his gaze away from the needle. "Sounds fair to me. I'm doing all the legwork. Taking most of the risk. Overseeing the day-to-day."

Top Dog chuckled. Beau probably thought that he, too, was a junkie, pumping heroin or worse into his veins, but what he had was pure human growth hormone. HGH. Athletes everywhere used it. He'd stumbled on it by accident, but combined with his new practice, he figured he had the balance just right.

"You know"—he plunged the needle into his arm and stood—"greed isn't good."

Beau jutted out his chin. "Something we agree on."

Top Dog went over to the tools and found a flathead screwdriver. He used it to wedge open a paint can, then scrounged around for a brush.

"You putting in some work?" Beau's attempt at being lighthearted was valiant, but his voice hitched, giving him away.

Top Dog traced a pattern on the floor. It was a symbol that had caught his keen eye when he first moved to New Orleans and stopped in a shop in the French Quarter. He had been there on a whim, but Top Dog knew power when he felt it, and he'd been drawn, pulled, to dig deeper. He paid someone online to teach him, waving off warnings about the dangers of practicing Voodoo without initiation.

He was not some backwater yokel. He was an educated man.

Top Dog carved out the *vèvè* from memory. Parallel horizontal slashes, connected by a single line crisscrossed with double-headed axes. A serpentine swirl along the right side. He stepped back, admiring his work. He momentarily wondered whether he'd gotten it right, but overconfidence silenced the doubt.

"Ah," he crooned when he turned to take in Beau's shocked expression. "You recognize it."

Before Beau could react, Top Dog snatched up a wooden plank and whacked him across the head. Enough force to stun, not kill. Beau fell and Top Dog moved in. He picked up some electrical wire and deftly bound Beau's arms behind him. He grabbed him beneath the armpits and hauled him into a chair.

"Wha—" the Snowman muttered, rousing. "What are you doing?"

Sweat poured off Top Dog's body. "Just wait."

He gestured at the symbol painted onto the floor. Smoke was curling around its axes. His heart pounded like a thousand feet stomping in an arena. The doubt had returned. He bit his lip, gaze flittering back and forth to Beau.

Tiny flames erupted from the axes. Top Dog pumped his fist.

The flames rippled across the vèvè until the whole thing was alight.

Beau's eyes widened. He fought against the restraints. "Man, what's going on? Let me go! You messing with some stuff here you don't understand."

"Don't understand?" Top Dog barked. "Why? Because I wasn't born in one of your backcountry swamps? Something else you want to say?"

Beau kept his flap shut. Smart, but too late.

"You tried to blackmail me. I can't have you going forward, talking to authorities. And you think because you and that lackey of yours run a few errands for me you're on my level?"

"Keep the money, all right? I don't care. Just let me go." The Snowman's thaw was complete. He was now a puddle.

"In truth, Snowman, you're right. This is just practice. Still, I gotta teach you a lesson. Now. Hold still."

Top Dog didn't let on to Beau about this, but he was struggling. The symbol pulsed in his eyes; the flames pulled on him in a way he found hard to contain or resist. He plunged ahead anyway. He raised a hand toward the vèvè, and this time, the flames shot out to meet his fingertips. Top Dog buckled, lurched forward, then straightened.

He was the Top Dog again.

His eyes were flames.

He stretched out a hand. "I'm not going to lie to you, old friend. This will hurt. Badly. You'll live, but you'll think twice before crossing me again."

Beau's mouth was open as if he wanted to cry out. To beg. But he had lost the ability to speak. He was probably angry. If he hadn't tried to elevate himself beyond his station, none of this would have happened. He could have continued making the easy money that bought him his ridiculous jerseys.

Top Dog brought his flame-tipped digits toward Beau. His index finger touched the other man's arm. Because his throat no longer worked, the Snowman moaned like a mute. The agony of unseen third-degree burns shot up his arm and only subsided when Top Dog removed his finger.

"I'm getting better," Top Dog said, congratulating himself. "Stronger."

He turned to the vèvè again and pulled on that flame, and it answered his call. Curled out, circled his hand, and settled along his fingers.

Tears were flowing from Beau's eyes, even though Top Dog figured the pain must have subsided. Wounded pride, maybe? He looked down at Beau's arm, and it appeared normal. No burns, nothing to show what had been done to him. The flame's work was internal.

Top Dog, giddy with excitement, called on the flames again and again.

He flattened his palm against Beau's chest and pressed. The Snowman jerked and sputtered against the saliva pooling in his mouth.

In that moment, Top Dog imagined what the Snowman was able to see beneath eyelids that were squeezed shut.

Top Dog could sense images of game-winning shots, crowds cheering, the adoring eyes of female fans. The deaths of his parents, one after another. The son he wouldn't see again. The images flashed before the Snowman's eyes in quick succession, until suddenly the flames doused, the vèvè stilled.

The power that had been coursing through Top Dog dissipated. He dropped to his knees with the impact of the loss. Breath came in ragged shards. The image carved on the floor began to disappear. He inhaled and exhaled deeply.

He cast a furtive glance over at Beau, whose head was bent forward. He wasn't moving.

What have I done?

Top Dog struggled to his feet, slowly regaining his strength. "Hey! Snowman," he said. "Come on, man, you okay?" He touched his friend's hand, then kicked at his leg. He checked for a pulse at the neck but, finding none, yanked his hand back.

The Snowman's skin looked untouched. It was only through his open mouth that Top Dog understood the damage he'd inflicted. The charred remains of his tongue. Teeth stark white against blackened and smoking gums.

Top Dog stumbled over and grabbed his jacket. With one last backward glance, he raced out the door.

CHAPTER TWO

Dèyè mòn, gen mòn.

(Beyond the mountains, more mountains.)

—Haitian proverb (author unknown)

I was drawn outside by the agitated whistles and croaks of a white-throated sparrow. In an effort to attract more feathered friends to my backyard, I'd planted a triad of elegant Savannah holly trees alongside the perimeter fence.

Hovering in the midst of the middle tree's glossy, green leaves, fiercely guarding a cluster of red berries, was the squat source of the fuss. Beneath the sparrow, whizzing aggressively around a pot of wisteria, a crimson-throated hummingbird.

All I'd wanted was to entice another note to my morning birdsong ensemble, and here I had introduced another problem. Like their human counterparts, always in a state of conflict, they would have to learn to coexist.

I strolled over and took a seat on the little canary-yellow bench outside my garage turned *peristil*, Le Petit Temple Vodoun. The glassy surface was cool and smooth beneath my touch. The crisp October morning was dawning with a mottled-gray sky that left the question of whether it would be a sunny or cloudy day as yet a mystery.

I inhaled the scents of the city yawning its way to life: sizzling fried eggs, the sharp lingering twang of freshly mown grass. Leaning my head back, I coaxed my pores to expand. My body was a sieve, sifting through gaseous muck. I cast away the nitrogen and carbon dioxide. Banished trace amounts of argon and neon.

All that remained was pure oxygen. With an almost-imperceptible suction, I sipped on those delicious morsels of moisture-laden air.

A full minute passed, maybe two. A flood of warmth surged, then peaked, screaming through hundreds of nerve endings. Fluidly free. The world's solidity quivered at the edges.

A tug pulled me back.

I was a servant of the *lwa*—more specifically, the spirit Erzulie. Though she ruled the rivers, water intoxication was a slim but ever-present danger, even for me. And what I did could also have cataclysmic effects on the weather.

With an effort that grew more difficult each time I feasted, I closed the draw, shrinking my pores.

Fully alert now, I took in my surroundings as if through laser-enhanced vision. Everything sharp as the dagger of sunlight that lacerated the last of the clouds. It wouldn't last, the effect a temporary one, but I'd enjoy it anyway.

From this vista, it was clear that inside a year or three, my home's exterior would need to be completely repainted. The royal-blue trim was in worse shape than the white siding. The yellow door, a tribute to the goddess, was in remarkably pristine shape. Channeling the damp from the air inside—battling the tenacious threat of mold and mildew—was within my control. Doing so outside was not.

Most bemoaned these inconvenient costs of homeownership, and even though I didn't have the money, had no idea how I would come up with it, I was grateful to count this among my life's challenges. The lwa wouldn't let me fall too far, after all.

If you have ever been uprooted, yanked away from your home in a frenzied rush, you crave the sort of permanence a home provides. The shotgun house and peristil, the creaky front door, even the rust stain in the aged claw-foot tub, were *mine*. At least, according to my rent-to-own agreement, they would be in a few years.

Few memories of my life atop Jacmel's bustling hillside remained. South of Port-au-Prince, the town was a coastal oasis virtually unknown to tourists. Aside from the Bassin-Bleu pools, what I recalled most was the dizzying blur of those elaborately trimmed gingerbread-style houses that we passed as my father ferried us to the airport.

When our family disembarked from the cool, stale-aired confines of the plane, the tastes and smells of Haiti still clung to us like the last vestiges of a second summer.

The early days and months passed, somehow both painfully and effortlessly. All that was familiar deserted me with a swiftness that was alarming. Those precious bits and pieces of our home—a nascent accent, the omnipresent rumble of packed tap-tap buses shuttling people up and down the road—shed like autumn leaves.

We eagerly embraced our new home as if we had been desperate exiles making land after weeks clinging to a flimsy rubber inner tube. New Orleans has its way of sinking beneath the skin and making itself comfortable.

Papa had agreed to New Orleans only because, with the exception of Haiti, and the source, Benin, there were few places where the god Bondye's spiritual messengers were more omnipresent. The lwa had sustained their followers on the brutal journey to the Americas and throughout the African diaspora. Here they were reshaped and venerated under the brilliantly cloaked guise of Catholic saints.

We lived. Eventually we thrived. But the spirits exacted their prices.

Rituals, both public and private, were at the heart of our tradition. In the public variety, our bodies were relinquished for brief or hourslong rides so that the spirits might walk the earth again. Public rituals had a place in my heart and my practice, but I was particularly fond of the more private displays of homage.

Above all, I served Erzulie. The goddess of love, champion of children, diviner of water and storms. The exacter of tolls. A sliver of her essence subsisted within me, unlike other duly initiated *mambos* and *houngans*. There was only one other person who had such a relationship: a rather pompous houngan and constant thorn in my side over in Uptown.

Months had passed, and the events of the French Quarter murder no longer disturbed my sleep. Shadows had grown less ominous. In an effort to help a fellow mambo, a *vodouisant* in dire need, I'd done things I wasn't proud of. Made choices I still only marginally regretted. I'd atoned for those trespasses.

My relationship with my patron was a two-way street, only she maintained control of the streetlights. Don't get me wrong: my life and decisions were my own, but I lived to *sèvi lwa*—to serve the spirits. Part of that duty was to occasionally show my gratitude for all that she'd gifted me. And I had.

But Erzulie had been oddly silent.

Customers even reported that some of my *sangswe* wine–enhanced tinctures were less potent.

To regain the goddess's favor, I would honor her with an *action de grâce* ritual.

This called for a clear mind *and* body. I turned on the tap and filled the bath. Steamy hot water infused with heady oils of lavender and bergamot, ground basil, and a handful of salts.

After a twenty-minute soak, I toweled off and used the last of my coconut oil to moisturize my skin to a sheen. I padded into the bedroom, where pale sunlight had won the standoff with the clouds flirting beneath my blackout curtains.

White attire was called for. I opted for a loose, white, long-sleeved blouse to warm me against the October chill. White linen pants, a white headband to match. My feet would remain bare.

When you expose negative energy, you don't want that energy bottled up within you. It is important to allow it an easy path of escape. So I cracked the window above the kitchen sink, then rummaged around for the smudge stick. Mine wasn't your everyday variety, but a blend with a magical boost that Papa procured from a contact back home. I snagged the bundle along with matches from the drawer near the stove before I made my way to the front of the house.

At my altar, I struck the match and lit it. After the cluster had burned down about a quarter of an inch, I blew out the flame with a small puff of air. The earthy bouquet, with notes of spice and pine, blossomed. Starting at the front door, I glided from room to room, directing the smoke east, south, west, north.

With an offering to the sky, the earth, and finally my heart, I was done. The entire house was smudged, and I set what remained on the fireplace mantel in the parlor, where it would continue to burn down.

I removed everything from the altar and gave each item a thorough cleaning. It was long overdue for a refresh. The candle stubs that had burned down would be disposed of properly later. They couldn't be just dumped in the trash.

After polishing the small table and covering it with a freshly laundered white tablecloth, I draped it with strings of golden beads and a broken but still serviceable gold chain I'd found on the sidewalk. A client had sewn a beautiful rendition of Erzulie's vèvè on a thick fabric like a woven mat, about the size of your standard picture frame. I set that up against the back edge of the table and propped it against the wall.

Next, I took out new candles in blues and yellows and pinks and whites. Tall and skinny, fat and round. I gave them each a once-over to make sure there weren't any nicks or imperfections, then dressed them all in Van Van oil, careful to avoid the wick. After a quick polish with a clean cloth, they gleamed. Each took their place in the crystal candleholders on the altar.

In a small porcelain bowl that I used for only this purpose went a thin slice of cooked ham and, beside it, a couple of tablespoons of fried bananas. These items I bought from a local restaurant, and I was certain Erzulie would understand. From a glass, I sprinkled fresh filtered water over the altar and a bit on the floor for good measure.

Finally, I held my right hand over the water glass, inhaled. It was time to add the watery, bloodred blessing that ran in my veins. My sangswe wine. Literally, blood sweat. My body heated and my palm throbbed. I gasped at the mini lacerations opening up along the life lines on my hand and urged the sangswe forth. One drop, two, three, and then I sealed off the flow.

The water took on a crimson hue, and slowly tiny bits of ruby crystallized and glistened. It sang to me in the language we shared, whispered notes of love.

I knelt and planted my knees on the cushion before the altar, clasped my hands together, and closed my eyes.

Erzulie, I greet you, your servant, Reina Dumond, daughter of Josué and Merline. I ask that you accept these offerings as a show of my love and dedication.

I honor you and all the lwa as I honor my ancestors all the way back to the source. I pay tribute to those who have sacrificed and suffered so that we are able to live in your traditions. I pray to you and the Seven African Powers.

As I began the prayer, calling out the first two names, Eleguá and Yemaya, a subtle feeling of discomfort flared against the nape of my neck. The skin on my palms, still tender, prickled and warmed. Then, starting from my toes and racing to my scalp, a jolt ripped its way through my body. I tottered from the cushion and landed on my behind.

A thin fog filled the darkness beneath my closed eyelids. When it cleared, a vision from a few months prior flittered across my mind. It was the client visit from Evangeline Stiles. Ms. Vangie. She had come to me for help with a decision—something about her husband, Arthur. Something amiss. In my mind's eye, there was an essence surrounding Ms. Vangie. And I had no doubt it was malevolent. I was yanked from the vision as quickly as it had begun.

I stood on unsteady legs. The vision—daydream, figment of my imagination—had left me with an undeniable twitch of unease. The spirits, in their infinite, if unorthodox, wisdom, were trying to send me a message. Whether they wanted me to stay away or plunge in headfirst wasn't certain. The lwa didn't speak in such definitive terms. The only way to find out would be to contact Ms. Vangie and follow the trail from there.

My client had been worried about five grand that had mysteriously appeared in the bank account she shared with her husband. She was an on-again, off-again hairstylist, so we had agreed that in lieu of a traditional payment, she would do my hair a few weeks after the appointment.

Only she had canceled at the last minute, sounding frazzled. I had my own worries, so I hadn't pressed her. I did eventually reach out and reschedule for a couple of weeks later, but then something had come up, and that time, I canceled. And then time passed, and the whole matter was forgotten.

Clearheaded now, I grabbed my snuffer and extinguished the candles after saying a final prayer of thanks. All the items on the altar aside from the food would remain just as they were. I went to the bedroom to change clothes. I took in the sorry state of my hair: fraying ends, single-strand knots, scalp as thirsty as a desert cactus.

I resolved to call Ms. Vangie after breakfast. It was time for our appointment.

CHAPTER THREE

I had to admit, the *action de grâce* ritual had left me shaken. Sleep paved the way for a semblance of clarity. If yesterday was a shock fully unmasked, today was more of a disturbance, sitting behind the confines of a veil.

The lwa had been clear, though. I was compelled to check on Ms. Vangie and, no matter how frayed the threads, follow them until they ended.

When I called, her tone was cool. Leery, even. That could be attributed to a number of things. An overflowing calendar. A smoldering resentment that I'd essentially blown off her plea for help. Or trouble with the husband who had brought her to my door in the first place.

A combination of the three made the most sense.

There remained the possibility that all she needed was an ear— someone to talk to off the record and without a tab. For her, I'd gladly do so.

It didn't hurt that I hadn't had my hair professionally done in years. The occasion for that last appointment? A first date with the detective I had met in jail. Detective Roman Frost had blindly, irrationally, pointed a finger at me and others in the vodouisant community for a crime committed by an interloper.

After we were all cleared, I'd allowed myself to acknowledge the mutual attraction. And against my better judgment, I'd accepted his dinner invitation.

I stood at the bathroom mirror now, taking in the sorry state of my raggedy ends. A real haircut to frame my face was in order. Maybe a blowout.

With the changing weather, I opted for a long skirt, T-shirt, and jean jacket. A patch of snakeskin at the bottom of the wardrobe caught my eye. A sort of reconciliation gift from Roman, the three-inch-heeled, knee-high boots that were as far from my style as humanly possible would remain right there, where they had been ever since he'd bought them.

Outside of a scattering of brisk days, fall had come on with a whimper; green leaves failed to yield to oranges and browns. The sun scorching everything in its path. Even before noon, I had to turn on the air conditioner in my car.

I drove out to the house where my client was still staying with her sister over in Bywater. A part of town nestled near the crook of the Mississippi River, the neighborhood Roman also called home. Houses and shops done up in bold and colorful Caribbean hues. All the restaurants were unique—none of the big chain variety. And after the nearby Crescent Park finally opened, Roman had brought me here to watch many a sunset. The whole area boasted kind of a laid-back, bohemian feel that, I had to admit, held a certain appeal.

A graveled patch served as the driveway that housed my client's car, a blue, late-model Toyota.

Halloween decorations were out in full force. Yards and doorways overrun with pumpkins, skeletons, and bats. Ms. Vangie's sister's place, though, was bare. It was a simple, single-story home, aged and in need of repair. A loose gutter. A cracked windowsill. The patch of land out front looked like the place where grass went to die. But the yard was clean, and the white steps leading up to the door were freshly swept.

"Come on out to the kitchen." Ms. Vangie opened the door and turned on her heel. The African-printed housedress she wore brushed at her well-oiled ankles. Plush pink slippers on her feet. Her own hair was done up in a sleek updo.

"Yes, ma'am," I said, coming in and then closing the door behind me.

I was bent over, untying my tennis shoes, when she glanced back over her shoulder. "Don't bother with them shoes."

I had dropped Ms. Vangie off at home once or twice but had never been to her sister's house. I was a firm believer that you didn't really know people until you saw not only where they lived, but how. The things they held dear told stories.

For her sister, that story was one of the past. Instead of abstract or African art, family photos filled the entire wood-paneled wall above the sofa. A yellowed wedding photo at the center featuring an unsmiling couple, stark against a plain white background. They stood side by side. Backs straight and hands clasped. Ms. Vangie's sister shared her eyes and nose. The pair and their two children—at every stage over what appeared to be the last couple of decades—were arrayed around that centerpiece.

Photos of my client and her family joined the display. Relocation was like a disease that had been let loose to run unchecked after the storm. Many had returned, but the couple's children were not among them. One to New York—Harlem—and the other to Atlanta. I had no idea if visits were frequent or nonexistent. I realized I hadn't thought to ask.

The sofa was of the variety that after a few minutes, one would find oneself asleep, nestled into a well-worn cushion. A matching chair in a maroon faded to brown by the sunlight streaming in from the front window. A wooden center table and end tables with Tiffany-style lamps.

Everything in the room said "antique."

"You coming?" Ms. Vangie called.

Lovingly scratched and scarred wooden floorboards creaked beneath my feet as I made a beeline for the kitchen. This was no hair salon, but the aromas permeating the air were one and the same. A smooth whiff of shampoo lingered, followed by a rich, fruity conditioner, both overwhelmed by the smell of frying hair. Vangie had already been working.

A few steps away, a voice snared me. It was a familiar one. Gruff, loud, and contrary. A cough, less pronounced than before, hanging on the end of every sentence. I rolled my eyes and steeled myself as I stepped into the doorway.

And did a double take. Was I even in the same house? I almost glanced over my shoulder to make sure I was. If the rest of the place was stuck firmly in 1960, this kitchen had leapfrogged a few decades into the future. Stainless steel appliances. Sunlight pouring through what appeared to be a recently enlarged window above a farmhouse sink. Granite countertops throughout. Fixtures and flooring that looked like they belonged in the home of someone very rich and very famous. A nursing assistant and a custodian were neither.

I looked down at something brushing against my leg. A brown tabby looked up at me, hissed, and scampered off. It was enough to snap me out of my kitchen-remodel contemplations.

"Look what the cat done dragged in," my across-the-street neighbor, Ms. Lucy, said. She sat in a diner-style metal chair in front of the stove; Ms. Vangie stood behind her. Ms. Lucy wore one of her customary eighties tracksuits, her wide hips filling the chair near to overflowing. Vangie took a hot comb from the blue flame on the stove, blew on it, and then ran it through a small section of hair.

"And good morning to you, too, Ms. Lucy," I said, pulling out a matching chair at the kitchen table before plopping down. "I didn't know you'd be here."

"Am I supposed to be keeping you up to date on my comings and goings?" I waited and was relieved when her cackle didn't end in racking coughs. She must have been taking the tincture I'd prepared for her and,

I hoped, staying away from bars. "I could ask about who's been sniffing back around your place but guess that ain't none of my business."

I rolled my eyes and sighed. Loudly.

"Watch what you say now," she warned.

This time, I kept my breathing unchanged. "Yes," I said, straightening. "Roman and I are seeing each other again."

"The cop?" Vangie asked as she put the hot comb back to the flame and parted another section of hair. She dabbed a bit of grease from the back of her hand onto the scalp.

"All right, all right. Roman is a police detective. Is that such a terrible thing? He's a decent man, that's what matters. And yes, we're trying again. Does it bother you so much that I want to see if we can work things out?" Too many words. Why was I getting defensive? I didn't have to explain anything to anyone.

"Just don't come complaining to me when things go wrong again," Ms. Lucy said. "And another thing, tell your customers to turn down their music when they drive down the damn street. Don't nobody want to hear all that loud thumping at all hours of the day and night."

"I'll tell them," I said.

I had never and never would complain to Ms. Lucy about my relationship with Roman. Okay, maybe just that once. He had stormed out of the house after one of our epic arguments, me trailing after him still yapping. When he'd zoomed away from the curb, Ms. Lucy had been standing there on her porch, foot tapping, head shaking. She'd beckoned me inside and plied me with tea.

"Why don't you stay out of this girl's business, Lucy?" Vangie said.

"I will when you learn to stay outta mine," Ms. Lucy countered.

"Just because I told you to quit being stubborn and call that son of yours don't mean I'm in your business. You talk about the boy all the time. He asked you to come visit, but you sit over there in that house all by yourself and stew instead," Vangie said.

"If he wants to see me, he knows my address. For all I know—ow!"

"Sorry about that," Vangie said and then winked at me. I stifled a laugh beneath a cough.

"Laugh if you want," Ms. Lucy said. "See how you feel when she tries to comb out that three-week-old afro of yours."

Ouch.

"You leave her alone," Vangie said, and the two old friends got back to trading barbs with each other while Vangie switched to a curling iron to put the finishing touches on the hairstyle.

"So is this man going to marry you or what?" Vangie asked.

I looked up from the window I'd been staring out of and found both women's eyes firmly planted on me. "We're not rushing," I said. "Baby steps."

"That just means he ain't asked yet," Ms. Lucy said. Then, after standing and fanning at her face, she added, "How long did you date before you broke up the first time?"

If only I could redirect this conversation away from me. "About a year," I said. "Maybe a year and a half."

"And why did you break up?" Vangie asked.

I squirmed, hating every minute of being under their spotlight, but there was no getting away from it. "Religious differences, and other couple stuff."

"If you want to have kids, you better do it soon," Ms. Lucy said. "Even if it ain't with that detective of yours. It takes too much energy to be chasing after a toddler past a certain age."

Despite myself, I agreed with her. And yes, I wanted at least one kid. Okay, I wanted three. I grew up an only child with parents who were also only children. Not a pattern that needed repeating, or there might be nothing left of the Dumonds. And what would that mean to the lwa?

"Don't you go rushing her," Vangie interjected, pulling me back from my internal dialogue. "She's gotta make sure he's the right one for her, and even then, they should wait a couple years, build up that foundation, because they gonna need it when the babies come."

"Look at you handing out advice, and you can't even leave that good-for-nothing husband of yours?" Ms. Lucy placed her hands on her hips as Vangie waved me over to the chair.

"I'm not talking about Arthur. Not one word," Vangie said as she removed the tie from my hair and pulled it apart, inspecting my roots and ends.

"You know who I saw him with at the bar?" Ms. Lucy said.

"I told you to stay out of that bar," I cut in. "It's bad for your cough."

"And I told you that I wasn't your child and to boss that man of yours or Sweet Belly around, not me," Ms. Lucy snapped, and then thought about it. "And I need another one of them cough syrups you made."

"Who did you see Arthur with?" Vangie had stopped working on my head. I felt her tense behind me.

Ms. Lucy paused, stringing her friend out a bit before she responded, "None other than Beau Winters."

If pictures are worth a thousand words, my neighbor's expression was worth triple that. Arms crossed, head leaned forward, lips pursed. One bushy eyebrow raised. Ms. Vangie whipped out a cape and secured it around my neck—a little too snugly.

When her friend didn't say anything, Ms. Lucy pressed on: "You gon' start a little war there you don't watch yourself."

"Not a chance," Vangie said, but her voice had lost its conviction.

War? I couldn't help but wonder at what was passing between the two friends.

"Who is—"

Vangie pressed a hand to my shoulder, willing me, at least I thought, not to keep the conversation going any further.

Ms. Lucy ambled over to the refrigerator, rooted around inside, and emerged with a can of soda. She popped the top and gulped down half the can. "Yeah, I guess you don't want to talk about that, huh?"

"Didn't you say your ride would be here by now?" Vangie looked up at the clock on the wall over the sink. Just then, a car horn sounded. "Come on, I'll walk you out."

The women trailed off toward the front of the house, and I sat there wondering about such a strange friendship. But then, that's kind of the way it went. Opposites did indeed attract.

"And don't forget what I said about that music," Ms. Lucy called before I heard the door shut and the sound of Ms. Vangie's footsteps heading my way. She came back into the kitchen and sat down at the small dinette set.

"You want something to eat? Drink?" she asked as she worked out the kinks in her fingers.

"Just some water," I said. "But you sit, I'll get it."

"Glasses in the top cabinet behind you. And tap is going to have to do," she said.

I didn't want tap water, but my body could sort out the bad stuff myself. I went to fill from the sink but was stopped. "Got cold water in the refrigerator."

My appliances were all white and what you might call vintage. But this—this was a gleaming stainless steel work of art. I filled my glass from a pitcher, went back to my seat, and took a few sips. The metal hit me first, a chaser of rust right behind it. Chlorine and something else. My body went to work, separating out the bad and absorbing the good. It did all this without me directing, as natural as the beat of my heart or the breath that pulled into my lungs.

"Took you long enough," Vangie said, lips pursed.

"You canceled first," I said.

"And you second," she shot back.

I felt a stab of guilt. I'd let my own troubles keep me from lending that helping hand. That wasn't the way this practice was supposed to work. "I'm sorry, but I'm here now."

"I'm worried about Arthur." Ms. Vangie had tapped a cigarette out of a pack. Granted, she wasn't what you would call a regular client, but I'd never smelled smoke on her, nor did it cling to the inside of her house like it did with most smokers. She didn't light it. "I don't really smoke them anymore," she added.

"Is it what you mentioned before?" I said. "The money? Has anything else happened?"

She was silent as she stared out the back door, rolling the cigarette between her palms before she answered: "That five thousand dollars is still there. He hasn't touched it. The only thing he'll say about it is that he's saving it to invest in some new business. I know it's a lie, and I'm hoping you can find out what it is."

"Why me?" I asked. "Why not just take him at his word?"

"First, I know that you know Arthur is no saint. Second, everybody knows that somehow, you helped get that French Quarter mambo out of that fix with the murder. That money is yours if you find out what's going on. I don't want any part of whatever his latest scam is. Donate it, use it to fix up your house. I don't care what you do, just as long as it's not here to cause us any trouble."

Could I use the money? Who couldn't? A nearly hundred-year-old house was never without need of repair. I had some cash set aside for emergencies that I plucked from occasionally, but with this amount, I could also put more money down on my rent-to-own agreement. And there was Jason, and other street children in need. But something about this already felt off. I didn't want any part of anything illegal. For Ms. Vangie, though, I'd do some digging and leave it at that. She and Arthur could work out their own lack of communication themselves.

"I can't commit to anything," I said. "But I will at least ask around."

With that, Ms. Vangie nodded and stood. "All right, then, come on over to the sink—let's get this hair washed first. Gotta always start with a clean slate."

CHAPTER FOUR

The rest of the visit with my client turned hairstylist passed with talk of parades and new restaurants and all things beauty. Surface-level minutiae that did little to provide insight into anything more than how to take better care of my hair between visits.

My instincts suggested there was something beneath the layers of furtive glances and coded language exchanged between her and my neighbor. Things that only those with shared history understood. It was easy to recognize because I shared the same undercurrents with my friends Darryl and Tyka.

One thing was clear. Evangeline Stiles had a past and a present all her own. Hidden parts of herself that she hadn't shown me and that, before now, I hadn't picked up on. The woman I knew today was just another piece in the puzzle that was her life. I wondered at what had passed between her and my neighbor, what I'd missed. That name, Beau Winters. If I recalled correctly, he was at the center of something—that much was for sure. Nothing else I could stick a pin in, though a note of acute disquiet wedged itself in the back of my mind, where I'd let my subconscious go to work on it. If there was something there for me to know, eventually it would be revealed.

Of course, there was that kitchen remodel too. That six-burner stove and what could have been marble flooring were no big-box-store standards. It stood to reason that there was more money involved than I knew, which meant that my client wasn't telling me everything. And that some of the money had found its way to her sister's hot little hands. It was also possible that if Ms. Vangie was considering leaving her husband for good, it wouldn't hurt to have a fancier place to do hair. Might justify a rate increase.

Ms. Vangie and me, we weren't what you would call friends. Yet she had been a client of mine for years, and I treasured her and her occasional counsel. For her, I would look into the source of this cash.

⁓

The direct approach was often the quickest path to resolution. It was so simple that I almost reached around and patted myself on the back. Arthur Stiles was due a visit. Pin him down, ask him about the money. Warn him that he was in serious danger of losing his wife this time.

Then, lwa and my annoying curiosity appeased, I could wrap all this up and get back to my practice.

As many siblings tend to do, Ms. Vangie and her sister lived less than a mile away from each other. This corner of the neighborhood was part industrial, part residential. It was a community in flux. A spattering of old factories and squat office buildings covered in colorful graffiti. Homes of every kind and hue: shotguns and cottages, pricey new condominiums and apartments.

I pulled up in front of the house on Saint Charles Street the Stiles had shared for the last twenty years. It stood across the way from an abandoned lot enclosed by a chain-link fence. A lone palm tree in need of a trim towered over the brush. Weeds had waged a holy war with the cracked concrete sidewalk and come out on the winning side. The air in this part of town always smelled of old, decaying wood.

In a way that I couldn't explain, things felt off.

An occupied, well-lived-in and well-loved home has a sort of energy to it. It becomes more than a structure crafted from dead trees and nails and is as much alive as its inhabitants. The Stileses' home felt flat, as if frozen in an aged and yellowed photograph. It was a single-shotgun affair. Not even one window adorned the front facade. The only source of light for what was likely the parlor was a glass arch above the door.

A narrow concrete porch extended the length of the house and ended at a short flight of steps on the side, not the front. The bottom step was crumbling, so I grabbed ahold of the railing to steady myself and hopped over it.

I rang the doorbell. A few moments later, I knocked.

No answer.

I was thinking about hauling something over to prop myself up to get a look through the arch when a voice rang out behind me: "You just hold it right there."

I spun around to find an elderly man planted at the curb, one eye closed, the other peering down the scope of a rifle pointed directly at me. His hands were as steady as his wide-legged stance.

No time to get to the potions in my purse. Even less time to summon any watery defense. A panicked blast of cold shot through my veins, and I shivered.

"Come on down from there." He gestured with the rifle.

I eyed the trash bins in the yard next door, considered diving behind them for cover to buy myself some time.

"Now," the man said, inching closer.

"I'm just looking for Arthur Stiles," I said, coming down the stairs. The rifle followed me every step.

"You some kind of kin?"

"Look," I said. "I'm a friend of his wife's. Ms. Vangie."

He took his eye off the scope. The whites of his eyes were yellowing; the pupils had a hint of whiteness. Cataracts. Likely within the year. "Well, why you looking for Art then?"

"You live around here?" I asked, sidestepping his question.

He motioned to the house beside the Stileses' place.

"I'm all of five foot three inches tall. The only weapons I have is my wry sense of humor and a rather heavy purse. Why don't you lower the rifle?"

Neither the rifle nor the man budged. However, my mind had started working again and my pores responded, drinking in the scant moisture from the air, just in case.

Time to spin a tale. I softened my features, let the annoyance slip away. Tilted my head just so and looked up at him with all the gentle concern I could muster. "Ms. Vangie is a friend. Well, she does my hair." I paused to run a hand over my freshly done style. "She's more like a mother to me, and I'm worried about her. About them."

The man lowered the rifle—an inch. "Like a mother, huh? Then why ain't I seen you round here before?"

He had me, but I recovered quickly. "Guess we just missed each other."

After eyeing me dubiously for longer than I thought was strictly called for, he lowered the weapon. "There's been some break-ins around here. Can't take any chances."

With the weapon tucked under his arm, he reached into his pants pocket and pulled out a pipe, tapped in some tobacco, and lit it up. After drawing in the smoke and releasing it, he said, "Keeps to themselves, them two. That fast-tailed mother figure of yours has been in and out too. Something's up, ain't it?"

Fast-tailed? Ms. Vangie? I almost laughed. I gave the rifleman a look that let him know what I thought about his insult and got back to my questions. "That's what I'm trying to find out."

"Ain't seen Art in a week, and last time I did, he was with that friend of his. That fella always walks by me like I ain't even here. How much you wanna bet he's one'a them New York folks that moved down here after the storm. Not even a shot glass full of manners."

"This guy—do you know his name? Can you describe him?"

"I just told you, he never so much as gave me a second look," the man said. "Tall fella. Look like he should'a been bouncing a ball on somebody's court instead of trailing after Art. Bad vibes off'a him too. Something in the way he carried himself, you know? 'Sides that, all I can say is that he always parked his car in front of my house. I spoke to Art about it, but he never stopped."

It was clear that I wasn't going to get anything else out of the man, but to leave now would be rude. We exchanged a few requisite pleasantries, me making up pertinent details about myself. With the pipe perched at the corner of his mouth, his lips barely moved as he talked. And in a feat of oral dexterity, he could even switch it to the other corner of his mouth without missing a syllable.

At the end of our exchange, he turned to leave but then stopped. He hoisted the rifle and chuckled. "You know it's only a pellet gun."

After I heard his door close, I went back up the stairs and checked the Stileses' mailbox. It was stuffed to overflowing. That had to be at least a few days' worth of mail. Ms. Vangie was at her sister's, but I think we'd both assumed Arthur was still at home. My senses prickled. He was up to no good, and it was time to find out what.

But I needed to gather myself, get my bearings. I'd stop home first and think about my next move.

CHAPTER FIVE

As soon as I pulled up at home, I saw the package I'd been waiting for propped up against the front door. I grabbed the box and checked the label. A Haitian botanica in Florida. *Yes!* I tucked the box under my arm, grabbed the rest of my mail, and hastened inside, where I dropped it all on the kitchen table.

I stepped into the bathroom and, after a quick use of the facilities, gazed into my scavenged and reclaimed bronze antique mirror.

Wow.

Growing up in the Dumond household, a compliment was a gift you gave to other people, not yourself. Humility, my parents preached, was a virtue. But there comes a time for all adults when they have to reassess the lessons their parents instilled. An opportunity to hold those nuggets up for evaluation and decide for themselves if they were worth keeping, tweaking, or dropping altogether.

Taking in my reflection, I decided there was no shame in saying it—I looked good. My hair had been all one length for years, but the new layered cut gave it a fuller look. Curly ringlets framed my face while others fanned out, ends tapered clean. Still long enough for a ponytail, though—that had been my only requirement.

My breath had gathered in an uncomfortable lump in my throat while Ms. Vangie outlined the extent of the neglect. I'd grieved, just shy of tears, as she'd trimmed a good couple of inches off my troubled ends. I was careful to sweep it all up and put every strand in a plastic bag for proper disposal. Hair was a powerful tool when used in the wrong hands. I didn't think I needed to worry about that with my client, but one could never be too sure.

I scooped up the package from the table and headed out back with a little sashay in my step. Something drew me to the side of the house, the walkway laid out with white stepping stones. I glanced at my little blue-and-white hand-painted sign: LE PETIT TEMPLE VODOUN, 1791. Memories of the vodouisant role in the slave revolt flooded my mind. And with it, a sense of pride in this centuries-old tradition.

I turned and went to my shop. Inside, I inhaled the scent of sandalwood, and my eyes alighted on the two most precious things in the space: the table that Darryl and Chicken had gifted me after I lost one to the hired hand the French Quarter killer had sicced on me, and the machete Papa gave me after training me in the art of *tire manchèt*. The machete was safely encased in glass again and hung up on the wall, where I planned for it to stay.

Violence was not part of my practice, but once cornered, even a gnat will try to save its own life. I was no different.

A light ripple in my veins told me that Erzulie agreed with me. In that moment, I felt that I'd been pardoned of all my previous transgressions. The goddess within drew my mind to that place at the bottom of a river where everything is a melody. It felt as if my peristil sucked in a cleansing breath and exhaled out all that negative energy right along with me.

Being a Vodou healer was no different from any other profession: ongoing training was always on the agenda. As certain ingredients became either unavailable or in low supply, one had to learn what to substitute. New interpretations of the old. Spells that could be enhanced or altered. The vodouisant art was not static; our practice was ever evolving.

I knew that every moment that passes, we die and are born again. Each new breath inhaled makes a person a heartbeat older, if not wiser. Gathered together, that collection of moments, everything that happens to us, shapes us.

A decade earlier, the hurricane had changed me forever. Swept away half the city and claimed my mother in the process.

The battle with Rashad was different, but it had spooked me—a devastating truth I hadn't shared with anyone. The events surrounding Virgil Dunn's murder exposed my vulnerability. There were limits to what even I could do. The lwa were not always available, nor was a ready water source to aid in my defenses.

After everything I'd gone through months prior, there was no way I was going to be caught unprepared again. A man had been murdered, a fellow vodouisant implicated. And I'd gotten myself involved, putting myself and my friends in danger in the process. Now here I was, finding myself at the wrong end of a gun—pellet or not, it looked like, once again, I could be stepping into a dangerous situation. I needed some safeguards in place.

So my plan was to work on a new spin on a general protection spell. And I had just the spell in mind. It had to be something in powder form, malleable enough to adapt to a myriad of circumstances. Thus the order that had taken months to arrive. Now it was here, I could practice.

I grabbed a pocketknife I kept in a drawer and set to work on the layer upon layer of tape that sealed the box. A few too many slashes later, and I had all the items I'd ordered laid out:

- Epsom salts for baths to soothe aches and pains and for a whole slew of other potions;
- rose absolute for anxiety and insomnia;
- agate, which alone didn't do a thing but, when combined with other ingredients, was a boon for overall general health;
- assorted candles in every size, shape, and hue.

And then my gaze alighted on the one ingredient I'd been most anticipating: John the Conqueror root. Named for the African American folk hero, the earthy-smelling brown nuggets were good for a number of magical works but were, most importantly for my purposes, a powerful boost to protection spells.

Many traditional Vodou potions and tinctures were now shared openly, documented in books or on the internet. Unfortunately, most recipes were wrong, some dangerously so. It boggled the mind how quick some people were to believe everything they read without question.

Serious practitioners learned the art through years of training. Mambos and houngans endured grueling initiation rites where spells were whispered, mouth to ear, like an invisible thread of silk. A hint of an ingredient or two might find its way onto a bit of paper or the back of a napkin, but that was the extent of it.

Papa, and to some degree, my grandfather, had trained me. Curious, then, that I hadn't told him what I was planning. Doing so would lead to inevitable questions.

Why?

What are you afraid of?

I coined my new spell the "Sphere of Protection." I had gotten the idea after catching the pointy end of an iron finial in the chest. If I'd been able to coat the finial with something that dulled the impact— shattered it, even—I wouldn't have wound up in the hospital.

I closed the blue curtains that covered the lone window and dimmed the lights. I lit a tall yellow candle dressed in clarity oil to keep my mind centered and focused on the task at hand.

My first two attempts without the root had failed miserably. For what would be my third attempt, I got out a little ceramic plate and tossed on a few rusty nails, then set that aside.

It was time to make the liquid base, war water. A mixture of Haitian and New Orleans magic made for a modern spin on this very old traditional recipe. Tap water was off limits. Ocean water too salty. The recipe called for water pulled from a natural source.

From the cupboard, I grabbed a mason jar filled with water from the Manchac swamplands, something picked up from my last visit with Papa. With my father's urging, I'd come to rely on my own good sense and not measuring cups, so I tilted the jar over and poured the liquid into a glass bowl.

When I reached five cups, I stopped, but my thoughts veered to the $5,000 that had caused Ms. Vangie to leave her husband. She'd said that none of the money had been spent, that Arthur was holding it to invest in some new business. But there was her sister's fancy kitchen remodel to consider. Where did that fit in? From what I knew of them, neither couple had much in the way of extra funds. And that kitchen cost way more than five bills. It just didn't make sense.

The next ingredient was a protection powerhouse. Alligator teeth, taken only from a deceased animal, were dried for months, then ground into a fine powder. I sprinkled in two pinches of the zoological curio, which amounted to a half teaspoon.

Ms. Lucy had mentioned something about Vangie starting a war. Arthur and another man. Much of the two women's banter was a walled and locked garden for which only they had the keys. But that name—Beau Winters—Ms. Lucy had flung it out like a welcome mat caked with mud. There was some dirt beneath that exchange. She had intended to rattle her friend—her so-called *fast-tailed* friend. Ms. Vangie wasn't telling me everything, but I sensed it was more out of fear than malice.

I looked around and realized I, too, had missed something. I went back to the cupboard and found the six-inch-wide polished brass box on the top shelf. Inside, only two of the very expensive obsidian stones remained. One more try before having to restock. I carefully grabbed one—dropping it on this concrete floor would shatter it, and that I couldn't afford. The smooth reflective surface of the volcanic glass felt cool in the palm of my hand. Known for its power to seek out and absorb, to shift patterns, it was often used to make weapons. Weapons for protection.

I brought the stone close to my lips and whispered a prayer, then added it to the glass bowl. It floated on the surface, turning until coated with the swamp water and glistening in the candlelight. Once fully covered, it drifted to the bottom of the bowl.

The spirits had been clear during the ritual: turning away from Ms. Vangie at this point would not be an option. But before things went as far as they had with the French Quarter murder, I'd step away and let the authorities handle it.

Resolved as I was, it was time for the final piece, my sangswe wine. Right hand held aloft over the bowl, I murmured to Erzulie. It began with a dull throb that ratcheted up with each second. With effort, I concentrated so that only the line closest to my thumb crease peeled open. I gritted my teeth through the pain. One, two, three drops dripped into the bowl before I stopped.

It wasn't much, not enough to drain me, but I still took a moment to grab a glass of water and sit down.

The loving slash near my thumb sealed as if by an invisible needle and thread, the pain gone with it. I turned my hands over, flexed my fingers. Like new. From friends, I'd heard that giving birth is like that. The pain gone as soon as you set eyes on your baby. The memory nothing more than a suggestion.

Now I waited.

I stared as the bloodred contents of the bowl sat there, unaltered. A full five minutes, then ten, passed with no reaction. I was about to toss everything out and start over again when something in the air shifted. The bowl itself, kind of a blur. I leaned in closer, eyes narrowed. Tiny bubbles erupted, the contents going from stagnant to a babbling brook in a few held breaths.

The liquid swirled, the obsidian stone dissolving more with each revolution. The concoction became more viscous with every turn.

Yes!

The first time, the mixture had exploded in a small puff. The second, it had curdled like spoiled milk. Now it was time for the final test.

I called to the water mixture, drawing it up with my left hand. I repeated the prayer: *Oh, Seven African Powers, who are so close to our Divine Savior, with great humility, I kneel before thee and implore your intercession before the Great Spirit. Hear my petition that I may glory in your powers to protect me, to help me and provide for my needs.*

I finished with *Ashe!*

With the index finger of my right hand, I touched the nails. The room had gone noticeably colder. I was nearly bursting with anticipation. What I'd hoped was that the nails would freeze. They felt only slightly cold to the touch, and then nothing.

The room's temperature, and the nails, both shifted back to stubbornly warm. I released the water mixture, disappointed with myself again. I had no idea what I was getting wrong. Still, I put the water base in a glass vial and stashed it away on a shelf. I had one obsidian stone left. I would try again, but later.

I cleaned the bowl at the sink and was going to put it away when my gaze flittered across the water-gazing bowl. Another failure. I'd used it countless times to try to find my mother, but she remained as lost to me now as she had been a decade ago.

Some days, when I thought of her, it was as if I'd made peace with not knowing. I'd remember a funny conversation, or standing beside her as a little girl, watching while she expertly layered on her makeup. Other times, like now, the pain would sneak up and sting me like a bee. For a moment, I allowed myself to sink into the self-pity, becoming familiar with it once again. Then I glanced out the window. A light rain had begun to fall. Fine drops of renewal, a signal that life always continues. And I came out on the other side.

I put everything else away. After the place was tidy and restored, I went back to the house. I would do as promised and ask around about Ms. Vangie's husband, and I couldn't think of a better place to start than the Lemon Drop.

First, it was time to try another one of Darryl "Sweet Belly" Boudreaux's recipes.

CHAPTER SIX

Though my kitchen was an abiding source of seemingly infinite culinary defeats, it never failed to give me comfort. For one, there was always a cup of tea or blessed water to be had. Walls a cozy pale yellow. A gas stove, lovingly scratched and scorched.

My table was angled such that I had a view of both the back door and the window over the sink. Part of this was Roman's influence. The detective in him had warned me to keep my eyes peeled on exits at all times. Cloak and dagger aside, I also loved that right from this spot, I could take in whatever the morning served up. Whether sunlight or streaks of gray, I could sit and let my mind awaken and prepare myself for the day ahead.

I typically avoided appointments before ten in the morning for a reason. My thoughts on alarm clocks were that they were evil. Whenever possible, a person should be allowed to wake up when their body told them it was time. I never hated early mornings, but I needed that time to connect with myself, to think before inviting anyone else into my head. Here in Tremé, fall mornings rose with a dramatic beauty. Summer showers on temporary hiatus, the sun shone brightly. It bled through the gauzy curtains over the sink, planted a kiss on the African violet on the windowsill, and swept across every surface in the room.

Those gentle rays were like a warm cuddle, soothing the letdown of my failed attempt at the spell.

Given the challenges I'd had in the kitchen and my already-souring mood, I questioned the wisdom of trying out a new recipe. A person could stand but so much disappointment in a day. But in order to get the 411 on Arthur Stiles, I would need to start at the Lemon Drop. And an offering of some kind would be expected. I didn't want to go hunting for candy, so perhaps a food offering would do. As long as I did it right, that was.

With effort, I rose and sought out my recipe box. It was right where I'd left it, grease smudge and all, in the cabinet beside the stove. When I opened the cabinet door, the handle came off in my hand. Yet another thing to fix. I tossed the piece in a drawer for another day.

Recipes in tow, I padded over to the sink, where the lighting was better, and flipped through the index cards that, at one point, Darryl had painstakingly organized by the type of dish and then alphabetized within each section. That didn't last long. All the attention to detail that went into organizing my supplies and tools in my peristil had apparently vanished as soon as I shut the door and turned the lock.

I stood there flipping back and forth through those cards for long enough that I considered giving up. Eventually, I found the recipe I had been thinking about for a week. Scrawled at the top of the index card in Darryl's disjointed script: *Sweet Belly's New Orleans Dirty Rice.*

1 pound ground pork
1 medium onion, bell pepper, and celery—slice 'em and dice 'em
5 cloves garlic—minced chopped up
2 teaspoons Cajun seasoning (I left some at the back of your spice cabinet)
3 teaspoons of plain old Morton's salt
1 1/2 cup'a white rice (not that five-minute mess and don't cook it till I say so)

4 cups of broth (chicken or beef, not vegetable)
A little parsley if you feeling fancy

Cook the pork up first and don't skimp, make sure it's done through and through. Add in ya chopped veg, the Cajun seasoning, and that heap 'a salt. Afterwhile, add the rice and broth and cover for on 'bout twenty minutes. Check your rice to make sure it's done. Then set aside a bowl for me and eat up.

And then at the bottom, as if he'd forgotten and later come back to add it:
Oh, gone 'head and sprinkle on that parsley.

First, I scrounged around in the cabinet to find Darryl's Cajun seasoning, and sure enough, there it was in a plain clear jar with a handwritten label. I set that on the table and then pulled out the ground pork that had been defrosting in the refrigerator. Two cartons of chicken broth: check. And the vegetables I'd chopped the day before and sealed together in a plastic container. I popped open the lid and frowned. The veggies swam uncomfortably in a pool of water and had taken on a washed-out pallor. Had that been yesterday or the day before that?

Whatever. So be it.

It was clear that my friend didn't think I knew what mincing was, and truth be told, I didn't. Either way, I wasn't mincing or chopping up any garlic. Who had time for all that, anyway? Was a family, home after a long day of school and work and soccer and dentist appointments, supposed to stop at the store, pick up fresh garlic, then get home and mince it? A small incredulous sound escaped my lips. The little bottle of garlic powder would have to do.

Pot on the stove, ingredients all laid out within arm's reach, just the way Darryl had taught me last time. Recipe front and center. I smiled, thoroughly impressed with myself. Before I got started, though, I'd have another cup of tea. Kettle filled and on the burner, a new rooibos tea bag and honey.

I paced tiny circles. Steps slow and tentative, but mind on full alert. Even cooking hadn't loosened the tightness in my shoulders. Whatever was going on with Ms. Vangie and her husband was bad business; I knew it. There was something she wasn't telling me. I supposed she'd asked him about the money straight out—that was the type of person she was. For her to ask me to get involved meant that she had been less than impressed with whatever story he had concocted. Sure, I was curious, but the bigger question was, Why would the lwa care? Why intrude on the ritual with that vision? I'd have to keep digging until I found out. The lwa had all but demanded it.

I was still pacing when the kettle whistled. Moments later, I sat down, and after a few delicious sips, my phone rang. It was Roman.

"How're you doing today, lovely lady?"

My stomach warmed, and not just because of the tea. Roman was loving in his way. A way that didn't usually involve overt shows of affection unless it was for foreplay, or pet names. Why now? Had he done something? Guilt? As much as I loved the sound of his voice, deep and murky like the ocean floor, those words sounded strange coming out of his mouth.

"Better if you tell me you'll be off tonight," I said, shaking off the doubt like a layer of dust.

"This ain't no nine-to-five. You catch a body at 4:59, you can't just pack up and go. You have to follow the trail while it's hot," he said as I made out another voice in the background; a car door slammed. "We just caught a new case. A homicide."

I sighed. I knew that was all he'd tell me about the case, and part of me was glad for it. A hand over the receiver, then. Muffled conversation.

"Darby sends his regards," Roman said.

"And tell him I return them with a bow." I was still pissed at both Darby and Darryl for hiding their friendship. It was bad enough that, by not mentioning it, Darryl had effectively lied to me for years about knowing my boyfriend's partner. The thought that their little information exchange could have included things about me, about Roman, had me spitting fire. But I had forgiven them both and vowed to never raise the issue again, and I would keep my word. Keeping my mouth shut but holding on to the hurt wasn't doing me any favors, though. They had their secrets and I had mine. It struck me, then, that you never really knew anyone, least of all yourself. It made me wonder what I didn't know about Roman.

"I just wanted to let you know in case I can't answer the phone," Roman said. Then he added, "Have a good one."

"You too," I said just as I heard the click of the disconnect. Professions of love were not Roman's style. Especially not within earshot of his partner, or anyone else. So while he didn't end his call the way other couples did, at least to my ears, love was there all the same.

My tea had cooled to just the right temperature for drinking without scalding. I drained the cup and turned my attention back to the recipe . . . and Ms. Vangie. I picked up the packet of pork and cursed as blood dripped onto my recipe. I set the packet in the sink, grabbed a napkin, and dabbed at the index card. Luckily none of the words were smeared. I blotted it dry with a bit of water and set it on the windowsill to dry.

Now, where was I?

Ms. Vangie and that money. I didn't know much about Arthur, other than the fact that he'd worked a series of odd jobs. They had married not too long after high school. Two kids I had never even met.

I took out another pot and filled it with water for the rice I probably should have started already. Despite what Darryl said, nobody has time to cook rice the old-fashioned way, so I grabbed two bags of five-minute rice and set them on to boil.

Unlike Ms. Lucy, I didn't know anything else about my client's earlier life and, now that I thought about it, little more about the last several years. In fact, it was through my nosy neighbor that I'd met her in the first place.

It had certainly not been a recommendation—no way Ms. Lucy would do that. It was an introduction. I had gone over to deliver a general wellness tincture—for free—and Vangie was there. Unlike my neighbor, she had been curious, respectful about my practice. She made an appointment immediately. Her first request? A spell for gambling luck with her numbers. Even then, I had found her open and evasive at the same time. At least that first time, she had paid with cash and a meal.

I poked the bags of rice with a fork and looked up at the clock. How long since I'd put the rice on the burner? It had to be long enough because the water was boiling, and the rice looked plump. Time to get the pork and other stuff cooking. I took the package from the sink and dumped it into the dutch oven on the stove, and if I remembered correctly, everything was pretty simple from there. I added in the spices and let that cook.

I combed my mind, trying to think of where and how one could legally find oneself in possession of what, at least to me, seemed a sizable windfall, especially for a couple I knew always lived on the edge of lack. Outside of the lottery, which wouldn't be worthy of hiding from one's spouse, there was nothing I could think of.

With the pork on, I turned off the rice and drained the water. I opened the bags and set them aside. The pork was sizzling nicely, so I turned my attention to stirring. Once no more pink was visible, I added the veggies and rice. Stirred and stirred some more.

From the corner of my eye, I saw the broth. Almost forgot. I emptied one, then the other container, placed the cover over the pot, and then turned the flame down a little lower and left it to cook.

Easy peasy. I had a good feeling about this one. It would be a winner.

While I waited, I washed up all the dishes, lamenting the fact that Roman had a modern kitchen with a brand-new, unused, dishwasher. I stacked the spices back in the cabinet and wiped off all the countertops. After my dish finished cooking, I would head over to the Lemon Drop to gather some intel and show off my handiwork. Darryl, I was sure, would be impressed.

CHAPTER SEVEN

I had to smile when I saw the Lemon Drop sign, gently swaying back and forth on the breeze like a swing. It was clear of the bird droppings that had drawn Darryl's ire and scrub brush on so many occasions.

There was, however, a big splotch of something red and sticky on the mural. It looked like one of the expertly painted bottles had been broken. Aside from cooking, cleaning was my friend's favorite pastime. He would see to it.

I arrived at the door in enough time to shift the pot of dirty rice to my hip and hold it open for a man pushing a dolly stacked with boxes so high that it didn't appear he could see over them. He nodded his thanks and maneuvered over to where Darryl stood near the swinging double doors that led to the kitchen. Darryl waved and motioned for me to take a seat at the bar.

The dolly wheels left a nasty mud trail in their wake. I had to chuckle when I looked over in the corner and saw Darryl's ever-present mop and bucket of soapy water. He was just waiting to annihilate the offending dirt.

As was the case most Saturdays, even early afternoon, the place was in full swing. Preparations underway for the band that would be playing this evening. A pack of musicians arranged drums, microphones, and other equipment, cramming them onto a stage the size of a small backyard patio.

My table by the picture window, or at least the one that was usually mine when I had the chance to swing by earlier in the day, was occupied by a couple who gazed into each other's eyes as if they were the only souls on an isolated island, instead of in the middle of all this activity.

Ceiling fans rotated slowly overhead, stirring up air that was already cool, thanks to a recent cold spell, and perfumed with the flavorful scents of fried and roasted meats. The sweet-and-sour spice of liquor topped it all off. And one of the people at the table to my left had been a little heavy-handed with a musky perfume. Talk ranged from low murmurs to loud guffaws, punctuated now and again with an anticipatory horn blow or drumroll. Summer's skimpy skirts and sports jerseys had given way to fall's longer pants and light sweaters. Jackets and colorful silk scarves were slung across chair backs.

I perched myself on a barstool, lamenting the loss of my preferred table.

"Tea for you, Mambo Dumond?" the bartender said. I couldn't remember his name. William? Warren? The next in a long line of bartenders Darryl employed. He was tight lipped about the turnover. The tips alone had made me consider a change in professions. But this wasn't your typical bar, and my guess was that Darryl's narrow interpretation of what it meant to clean drove them off. Clad in a black turtleneck, jeans, and snazzy glasses I suspected were more for show, this one looked like he'd stepped out of a magazine ad. He must have read the blank look on my face.

"Wes." He chuckled. "It's okay. You look like a lady with stuff on her mind. Remembering my name must be at the bottom of your list."

That earned a smile from me. Wes was more perceptive than the last one, Jimmy, if I recalled correctly. "Thank you, Wes. And no, I won't be that long today." He nodded but hovered nearby, polishing a glass, giving the impression that if I changed my mind, he wanted to be ready to spring into action.

I fished around in my purse for the pain relief tincture I'd prepared for Darryl. When asked, he'd dodge and dive questions about what had been ailing him. Even Chicken, his other best friend, had come up short. And would Chicken tell me if he did know? Not for the first time, it struck me how little I knew of the man. Not guarded, just not forthcoming. An enigma who had been there for me and for Darryl when we most needed him. All sorts of things ran through my head, each worse than the former. My prayers to the lwa included desperate pleas for the well-being of the crotchety coveter of sweets.

"I see that detective fella of yours has let you out for the day," Darryl said, coming up behind me.

I'd heard the soft squish of his favored orthopedic shoes against the unnaturally clean wooden floor, polished to a shine. "To what do I owe this greatest of all gifts?" he said. "Ah, I see, you got something for me. Hand it over."

Beaming, I presented him with the dutch oven. "What are you getting delivered today?" I said, gesturing at the last of the delivery rolling by. "You sure ordered enough of it."

"All courtesy of Grip," Wes offered, a glint in his eye. He was, of course, referring to the third rung in our trio, one Tyka "Grip" Guibert. She'd earned the nickname as a wrestling phenom in high school. Something I wished I had been able to witness.

"That lil' old gal." Darryl sighed and waved Wes off to help another customer. He didn't walk, but slid sideways with a flourish, earning an eye roll from his employer.

Darryl reached beneath the counter and emerged with a fork and salad plate. "Some ribs she won't say how she came into possession of. Swears she didn't do anything wrong, just happened to stumble across 'em. She went on and on about how it didn't make sense to let it go to waste and all. What was I supposed to do? You know how sensitive that gal is. Ask a question or turn it away, and she would get herself all tied up in a fisherman's knot."

He was right. It wouldn't do to argue with Tyka about where she got the goods because when she offered, you accepted, or you risked hurting her feelings. There was nothing more dangerous, more fraught with complication, than hurting Tyka's feelings.

"Whoever did your hair did a good job," Darryl said. "I know it wasn't you."

I accepted the compliment—and insult—with a head toss for effect. I couldn't help thinking about how Roman noticed things, mentioned them, but praise and flattery weren't his thing.

"Go on," I nudged, gesturing at the pot. "Taste it."

Darryl raised an eyebrow. "Sound like you done went and put your foot in this one, huh?" I still didn't understand that expression. Some things about the English language made no sense. He opened the lid and frowned. He looked down in the pot and then back up at me.

"What?" I said. I'd been so overconfident that I hadn't even looked at the dish. I checked the recipe after everything was done, and I'd taken it off the burner at the right time. It couldn't have been overcooked. Darryl spooned a bit out. Shoved a forkful in his mouth. He chewed, gaze skyward, eyes narrowed. After a showy swallow, he shook his head and handed me a fork.

"You got the taste right, but something else wrong," he said. "And you broke the first rule." He paused and then said, "Well, maybe the second. First, you probably didn't follow the recipe. Second, you didn't taste your own food before you gave it to somebody else, now did you?"

Well, no, I hadn't. But I had been so sure.

"You try it," he said.

He was right. It didn't exactly taste bad, but my rice was all mush. It may as well have been mashed potatoes. "So what?" I asked. "Too much broth?"

"Too much broth would have made it soupy," Darryl said. "No, you didn't use good rice and you cooked it first, didn't you?"

Well, come to think of it . . . "I guess I did. I mean, I don't have time to wait for that rice in the sack to cook for an hour. I have clients. A life, you know."

"Even if you had dumped in that mess when the recipe told you, it would have been better than this. Lawd, it's back to the drawing board again."

At that point someone waved Darryl over, and he shook his head and shuffled off. "I'm going to the back," I said.

Through the double doors, I nodded to the two folks who now made up Darryl's expanding kitchen staff. He couldn't handle the load by himself anymore. One was loading Tyka's ribs into the freezer, the other hovering over the stove, stirring something in a very large pot.

Darryl's office was cozy small, not cozy cramped. Filled with gently used things, donated piece by piece since he'd opened a couple of years after the storm. As meticulous as he was about the rest of the bar, the office was the one place where he relaxed his over-the-top standards.

Scratches and scuffs marred the white walls I had begged him to paint. He balked about how much trouble it would be to move everything out, so he occasionally painted over the marks, creating a sort of polka-dot effect, as none of the paints were the same shade.

The lumpy love seat sported the new addition of a couple of simple decorative pillows. The room was dominated by the overlarge maple desk that had to have been made at the turn of the last century. Stacks of invoices and bills were smaller and neater. The slim cupboard we'd picked up from a trash pile was jammed into the corner. It probably hid all the untold horrors that used to sit on his desk.

The smell of something synthetic, unnatural, nagged at me, and after a bit of fishing around, I found an air freshener plugged into the outlet behind the love seat. I yanked it out and tossed it in the trash just as Darryl entered the room.

"Hey," he said, shuffling over to try to grab it out of the can. "I just bought that."

I smacked his hand away. "Those things are poison." I stood my ground over the trash can, and he huffed over to his chair. "Essential oils, beeswax candles, incense. Use any one of them."

"Yeah, whatever." Darryl had to turn sideways to slide behind his desk. He rolled out the overlarge, peeling chair and eased down, joint by cracking joint. He leaned over, pulled out a drawer, and set out three of the same toxic air fresheners.

"You may as well toss these too," he said with an exaggerated sigh.

His eyes and fingernails were clear. Skin a bit ashy but otherwise unblemished. I wanted to ask about his urine. If there was blood, if it was foamy maybe. But he'd bite my head off and hand it to me on a plate.

From my seat, I took aim and shot each of the air poisoners into the trash, then took out the tincture from my purse and set it down in front of him. "You going to tell me what's wrong?"

"I never got to see Luther Vandross in concert. Mustard-based barbecue sauce. The fact that these here suspenders can't be found anywhere anymore." Darryl held a grim expression as he counted off each offense.

"Don't get cute."

"You seen my profile." He turned his face to the side and lifted his chin. "It's hard not to call all this cute."

I stared at him, unblinking. Even tapped my foot, though he couldn't see it. I pointed to the vial. "This is just for general pain, but if you'd tell me—"

"Nothing to tell. You tweak a knee or back and folks assume you on your deathbed. You just as bad as Chicken." He said all this and didn't touch the tincture.

I eyed him for a few more minutes but couldn't tell if he was telling me the truth or not, so for the time being, I'd have to drop it.

"Hey," I said, switching subjects. "Do you know Arthur Stiles?"

"Married to Vangine, Tangene . . . ?"

"Evangeline," I corrected. "Vangie."

Darryl whistled. "Yeah, I know him *and* her. Why you asking? What kinda trouble has she gotten into?"

Curious that he thought Ms. Vangie was the subject of my inquiry, not her husband, the petty criminal.

Like a medical doctor, I didn't share details of who my clients were or what they came to see me about. Confidentiality was essential to my practice. And my friend took his role as community fountain of knowledge just as seriously. He didn't share his sources. That's how he'd been able to keep his relationship with Darby a secret for so long.

"Well . . ." I had to figure out just how much I was willing to share. I was going to get to the bottom of this. The lwa had been clear; that wasn't a matter up for debate. But the confidentiality thing meant I had to think carefully about what I said next. "She's a little worried about Arthur. Okay, more than a little."

Darryl sat up. "Worried how?"

I squirmed under the intensity of his gaze. "She thinks he may be into something. Some kind of trouble."

"Oooh," Darryl crooned. "This here is official business. And besides that pot of mushy rice out there, I don't even see so much as a penny candy in your hand."

"I just thought . . ." I stumbled. "Fine. Can I get you the candy tomorrow?"

"Do you want your information tomorrow?"

I glowered at Darryl. "What about the tincture?"

"Unless you tell me it's fruity flavored, I have no idea why you bringing it up."

"Have you ever thought that because we're, like, you know, best friends, you could cut me a little slack every now and again? Where

51

am I supposed to get candy at this time? Candy that's good enough for you, anyway?"

"You solved the French Quarter murder," Darryl said, rising. "I expect you'll figure that out in time. I'll be here."

With that he rose and left. Minutes later, seething, so did I.

CHAPTER EIGHT

Though Darryl's obstinance annoyed me to no end, I had nobody to blame but myself. Everyone in my friend's small network knew that a sweet treat was the price for information—and not just any old candy either. Darryl's sweet tooth was refined and snooty. And because I'd chosen to ignore the rules, I now found myself trying to find someplace to buy just the right kind of candy in the middle of a busy Saturday afternoon.

The fancy chocolate shops would be packed. No time, of course, to order anything online. The last and most obvious options were a drugstore or supermarket. I'd lose an hour just parking and walking around the latter. Decision made: drugstore. I drove to one of the national chains on Decatur Street and wedged my car into a space where the cars on either side had parked over the lines. After sucking in my stomach and shuffling sideways, I made it inside.

I returned the hello from the clerk at the counter and had just resisted the urge to venture down the makeup aisle when a hush—a weighted one, full of presence—crept up behind me.

"Mambo Dumond." The voice was all wrong, like wearing Mardi Gras beads outside carnival season.

I pivoted. His build was as average and unremarkable as his face. The set to his jaw and slightly jutted chin said he was as wary of me as I was of him. We took each other in as if running through a low-level background check. But I sensed something about him. Maybe the strange charge in the air was just the lwa alerting me that another servant was near.

I took his hand. "Seems I'm at a disadvantage."

"Houngan Cyrus Walters," he said. "From Queens, New York."

"Ah, the new houngan," I said. Word was that he'd apprenticed in New York but traveled to Haiti for initiation. I couldn't take my eyes off his red tie, nor the navy-blue suit. And were those cuff links? On a Saturday? The word "overkill" came to mind.

"New to town, but not new. You've got that practice over in Tremé, right?"

He'd done his homework. I was cordial, if not close, with the other members of the community. Here was a chance for the camaraderie that, I had to admit, I desperately craved. "That's right," I said. "What part of town has claimed you? You doing a storefront or home shop?"

He glanced away before he answered. "Still thinking about that," he said. For some reason, I got the sense that he knew exactly where he was going to set up shop but didn't want to tell me.

"What brings you to New Orleans?"

"The question is, Why didn't I come sooner?" he said. "You got your hurricanes to contend with, but what else isn't there to like?"

I felt much the same and appreciated him saying so.

"Well, let's get together sometime," he said, and turned to go. He hadn't offered his contact information, and I didn't stop him to ask for it. The vodouisant population was sizable. Public ritual or in passing, like just now, in time, we'd see each other again.

The candy aisle was a puzzle with too many pieces. I always got overwhelmed when I had too many choices, and perusing everything crammed onto the shelves threatened to give me a headache. Sugar-free anything was not an option. I perused the rest of the offerings and quickly discarded thoughts of snagging one of the cheaper chocolate brands. Darryl wasn't a fan of anything gummy. Licorice was a possibility . . . but then my gaze alighted upon something that made even me smile.

A packaged blast from the past. Little round disks of multicolored pure sugar. Individually wrapped in cellophane. A delicacy that occasionally graced the candy trays my friend set out around Christmastime. Smarties.

I snagged several packages and then, because I always had a petty side, put one back. Darryl wouldn't be getting anything over the minimum. Plus, he'd trashed my dirty rice. The voice that told me I'd screwed up the rice myself was quickly shushed.

Back at the Lemon Drop, I heard the music before I even opened the door. It was a cover of a tune I loved, Kermit Ruffins's "Drop Me Off in New Orleans." Jazz, R&B, reggae, or classical—for me, the kind of music didn't matter, because when good music hit you, it plucked on the strings deep within that spoke a language without words. Food for the soul.

Darryl was setting plates of gumbo on a table intended for two but crowded with four. He flicked his head back toward his office. I stood to listen to the music for a minute before weaving through the crowd of drinkers and dancers to the back.

The Lemon Drop's kitchen was a buffet for the senses. The smells wafting around the room made my mouth water. The gleaming surfaces, even in the midst of all the hustle and bustle, enviable. Darryl's handiwork.

One of the cooks hovered over the commercial oven in the corner, somehow reigning over pots on three of the six burners. The man moved as if he had a dozen sets of arms. Meanwhile, the new sous chef was chopping vegetables at the stainless steel table that nearly spanned the length of the room and simultaneously bouncing to the music from the front room. He greeted me with a chin lift. I waved and left them to their work.

In the office, I checked the trash to make sure Darryl hadn't snuck behind me and recovered his precious air fresheners. Luckily for him, he hadn't.

When he was seated opposite me, I whipped out the Smarties and plastered on my best grin. His eyes positively exploded. I tossed the package onto the desk.

"I can't believe you made me go out and get something."

"Aw, man," Darryl said, ignoring me. "I can't believe you found these." He immediately ripped open the package, took out not one but two of the small rolls of candies, and tossed them both back. I got up and called for someone in the kitchen to get him a glass of water while he inhaled a third.

"All right." Darryl leaned forward and said, "What is it you want to know about Arthur Stiles?"

"More like what does his wife want to know?" I said.

"Come again?"

At that moment, one of the kitchen staff knocked and popped his head in the door. "Two Sazeracs with an extra shot of cognac coming right up." By my guess he was a few years my junior, so the gold tooth must have been more for show than function. When neither his employer nor I shared in his laugh, he clamped his mouth shut and went to set down two glasses of water. Darryl shot him a murderous glare. The man mumbled something, left, then returned with coasters.

Darryl shook his head. "That boy's been angling to get up onstage. Fancies himself a comedian."

"She says she found some money," I explained, picking back up where we'd left off. "A lot of money in their bank account. See, she never checks it. He handles the bills; she handles everything else. It was only by chance that she saw the statement. She's wondering at the source of their sudden good luck."

"Back in the day, he was one hell of a ballplayer, you know. Point guard. Could shoot the lights out of the gym. But like so many, that all went away when he busted up his body. Can't remember if it was a knee or ankle or what, but long story short, he couldn't play no more. No college, no NBA, and then I kinda lost track of him."

Darryl leaned back in his chair and propped a leg up on the edge of the desk. His gaze skyward, the fingers of his right hand thrumming.

"Until . . . ," I goaded.

"Until he started getting into trouble. Wasn't the first, but the second scam that got him locked up. If I recall, it was a pretty short stint, though."

"And what kind of scams are we talking about then?" I asked. "If it's enough to land him in jail, what was it?"

"You want the short version or the long version?"

I thought for a minute, then said, "The important parts."

Darryl took a few sips of water and tore through another pack of Smarties before he spoke. "Arthur is small-time, tryin' hard to be big-time. Funny thing is, I just don't think he's got it in 'im. First time he got sent up, he was just the fall guy. You ain't gon' believe this one. He was going around trying to sell stuff door-to-door. Take the money, promise to deliver, and disappear."

"Okay, so they got him on theft," I interjected. "But was that enough to land him in these overcrowded jails?"

"No," Darryl agreed. "Not by itself, but when you get that somebody who doesn't like being scammed, and that somebody hunts you and your partner down and threatens you—well, when that partner beats this person to within an inch of their life, that assault charge *will* land you in jail."

"Huh," was all I could say.

"Next time," Darryl charged on. "This next scam, I gotta admit, was a good one: call old people up, get them declared incompetent, and then steal everything they have."

That would account for the cash. I wondered if perhaps Arthur had revamped his old scam again. "And he got caught."

"You bet he did. One lady he did this to had a daughter that was out of the country, over in Namibia or some such place. And when she came home to visit her mama and found out what happened?" Darryl stopped to whistle. "That lady lost her wig! She didn't stop until she'd figured out what happened. Hounded the police into finding the culprits and prosecuting. She packed up her mother and took her back on where she came from, and our man, Art Stiles, landed back in lockdown."

I had to shake my head. Would it have killed the man to get a regular job? Learn a trade? Why was beating good people out of their money the only thing he could come up with to survive?

"And now he's back at it again?" I asked.

"Seem that way," Darryl said. "But I don't know what he's up to. And this time, if he gets caught, he's gonna be sent up on that three-strike rule. He'll be put away for longer than these minute bits he's done before."

I sipped my water, relishing the liquid as it refilled my dwindling reserves. "Okay, I know this will sound lame, but is it possible that he's come by this money in some legitimate way this time?"

Darryl sipped his water, then plowed through another pack of Smarties. "I suppose lots of thangs is possible. Jesus could raise up, slap him across the face, and teach him a lesson."

"And he could confess and turn himself in."

"And I could successfully guess all the lottery numbers for this week."

"We could go on." I chuckled.

"But won't change the fact that Art is shady. If you want to know what he's up to now, though, there's one person who will know what the latest scams are and if your man is involved." Darryl paused for effect. "Remember our former mayor?"

I blinked. The former mayor, the poster boy for everything wrong done after the storm, was serving time for corruption in the Federal

Correctional Institution in Texarkana, Texas. "You want me to go to the state penitentiary and talk to Ray Nagin?"

Darryl frowned. "Naw, not Ray. His cousin. Was raised up in New York 'fore his folks brought him down here. When he came, he brought every scam he learned up north with him. But he's a preacher now. Who you need to talk to is the man with the plan. The fella who has all the answers. The devil in a three-piece suit. You need to talk to 'Juju' Lejune."

CHAPTER NINE

The air outside was as sweet and tasty as a Mardi Gras king cake. Pumpkins, cinnamon, nutmeg—it was almost as if I could open my pores and suck in the sugar directly. All these scents and more portended a New Orleans favorite: Halloween.

I intended to head straight home to salvage what I could of the dirty rice Darryl had refused to keep. But something made me pause. My gaze followed the flow of a trickle of foot traffic. Being so close to the French Quarter, I figured that was where they were heading. My thoughts turned to Salimah Grenade.

I hadn't seen her in months. Not since she'd stormed out of Lucien's office. Understandably, her nerves had been raw. The poor woman had just been released from prison. We had intended to confront Lucien about his involvement—or more pointedly, his *lack* of involvement—in helping a fellow vodouisant who had been wrongly accused of murder. But that encounter had ended badly when the houngan to the stars raised the issue of a Voodoo council—and his place at the head of it.

The vodouisant grapevine suggested that Salimah had recovered nicely from the murder scandal, at least financially, her shop overflowing with customers old and new. Publicity, good or bad, had that effect on a business sometimes.

Halloween, guilt, curiosity. Probably a mix of them all. I stashed the dirty rice in the back seat and closed the door. Traffic would be insane, parking lots as hard to find as a hand free of a cocktail. I left my car where it was and braved the short walk to the French Quarter.

After the residential portion of Saint Louis Street gave way and the noise and clutter pressed in, the sidewalks became as congested as the narrow streets, jam-packed with cars.

I passed a pair of performers. Something about their manner suggested they were a couple. The woman was strumming a ukulele, while the man sang a tune in accented English. From Australia? New Zealand? Either way, they were a hit. A glass donation jar was stuffed with bills. By my estimation, it sat far enough away from them for someone, running at a good-enough clip, to zoom past, swoop it up, and keep on motoring. They'd learn.

Across the street, competing for tourist coins, was another duo, father and son from the looks of them. The boy appeared to be no more than ten years old but played a saxophone with skill that belied his age. His father took the role of cheerleader, urging people to add some money to their growing pile.

Though the French Quarter hadn't sustained as much damage as other parts of the city during the storm, the yearslong slowdown in tourist traffic could still be seen a decade later. The homes were mostly occupied again, but some long-standing businesses had closed, replaced by newer, flashier varieties.

At Dauphine Street, I stopped to pop a few bills in an open guitar case. The handwritten sign next to the owner proclaimed him to be newly arrived in the city and homeless. And I believed him. As I hung a left, the sounds of music, trucks unloading, and rowdy vacationers carried me on to Dumaine, where I took a right and, in a few minutes, stood in front of Voodoo Real.

From a bar across the street, partygoers spilled out cloaked in sports paraphernalia, either football or basketball, and good cheer. Halloween decorations were in full display: pumpkins, witches' brooms, string lights, and signs announcing the Krewe of BOO! parade, the annual event that, though less famous than some of the other parades, always managed to generate huge crowds. It was something else to look forward to, especially as it was toward the end of hurricane season.

I knew I was stalling. I inhaled and blew out a deep breath, then pushed open the shop's door to be greeted by a sizable horde of customers. Business was indeed still good. The locals were marked by their normal dress and the intent with which they browsed. The visitors, though, were colorfully beaded, purses casually dangling from arms, just ripe for snatching. Some wore shoes more fit for a club and general wide-eyed expressions that told me this was the first time they'd been in such a place.

The store was painted a crisp white that still felt warm thanks to the colorful African artwork adorning the walls. The counter was right where it had been, but it seemed like everything else was different. I suspected that after everything that had happened to her, Salimah had wanted a fresh start.

Inadvertently, I gave a wide berth to the place where I'd seen Tyka's blood on the floor. Where she'd struggled for her life. The culprit, Salimah's nefarious cousin and former employee, the very late Rashad Grenade.

Another person, clad in all black, with a name tag that I couldn't read marking him as an employee. Rashad's replacement, then. A small group of customers huddled around him as he seemed to explain the merits of a poppet.

Salimah was attending to another client at the register. She must have sensed me watching her because she stopped midsentence and flicked her gaze in my direction. When she caught sight of me, instead of the hostility I'd expected, her expression—raised eyebrows, a question in her dark-brown eyes—was purely one of curiosity.

I smiled, offered a small wave. She returned the gesture, coolly, then motioned in the direction of the back room.

The beaded curtain remained, and I pushed it aside before making my way to the windowless break room. Here things had stayed the same: the college-size refrigerator with a microwave on top, the small dinette. A coffee maker in the snug corner beside the sink.

From the corner of my eye, the stairway leading to the upstairs apartment loomed like a thing returned from the dead. It was where Virgil Dunn's dismembered remains had been found. The scene Rashad had staged to look like a ritual killing.

"Didn't expect to see you here again," Salimah said as she pushed through the beaded doorway behind me, drawing me back to the present. Like her new assistant, she was clad in all black: snug jeans and fitted T-shirt, the only adornment a kente cloth headband. Her hair was different, short. It looked good on her. But the toll of the last several months was evident in the weariness that had settled into the premature lines across her forehead. Her lips twisted in what appeared to be a permanent purse.

I paused. I had to choose my words carefully. Salimah didn't know how, but she knew that her cousin Rashad wasn't coming back—ever. And that I was the reason why. Despite the fact that he'd killed a man and tried to frame her for the murder, some part of her—mother, aunt, family—that part still took issue with what I'd done. Even if it had seen her released from prison and her struggling business now thriving.

"It was time." With the words out, I thought I'd chosen wisely.

"You here about the Voodoo council? You and Houngan Alexander still trying to take over and lead us?"

I had my purse in a death grip. Being in this space, under Salimah's unblinking gaze, made me nervous. With effort, I let my hands fall to my sides. "Haven't heard anything more about the council than you."

Salimah crossed her arms. "I'm going to challenge Lucien for leadership, since it seems like you're afraid to." She thought for a moment, then said, "I take that back: he's probably just got you under his thumb, like everybody else in this city."

Where she got the idea that Lucien and I were allies of a sort, I had no idea, and I didn't feel in the least like I needed to explain this to her. Sometimes people made up their minds, and there was little you could do to change them. True maturity, I'd learned, was in understanding you didn't need to.

Salimah pointed at my chest. "What about that, uh, injury of yours? Guessing a healer like you has taken care of that, and you're pretty much good as new."

I was, and I told her so.

"Did you send Rashad away temporarily, or . . ." She paused. "Permanently?"

I sighed. Hadn't we been over this? "Are you worried about him?"

"You think you know me, but you don't." Salimah stomped over to the refrigerator and took out a bottle of green juice. "You think I don't know what Rashad is . . . was. Spoiled, angry, foolish. I cared for him like he was my brother, but all he had for me was envy. I don't care anymore what happened to him—I just don't want to be looking over my shoulder, wondering where the next attack is coming from."

The fact that this confession could be a trap crossed my mind. Erzulie, though, she only rushed normal currents through my veins. No warning signs. "All I can say is, I'm certain that out of all your worries, that doesn't have to be one of them."

Salimah regarded me for a long while without speaking, her face a merry-go-round of emotion. I'd just confirmed her suspicions: her cousin was dead. She was part relieved, part angry, and probably, if she wanted to admit it, a little envious herself. But she'd never ask another vodouisant of her methods of defense. She twisted the cap off the bottle and drank deeply. She didn't offer me anything. Impolite but not unexpected.

Finally, she shrugged. "So, if you're not here about the council, you come to ask after my health? In case you didn't see, I've got customers. Lots of them."

I suddenly didn't know why I'd come. I fumbled around for something and finally settled on the one thing I didn't need, which I'd just unpacked. "Supplies," I said. "May as well get them locally when I can."

Salimah eyed me dubiously. But then her enterprising nature took over. "What do you need? If I don't have it, I can order it for you."

My mind was a blank. I hadn't come here at all to order anything, but my mouth and my discomfort had painted me into a corner. One where Salimah both tested me and was determined to at least make a profit off my lie.

"Angelica root," I blurted out. It was the first thing that came to mind when the fog cleared.

"Guessing by the way you tidied things up for yourself, you're not the one in need of protection. For your clients, then?" she asked and then turned to walk back out to the storefront.

I followed behind her and muttered, "Of course."

The crowd had thinned, but the door opened, spilling in a couple more. There was something to be said for having a storefront where walk-in sales supplemented regular client appointments. But I didn't necessarily want to be tied to one place all day either. Sometimes, in not getting what you wanted, you got exactly what you needed.

"I'll ring you up over here," Salimah called.

At the register, I raised an eyebrow at the inflated price, but I swiped my card, the price for my guilt.

"You heard of any new scams going on in the Quarter?" I asked. The French Quarter was the hotbed of scams. May as well see if Arthur Stiles's exploits extended here.

"Nothing more than the usual stuff," she said. "I stand at the window sometimes and watch the same scams succeed over and over. You think people would read up on this sort of thing before they come."

I pondered that dead end while Salimah packaged my order and handed it to me. Just as I was turning to leave, I saw something that caught my eye. There, sandwiched between a few other packages on the counter behind the register, was a carved figure of a woman holding a gift to the gods with a double-bladed axe sticking up from the woman's head. This figure was for a follower of the lwa.

I thrust my chin in the direction. "A new vodouisant in town?"

Salimah's calm visage faltered for a second as her gaze flickered over to the statue. She quickly covered it up and shook her head. "Customer order placed online," she said. "Never even seen him in person."

"Shipping here or out of town?" I asked. The new houngan—Walters. I wondered if this was for him.

Salimah's face turned ugly. "And why do you think I would tell you anything about my business?"

What is she hiding? I felt my sangswe stir, and with it, my anger. Salimah had never been a fan of mine, not even when I got her behind out of jail, but if she was hiding something dangerous . . .

The air in the shop changed. The customers even seemed to notice. All eyes turned to the two vodouisants eyeing each other. Me considering going in my purse and whipping out something to take that sneer off her face.

"Everything all right over here?" It was her new employee. I looked at him for the first time. Concern, not malice, in his features.

"Mambo Dumond was just leaving."

I clutched the ingredient I didn't need, settled myself, and shook it off. I left without saying another word to Salimah.

Walking down the street back to the bar where I'd parked, I realized I didn't owe her anything. Any guilt I was nursing was done. I'd wasted enough time.

As I left the shop and the Quarter, my thoughts returned to Vangie and Arthur Stiles. Before I pulled away, I called the number Darryl had given me and made an appointment to see "Juju" Lejune the next day.

CHAPTER TEN

The man had hidden behind a group of obnoxious tourists while he watched the woman from the corner of the shop—Voodoo Real. He chuckled to himself at the banality of that name. Probably pandering to the drunk and ignorant throng who frequented the French Quarter in search of a few religious trinkets to take home and show their bored suburban neighbors.

The woman was short and had a halo of kinks held back by a headband. Her face was at least a decade younger than she appeared in that ridiculous garb she wore. Still, he couldn't deny that she walked with her back straight, a certain powerful confidence in her stride. She had glanced in his direction and let her gaze bounce off as if he were unremarkable. *Good,* the man thought. *Underestimate me.* He had been discounted before. It was a most effective camouflage.

The shop owner's demeanor had changed as soon as the other woman walked in. A tendon on the right side of her neck throbbed. Shoulders gone tight as a shoe two sizes too small. She did a serviceable job at trying to hide it, but beneath that impressive scowl of hers was fear. As plain as day.

When they moved off to a room behind a beaded curtain, he followed, hovering nearby. He busied himself with a wall of gris-gris bags and shooed away the employee who harassed him. The man couldn't make out what they talked about, thanks to the rowdy crowd who had piled into the shop.

There was a current flowing between them. Some sordid history. He recognized bad blood when he saw it. The short woman had a way about her, though. He had come to recognize it.

He could see it in the way she carried herself. She was a mambo, and one who thought highly of herself. He imagined the both of them thought they knew more than he did. But the short one in the skirt—if instincts were right, she would be his competition.

She might be capable, even powerful. But if she got in his way, he would stop her. Maybe he could even practice on her. The man was sure she wouldn't give out so quickly as the Snowman had. Yes, that would suit him just fine.

On the way out, the woman had asked about the statue—*his* statue. The owner brushed it off, but still he left without his package. No need to draw attention to himself. He would call later and have it mailed.

The citizens of this bathtub of a city were talkative, if nothing else. It hadn't taken long for him to find out who the top Voodoo pros were. Lucien Alexander, a priest with a practice that, from the way people talked about it, rivaled the pope's. He had the house, the car, and the wardrobe of a pimp to go along with it.

And another, the woman. Reina Dumond. She took houseplants and plates of rice as payment. Operated a business out of a backyard garage. But she was from Haiti. Voodoo wasn't just a religion but a way of life in that place. As much as Top Dog wanted to dismiss her, with that kind of history, he knew that he couldn't.

There was someone else, a newer man in town, Walters, or Watson. Another Haitian initiate. But not much else was known about him.

He scouted the man, Lucien, first. Some might mistake those tailored suits and cushy cars for someone unpracticed, but the Top Dog saw through the glam. The man had power, but he cared about money, maybe more than his practice. Top Dog cataloged that for future use. Money was the great equalizer.

He asked around until he found the woman. The much-heralded Tremé neighborhood. He had to admit that the place had a certain vibe. Birthplace of jazz, home to freed slaves and the lovely Marie Laveau. Haunt for late-night music and booze.

A sign pointed him to where she operated her shop. He felt powerful protections around the place, so he didn't go farther, but he would look up a few ways to thwart them. He knew that even the strongest spells wore off if not constantly tended. If he ever needed to break through, all he had to do was time it right.

She was intriguing. If he could take her, he could find out what was so all-fired important about being from Haiti. He thought it was all hype, but he would find out.

The Top Dog had plans. Big plans. And neither a political schmoozer nor a backwater mambo would stop him.

CHAPTER ELEVEN

According to Darryl, Lamar Lejune, "Juju" to some, was a New Orleans king of cons. Anxious to revel in his hard-earned reputation, he'd readily agreed to meet me at a Magazine Street coffee shop we both liked. I avoided the meters and found a parking spot on a side street. Fifteen minutes early, I took the time to scan my surroundings before I got out of the car—a new, most unsettling habit I'd gained as a result of the previous months' activities.

Parallel to the Mississippi River, the six-mile stretch of road ran through several eclectic neighborhoods spanning the Central Business District all the way to Uptown. Knots of homes, clusters of shops and restaurants, all blended seamlessly into this area of town that most tourists thankfully missed.

The coffee shop was a two-story affair painted a loud magenta. The shop was downstairs, an apartment with a nice iron-gated porch upstairs. On hot summer days, the striped awning protected those sitting near the glass front windows from the worst of the sun.

Next door, a new café, and someone, likely the owner, busy cleaning off the tables outside. Across the street, a pair of painters stood at a slatted wooden fence, sloshing sky-blue paint over graffiti that would likely be back within a week.

An old-fashioned door chime greeted me along with several pairs of eyes as I walked in.

The interior was on the smaller side. The chairs and tables were stark-white modern affairs, smudged here and there with remnants from the pastry case. Everything else screamed old French Quarter flair: masks, beads, and regal black-and-white photographs in silver frames covered the walls. A tall bookshelf to the left of the counter was reserved for books and magazines that in one way or another featured the state of Louisiana and her rich history.

As usual, the place was packed with patrons. A mother with two babbling toddlers, faces smeared with crumbs that looked like little jewels against their skin. When she leaned in to wipe away the delightful mess from the smaller child, he reached out a pudgy hand and stroked her face. She seemed so accustomed to that soul-stirring show of affection that she barely took notice. What she took for granted was my most persistent, yet unanswered, wish. I turned away.

The air was laden with the aroma of Brazilian coffee beans intermingled with the tempting scents of all manner of confections: cakes and muffins and beignets and macarons.

My mouth and stomach responded accordingly, and I soon found myself drifting toward the line to order junk my waistline didn't need with the few crumpled dollars I had left to my name.

Until I spotted Hezekiah Verboze.

His locs were pulled back away from his face and tied at the nape of his neck. He still sported that long black coat, the machete he carried visible at his hip when he turned. Without his customary scowl, I could still see evidence of the carefree kid he used to be when we were in grade school. The one who played with his little sister and had eyes as bright as the North Star. Back before the bullies stole his childhood from him.

Straight out of a kitschy movie, we sensed and spotted each other at the same time. Our eyes locked. We both stiffened. Him standing there with a cup and a bag, me, mouth hanging open. The last time we'd seen each other had been months earlier at the cemetery—where Rashad had lured us all. The clang of our machetes coming together in what I later learned had been a staged fight: he'd been sent to stall me. Neither of us had been hurt, but it had done little to improve our standing with each other.

I steeled myself and decided to let bygones be bygones.

"I see this place is getting popular with everybody," I said. I attempted a smile, but that was pushing it, and I abandoned the effort accordingly.

Kiah hesitated, probably weighing the same choice I had just made. "Guess so," was all he could muster. At least he didn't plaster on his scowl. Through his work for Houngan Alexander, Kiah had an ear to the streets as much as anyone. In the silent gap that lingered between us, I figured why not ask.

"You a sports fan?"

He actually looked uncomfortable. "I am."

"Do you know a local basketball star? Some years back? Name of Arthur Stiles?"

"I've heard of him." Suspicion had crept back into Kiah's voice.

"Have you heard about him being involved in anything?"

He looked around to make sure nobody was watching us before he answered. "Only that him and the wife broke up. Why you asking?"

Time to spin a tale. "He made an appointment with me and canceled. I know he has some troubles. I'm just worried about him."

"He's a grown man," Kiah said and then checked his tone. "I mean, from what I hear, he can take care of himself."

I'd done it. Though he didn't have any useful information, Kiah Verboze and I had had a civil conversation. I thanked him, and as he turned to leave, I called out, "It looks like Chavonne did the right thing. She's all settled and doing well in Austin." As soon as the last word had tripped over my tongue, I wanted to bite it off.

Kiah spun. Eyes narrowed. The scowl was back in all its glory. "How do you know my cousin?"

Knowing how uncomfortable Kiah would be with his cousin seeing me, Chavonne and I had kept our client-friend relationship a secret for years, and in the span of a few seconds, I'd ruined it. My mouth, previously so forthcoming with words, became dispossessed of the ability to utter anything other than, "Uh."

"I should have known," he charged on. "She was probably telling you all my family business. I should have done some more damage at that cemetery when I had the chance. I hope you know I held back on you."

That last bit unlocked my tongue. "Bring that thing out against me again and I'll carve you a new smile with it."

By now, we'd drawn stares and even a few whispers. One concerned man, about my height but with a determination in his gaze matching that of an Olympic boxer, started toward us.

"Everything okay over here?" he asked. I didn't need rescuing but appreciated the gesture nonetheless.

"Just chatting with an old friend." I glared at Kiah.

The concerned man backed away, and I headed toward the line. I was trying to put the exchange out of my mind when Kiah's words clawed at my back.

"Since we sharing secrets, guess you should know about where your man spends his time. Cops love strip clubs. Did you know that? Word is your Detective Roman Frost is kinda particular on one of the dancers. Fine as hell." He paused then, probably for effect. "May want to ask him about it. Or maybe you got what they call one of them *open* relationships."

I didn't give him the courtesy of turning around to argue or to show the anguish plainly on my face. But I imagined he saw the stiffening in my back, the falter of my steps.

Kiah had gotten the best of me. I'd let my guard down with him—a mistake I wouldn't make again. And because of that I would have to warn Chavonne that I had let the cat out of the bag and then poked it to rile it up even more in the process.

As far as Roman was concerned, who knew? It was difficult to admit, but would I have been so rattled if some part of me didn't think that Kiah had spoken true? A decision about what to do with that unwanted bit of information would have to come later.

I dragged myself forward and stood in line behind the lone customer at the counter.

"Hey, sugar." Sarah's knitted brow smoothed at the sight of me. The man ahead of me, the recipient of said frown, cut his eyes at her and stalked off with his espresso. Baristas were tricky. The same as other service workers. These were tough jobs—the toughest. They had razor-sharp memories. And if you approached them with just a modicum of respect and kindness for their hard work, they wouldn't forget it. That all but guaranteed perfect service every time.

"How are you, Sarah?" I greeted her with an equally warm smile. The shop had opened to much fanfare a couple of years prior. Sarah had been one of the first baristas, and I one of the first customers. We had been on friendly terms ever since.

"Making it," the barista said. "Got somebody I'll be sending your way soon."

Sarah wasn't one of my customers. She never said so outright, but I suspected she didn't believe in what I did. But that respect thing? It went both ways with us. She didn't have to believe. Working at a coffee shop, with its steady stream of patrons, she was in a position to funnel several believers my way. She did so often.

I marveled at how she wore her hoop-shaped nose ring without getting it snagged on something. "A new customer will be a welcome sight."

"And how's Sweet Belly doing?" There was a grunt from the man behind me. A woman, professional, judging by the heels and suit, was losing patience for our small talk. Sarah glared at her, and she turned her attention back to her phone.

The barista used to live in Tremé and had been a relative fixture at the Lemon Drop. She'd been known to put away an entire slab of Darryl's ribs in one sitting. Hadn't seen her much since she married and moved to Faubourg Marigny. Her inquiry resurfaced my fears about his health.

"He's the same as always," I said. "Loud, contrary, bossy."

"And still acting like you don't already have a daddy," Sarah added.

I chuckled. "He doesn't know any other way to be."

"What'll you have, sugar?" Sarah was one of the few people who didn't address me by the honorific "Mambo." She didn't have to.

After a quick scan of the pastry case, I said, "Blueberry muffin and a black tea."

Sarah's rail-thin form moved with practiced and graceful fluidity. She grabbed the muffin with a pair of tongs and had it on a plate and in the toaster oven in a blink. When she rang up the order, I offered her my debit card. After that unexpected purchase at Voodoo Real, I hoped I had enough.

Sarah waved it off. "On the house."

Ms. Impatience looked up from her phone then as if Sarah had offered me the contents of the cash register. No matter, though—she'd be back; we all would. I wasn't a coffee drinker, but I'd heard there wasn't a better cup to be had in the city. The baked goods were top notch too. I thanked Sarah, then dropped a dollar bill and the last of my pocket change in the tip jar when she wasn't looking.

I took my order and squeezed into a corner table, where I had a good view of the entrance. There was no honey, so I opted for one packet of sugar in my tea. I watched the other patrons as I ate and sipped.

Judging by the profusion of laptops and sketch pads, and even one simpleton conducting what looked like a video call in the corner, the place was overflowing with a hodgepodge of digital nomads, creatives, or those like me, eking out a living for themselves. Some people found coffee shops a suitable environment in which to read or perhaps get some work done. I didn't know how they did it. The strident rise and flow of chatter and laughter. The clamor of blenders, coffee grinders. Oftentimes the music a few decibels too loud. What they called ambient sound, I called grating.

To each her own.

At the table closest to the door, a girl sat with books spread over the table and her fingers pecking away at her laptop keyboard. Headphones covered her ears. Her feet propped up in the chair opposite her. Some people had no home training.

Next to the bookshelf was an older couple. Their hands were clasped together on the tabletop next to discarded wrappers and napkins. In his other hand, the gentleman with glasses held a tablet, while his companion hunched over, his head buried in a paperback novel.

Others hovered within arm's reach, prepared to wage holy war for the next open table.

The door chime sounded. In walked a man with a stylish, if gaudy, cane. Chemically straightened black hair was combed away from his high forehead and brushed his coat collar. His navy suit was neat and clean, but slightly ill fitting.

Our gazes met in the way of people searching for someone they've never seen before. This had to be Mr. Lejune.

After affirming head nods, he hustled over to my table and dumped his pimp cane on the floor by the chair across from me.

"Ms. Dumond, right?" Mr. Lejune offered me his hand.

"Mr. Lejune," I said. Already annoyed, I shook his hand. "Mambo Dumond."

"Oh, I see, you need the title." He smirked. "I don't. You know, even my flock calls me Juju. Anyway, mind if I get something?" I motioned for him to do just that. I didn't *need* the title; I'd earned it. And damned if he didn't traipse off without offering to get me another cup of tea. Mr. Lejune, or Juju, so far had done little to earn his way out of the negative balance he had started with.

Soon enough, the scam artist turned preacher returned with iced coffee and banana bread—for himself.

"Appreciate you meeting with me," I said, downing the last dregs of my lukewarm tea.

He took a bite of his breakfast, then wiped the corner of his mouth with the back of his hand. His expression pivoted from open to wary. "How'd you get my name?"

"I've got my secrets, as I'm sure you've got yours. Best to leave it that way, don't you think?"

"Touché." He grinned the grin of an animal intent on a new kill. "Today I get to minister to one suspected murderer, two confirmed thieves, one bad-check writer." He paused to add a sugar to his iced coffee. Gross. "And one—just one—decent person. A woman who's just trying to figure out her bad luck with men."

I wondered why he'd chosen the life of scam artist. Had he felt like no other choices were open to him? Had he just been lazy? And what had turned him toward the ministry? "Does this work suit you better?"

Juju leaned back and shrugged. His skin was shiny with an off-putting combination of oil and sweat. "I'm a new man. I take my clients just as you take yours. I preach the word of Jesus and leave the judgments for somebody else."

To a degree, he had a point. I'd been desperate enough to take money from many an unscrupulous character in my time. But I still had a choice, and I'd turned away more than a handful.

"As I said on the phone," I said, switching gears, "I'm here to talk about what types of scams are going on in the city now."

78

He watched me for a while without responding. "Before we begin," he said, "there's the matter of my church. I'm spinning up this after-school program, and we need supplies. Would you be willing to make a donation?"

"A donation." I was shocked but shouldn't have been. I did my part to serve the people of this city, and apparently, so did Juju. I counted out the three bills I had left in my wallet. "Will this do for now?"

"This will barely cover a few jugs of juice." He took my meager offering and stuffed the bills in his inner coat pocket. "How about you see what else you can put together—what you feel this information is worth—and drop that off in a couple weeks?"

"Deal."

"First I have to know who you're talking about."

"Why?"

"Cons are like cars: certain ones fit certain people. It wouldn't make sense for me to go off telling you about a scam that doesn't fit the perpetrator."

I couldn't argue his logic—again. "Arthur Stiles."

A slow smile spread across Juju's face. "I used to run with Art back in the day. Not a bad man, but that injury messed with his head. He had a life all planned out for himself, and when it didn't work . . . Let's just say he didn't believe in backup plans."

"So, knowing Arthur, which of the scams running now would he be involved in?"

Juju clapped his palms together and interlaced his fingers. "Art's small-time. He won't get into nothing too dangerous. Let me think."

In a minute, Juju tapped the table. "I got it. You seen these hand-made signs all over the place? Nailed or taped up near every stoplight? Usually says something along the lines of, 'We'll buy your shit house for fast cash'?"

I told him I had.

"It's all about house flipping. Now, I'm not saying they don't actually flip a property or two . . ."

I was intrigued. "But . . ."

"But," Juju continued, "but more often than not, they go in and haggle the price down to nothing or, even worse, get people to sign over the property, force them out, and then slap some paint on it and resell for three times that price. A wise man would see that this scam could reach pretty high. Somebody down at City Hall has got to be rubber-stamping these title transfers. You feel me?"

"Wow," I said, truly shocked. "You actually think politicians are involved in this?"

"Art may be small-time, but for some of these corporations, you're talking big money. And I mean 'nobody get in our way or else' kinda cash."

"And you think Arthur is involved in this scam?"

"Can't say for sho', but it makes sense," Juju said. "Arthur wasn't never really into anything violent. And an associate of mine spotted him at the airport recently. Not leaving, just lingering. Who knows—maybe he was picking up one of the big-timers?"

It all sounded reasonable to me. If Arthur was involved in what sounded like a pretty lucrative scheme, then perhaps that money was from a payment.

"I have to thank you for sharing this information," I said.

"All in service to the community," Juju said. "And my church."

As I was about to leave, Juju said something else. "You know, I saw Art with a lady. Name of Judge Gwen Guillory. Not saying there's anything going on—just saying."

Ah, monogamy. The ever-elusive institution we all strived for. I didn't know whether Arthur was seeing this Gwen, but if he was, I wouldn't have been surprised. Still, I knew a fair trade when I saw one, and I told Juju I'd make that extra donation to his church within the month.

His phone chirped. He checked it and turned back to me. "If word of how you received this information gets out, I'll deny it. I'll ruin your good name. If I see you begging on the street afterward, I'll pay a street kid to rob your cup. We clear?"

I wanted nothing more than to reach across the table and slap this man. I wouldn't even need a spell: I bet between Sarah and me, we could beat him into submission for talking to me this way. But this wasn't about me, was it? I nodded my agreement.

"Always nice to meet another hustler. Maybe next time you can share some of your tips with me."

With that, Mr. Lejune—I had no desire to know him well enough to call him Juju—swept up his crumbs and coffee and deposited them in the trash bin by the door on his way out. I grabbed my purse and kept my rebuttal cataloged in the back of my mind for when I'd have the chance to unleash it. I waved goodbye to Sarah and walked out into the midmorning heat and humidity. Based on that last nugget of information, I had something else to check out today.

CHAPTER TWELVE

My parents and I settled into a shoebox of an apartment in New Orleans East when we first arrived. We had nothing but the clothes we wore and the few pieces shoved into the one trunk we all shared. Heat that may have felt stifling to some welcomed me like a big damp hug and a wet, sloppy kiss. The pacing was different, though. Everything moved faster than it did at home. In time I adjusted, as did Manman, but I don't think my father ever did. And that's probably what eventually drove him out to Manchac.

Along with a relic of a television and a used but serviceable mattress, the previous residents left a treasure in that apartment—a half set of encyclopedias.

I wasn't a huge reader as a kid, only the occasional text I was forced to read for a school assignment. But the smooth feel of the leather cover beneath my hands, the edges of the pages gilded in gold . . . I couldn't help but be drawn in. I found myself caught up in the web of images and snapshots from places I'd never been. And I was intrigued. I went from skeptic to convert and read through each of those volumes ten times over. When we moved, I left the encyclopedias behind: I thought it best to leave them for the next child, as the set had been gifted to me.

I still wasn't an avid reader. I didn't have the disposable cash to buy books. Every now and then, I picked up something from the Nora

Navra Library that I rarely finished. It didn't make me proud to admit it; I determined to change this bad habit when I had time. But on one visit, a librarian there had taken the time to show me how to use the internet for a quick bit of fact-finding on permits and the like.

Research, I was learning, was an art form. When in search of information, a number of options were at your disposal. You'd be surprised by what you could learn from just asking the right person. Listening—okay, eavesdropping—was another seriously underrated skill that netted all kinds of fascinating tidbits. Some research had to be done with a dedicated afternoon visit to the library, using good old-fashioned books. But for certain types of information, the internet was a great place to start.

Back at home, I began simply: power up my computer, open browser, pull up search engine, and type in the name: Gwen. *Hmm, how to spell the last name?* I chided myself for not asking Juju and writing it down.

Gillary. Gilrey. Gelry. I tried each of them and came up with nothing that seemed relevant. *Gwen.* I wondered if that was short for Gwendolyn. I tried the search engine again. Gwendolyn Gilrey.

Bam. An article, three down from the top of the search results. My spelling was wrong, but this had to be her. Gwendolyn Guillory. The piece raved about how Ms. Guillory—correction, *Judge* Guillory—in partnership with the NCAA and NBA, had sponsored an after-school sports program for at-risk youth. The pictures featured eager-looking children staring at the players with open adoration. No images of the judge.

I navigated back to the results page and scanned the next couple of entries.

Another article talked about Gwen and other judges' stances on juvenile sentencing. It seemed she was a juvenile court justice—one who took the hard line, suggesting that juveniles who committed certain crimes should be tried as adults. I disagreed with her. For one, the system was biased and didn't take a child's environmental factors into consideration. And jailing children made them worse, not better. Rabbit hole aside, the more I read, the more it struck me that she was not exactly the kind of person one would expect to be running in the same circles with someone like Ms. Vangie's husband.

Back to the results page again, forefinger planted on the scroll wheel. I sorted through several more entries and landed on an article that changed that hastily drawn conclusion.

The judge's picture set the tone before I had read one word. It was the kind where you could tell the paper had tried extra hard to make someone look guilty. The lighting was dark, her expression flat and lifeless. I could tell the judge was a formidable woman; it was that hint of defiance in her eyes. The article said that she'd stepped down from the bench after a lengthy tenure in order to focus on other matters. Some suspicion as to whether she'd been forced out.

A *former* judge, then. You never really knew people, did you?

A quote from her daughter, who worked at the school where my mother had been a lunch aide for a time, proclaimed Gwen's impeccable character and brilliance. A near-embarrassing amount of praise later, she went on to say how her mother planned to dedicate her life to her first love, children, and would be working in some philanthropic capacity.

Having her daughter make the statement was a nice touch, but I saw straight through it. That former judge Gwen had been forced out was a given, but why, still a mystery. After what I'd heard from Mr. Lejune, I wondered if her philanthropic activity involved swindling people out of their homes and flipping them for profit.

I leaned back in my chair, thinking. Even ousted, we were talking about a former judge. Her records, if they even still existed, would be locked down as tight as a pit bull on a chicken bone.

Unless.

There was one person I knew who rubbed elbows with the city's elite. Judges, politicians, Uptown businessmen who had him on speed dial for their in-home Vodou services and *wangas*.

The more I dug, the more difficult it became to ignore my nagging sense that this whole thing was bigger than Ms. Vangie knew—or than she had let on, at least. Plus, I had no desire to go asking for favors from that preening peacock. I shut off my computer and stood up. The kitchen wasn't going to clean itself.

Byen vini pa respekte zo rèk.

Another of Manman's proverbs stopped me in my tracks. Roughly, it meant that you can't just go around worrying about yourself; you have to take an interest in helping others too. The lwa had laid out this path for me for a reason. Even if I tried to turn away—and I knew that I shouldn't—I had no doubt that they would find a way to draw me back.

I blew out an exasperated breath and grabbed my phone.

"Alexander House of Healing," the melodic baritone on the other end of the line said. "How may the lwa serve you today?"

"Mambo Reina Dumond for Houngan Alexander," I said.

After a brief pause in which I heard pages shuffling, he said, "Hold a moment, please."

That moment turned into ten minutes, during which I sank onto the sofa, turned on the television, and mindlessly watched a string of commercials, each louder and more senseless than the last. Once I realized how long I had been on hold, I huffed and was about to hang up when Lucien's voice came on the line. I could almost guarantee he'd sat there twiddling his thumbs while making me wait on purpose.

"Why did you have to go and pick a fight with Hezekiah?"

I sat up straight and balked. "I did nothing of the sort. Kiah has been angry at me since he was ten years old. You ever asked him why?"

"Don't need to. I get it. The man's got a past, history. We all do. You know, that history is like a bag of Halloween treats, some sweet, some sour. The thing is, we understand that and how it impacts a man's actions. You're a mambo—"

"Duly initiated," I finished for him.

"What I'm trying to say is, you're above these petty squabbles." He stopped and said something to someone. "Don't take the bait is all I'm saying."

It was as if the man thought he ruled from the top of an ancient Egyptian pyramid, peering down, barely tolerating the rest of the world as his childish subjects. "Then take your own advice and stop biting my head off every time you see me."

"What can I do for you? I have clients waiting."

The dismissal. The chastising. I hated it. And I despised him. Why had I even called?

We didn't argue about it anymore—okay, we didn't argue *as much* about it anymore—but the source of our earliest conflict centered around our practices. He was raised in the Voodoo tradition; me, Vodou. One New Orleans based, the other Haitian. The only real difference that I could see was that the New Orleans tradition incorporated more of the rootwork and hoodoo created by the enslaved brought to the southern states, while the Haitian style retained more of the West African tradition.

Lucien saw the American evolution as superior. I, of course, took issue with that.

"Hello. You there?"

I snapped back to the present and gathered myself. "Wanted to ask for your—" I nearly choked on the word. My tongue flat out refused to say it. I'd begun to sweat even trying. "I need to know about a former judge, Gwendolyn Guillory. I'm wondering whether she retired on her own or if someone made her."

"Why do you want to know?"

"It's about a case." Why did I say that? There was no case, only an inquiry for a friend. "Funny thing is, her daughter is—or was—a teacher at the school where my mother worked for a short while."

Silence.

"You thinking or ignoring me?"

"I'm listening," Lucien said, sounding distracted. I *had* called him during the middle of the day.

Lucien recovered without a hitch. "I'll need a favor in return." His assistance, if one could call it that with all the booby traps attached, always came with a price.

"Dare I ask?" I asked, steeling myself.

"Guess you should know first. I'm going to revive talks on the Voodoo council. I want to lead it and I want you *not* to want to lead it. In fact, I need you to back me. Publicly," he said. "That new houngan, Walters, he may make a play, but he doesn't have the support yet."

In my attempt to help Vangie, I had laid a nice little trap for myself. Point to Lucien, again.

I'd forgotten about the new houngan. He hadn't left a strong impression after our chance meeting at the drugstore, and I got the sense he preferred it that way. But now, thinking back to the statue Salimah had tried to hide over at Voodoo Real, I wondered if it was for him or another follower. Many people didn't realize that in Vodou, there were an infinite number of lwa, many with overlapping abilities. That made it hard to pin down someone's patron unless you asked outright. But if I wasn't mistaken, that statue would mark him as a follower of Shango—the lwa of thunder, lightning, and fire.

I'd be lying if I said I hadn't entertained the thought that I'd be a better, more impartial, leader than Lucien. But the other part of me didn't want the responsibility. I was too private. Too intent on my practice and my peace. Bureaucracy and long speeches—those were Lucien's territory. Still, I'd decided that if he ever raised the council idea again, I'd consider running simply to irritate him.

"Agreed," I said after an extended silence, leaving out the part where Salimah *would* challenge him, and with her newfound fame, she'd have a good chance of winning. Let him figure that out for himself. I'd pay good money to see the shock on his face if she followed through on her threat and won.

"I'm not going to lie," Lucien said. "That was much easier than I thought. But it's good to know one's limit, to understand and accept your place."

I wanted to drown this man. "My place is wherever I choose to be, thank you. And I'm comfortable with that. What do you want this council to look like, anyway?"

"I've given it some thought, and I'm thinking an exilarchy," he said as if it were the most understood term in the world. I refused to ask him what it meant; I would look it up later. But being the blowhard that he was, he couldn't resist explaining: "We have a president—me—and a leadership team. Your typical roles, VP, treasurer, secretary. We have a code of conduct, a set of sanctions."

"An educational component," I added, despite myself. "And a voting system. No decisions made in a vacuum."

"We can talk more about that later," Lucien said. "I'll get back to you on your inquiry."

CHAPTER THIRTEEN

With Lucien tapping his contacts for information on Gwendolyn Guillory, I gladly completed a few poppet and gris-gris bag sales, along with a couple of virtual consultations. My coffers weren't overflowing but were in much better shape now.

The phone rang. I glanced at the caller ID: it was Roman. An unbidden but welcome smile lit up my face. He didn't often get a chance to call me during the day. "If you're calling to tell me you're on your way over, fine. Otherwise I'm not sure I want to hear anything else you have to say, Mr. Frost."

His pause yielded to a laugh that was like a bright light breaking through shadow. I often found myself thinking of ways to pry it from him again and again. To relieve the tiniest bit of the stress the job caused him.

"Been waiting an hour for one simple forensics report. I wanted to hear your voice. Either that or the lab rats are going to catch it."

"My voice has that much power over you, does it?"

"Among other things." Roman chuckled. "I didn't interrupt an appointment, did I?"

"Just finished up," I said. "Can I bring you some lunch?"

"No need," he said. I heard raised voices in the background. "Listen, I gotta run. And delivery is on its way to you. Hope you like it."

I grinned like a teenager. "Anything will beat this boiled egg in the refrigerator."

"All right, *cher*. I'll hit you up later."

I hung up, and soon enough, lunch arrived from the Caribbean spot a few minutes away. Jerk salmon on a bed of yellow rice. Mixed greens on the side. I ate, happy that once again, Roman and I were working our way back to solid footing.

I just had to find a way to keep us there. Forces, outside and in, had put us at odds before. Our religions, his schedule. I wouldn't let my fear keep me too focused on all that, though. We were moving forward.

Stomach and heart full, it was time to get back to the case. And for that, I'd want my friend with me. Wrestler, hustler, caretaker to an alcoholic father. Self-proclaimed protector of Darryl and me. Smart and sensitive and prone to take your head off if you suggested either of these things. It was time to find Tyka.

⸺

Ever since she'd almost died at Saint Louis Cemetery No. 2, Tyka had made herself scarce. Of course, I'd seen her a few times since and had been on the receiving end of a few text message check-ins, but things were still tense between us. Being overpowered and subdued by Rashad . . . it had to have left her feeling vulnerable. An emotion that was anathema to her, and she was still coming to terms with it.

As a witness to her shame, I was still being held at arm's length. And there was something else. In her eyes, I'd made a choice. She and Roman weren't on the best of terms either. And with us trying to work things out, it only served to keep my friend away more. Why I couldn't get the people I loved to all love each other at the same time was something even the lwa had not been able to help me figure out.

Pride was the ever-present culprit. Unfortunately, those who were most prideful rarely saw the damage it caused. I wasn't one to quote scripture, but I couldn't help thinking about a Bible verse that summed it up nicely: Proverbs 16:18. *Pride goes before destruction, a haughty spirit before a fall.*

I dialed Tyka's last known phone number, the one she'd given to me a month prior, when she'd brought me a Southern University sweatshirt. Asking her where she'd come by it had only yielded me a tongue-lashing about knowing how to graciously accept a gift.

"What up, Mambo?" Assessing Tyka's vocal intonations provided the road map one needed to guide one's conversation. It was an art form honed over time, not rushed. From wired, to flat, to alert, her reactions were as dense as the Amazon jungle. Today, her voice was soft but not curt. An invitation.

"Reina," I said, and I spelled out my name for her.

"Reina Dumond?" Tyka said. "The one always so quick to tell somebody how 'duly initiated' she is? That one?"

We shared a giggle that felt good. One that in my mind took a sledgehammer and knocked away a boulder-size chunk of the wall she had erected between us.

"Can I come by and talk to you about something?"

"As long as it ain't about my future," she quipped. "You gotta learn to live more in the moment. I read that shit somewhere."

"It's not about school," I said, but at some point in the conversation, it would be. She rattled off an address on North Prieur Street.

"Wait. That's in—"

"Tremé. Give me about an hour."

I knew the street. I searched my memory, running through all the For Sale or For Rent signs that graced lawns and windows last time I drove by, wondering in which place Tyka and, likely, her father, Eddie, now lived. They had been known to squat in empty places until caught and then run off. Had they rented legitimately this time?

I wondered if this was what motherhood was like. That ceaseless worry. Even after your children were technically grown, I suspected (feared) it never fully went away. It must be a difficult existence, having to get on with life and not knowing if the little human you'd birthed was all right. The whole thing terrified me. But as stressful as it seemed, I'd welcome it if I ever had a child of my own.

Tyka was a survivor, and that gave me some comfort. Aside from Darryl and myself, she had friends. That future, though—no way was I ever going to stop hounding her about it. No matter how often she got angry and pulled one of her disappearing acts.

They didn't last for long, and once she reappeared, we rarely discussed what had caused the separation in the first place. Sometimes not talking was easier with her.

Thanks to my appointments, I had extra cash on hand. The house needed things, and my shoes could use another sole. But all that could wait. I made a pit stop at Gabrielle, a new Cajun restaurant, and ordered two shrimp and grits dinners for Tyka and Eddie.

The wait was long enough that by the time I got the food, almost an hour had passed. I was carefully setting the two Styrofoam containers in my back seat when my phone rang. It was Tyka.

Noise and shouts in the background. Wind, heavy breathing. "Change of plans. Pick me up near Saint Ann's."

The line went dead.

My blood froze. A memory. Tyka going to investigate something she had seen at Voodoo Real. The blood I found later. The cemetery.

I slammed the door and raced around to the driver's side. The city was a blur. I sped around cars, dodged two men crossing the street, their curses and blaring car horns dying on the breeze behind me.

I hurtled around the corner and saw Tyka and another woman sprinting toward me. I reached over and opened the passenger door. At the last minute, the other woman veered off on foot in another direction. A split second later, Tyka leaped in and banged on the dash, shouting, "Let's go!"

Unaware of what or who was in pursuit, I threw the car in reverse and peeled down a side street. I was sweating. Heart thundering like a rake drum in my chest. Tyka looked over her shoulder, out the back window once or twice, and then . . . laughed.

I was half a mile away before I pulled into a parking spot, cut the engine, and turned to her. "What is so freaking funny? I thought somebody was after you."

"Don't anybody read the internet anymore?" she said. "I can't believe tourists still fall for this one."

I caught my breath. "I'm confused."

Tyka looked at me then. Her face was much the same, her hair in its usual ponytail, only low and pulled over her left shoulder. And was that mascara?

"Man, this scam is an old one. You drive up beside somebody and get them to let their window down. You look concerned and all, like a good citizen, you feel me?"

I nodded.

"You tell them something is sparking under their car. You lay it on and tell them it looks really scary. But luckily, you know cars and can maybe fix it for them. They pull over, you pop the engine. Tinker around for a bit, doing much of nothing. Then you charge a mint for your timely help and get the hell out of Dodge before they figure out they've been had."

I fumed. "Why? Why would you waste your time on something like this? There are a million other ways I can think of for you to earn money less dangerously."

Tyka pulled a wad of bills out of her pocket. "Am I gonna make this much at the McDonald's drive-through?"

"At least nobody will shoot at you."

"I saw somebody take a beatdown over not having enough change in their drawer. That sounds just as dangerous to me."

I hated it when she made these kinds of points.

"If it worked so well, why were you running?"

"This lady, guess she was a little smarter than she looked. She figured out we were scamming her. When she said as much and made a beeline for that glove compartment, figured the jig was up. She paid first, though. That was her mistake."

In a few days' time, two scams had been brought to my attention. I couldn't help thinking about Arthur.

I started driving again, taking Tyka home. We argued back and forth for way longer than we should have before we finally got to their new place. It was only about ten minutes from my house, and I was glad to have her so close. The place had been abandoned. From what I'd heard, the owners were unable to keep up with the increasing property taxes. Maybe her father had used some of those disability checks he typically reserved for women and bars to actually rent the place, but I knew better than to ask Tyka about the specifics.

"What is it you wanted, anyway?" she said after I'd parked a few doors down.

"I need you to find a man by the name of Arthur Stiles."

Tyka typed the name into her phone. When I raised my eyebrow, she said, "I'll wipe it. And it's about time to change this one out anyway."

"I just need a line on where he is. He hasn't been home in a while."

She slipped the phone in her pocket; then, in one of her tones that said she was dead serious—a little worried, even—but didn't really want to alert you to the fact, she asked, "He do something to hurt you?"

"No," I said. "Nothing like that at all. Just doing a favor for a client."

"All right," she said, watching me with narrowed eyes. Searching for any hint of deception. Finally, she got out of the car and leaned back before shutting the door. "I'll let you know when I got something for you. Thanks for the ride."

"Oh," I said, gesturing toward the back seat at the containers. "I tried out that new place on Saint Bernard Street and, since I was coming to get you, brought something for you and Eddie."

"I got food in the refrigerator. Take this on down to the homeless shelter or something." She turned her back and walked toward her front door.

I didn't argue. This was how things went sometimes. But when she went inside and closed the door, I went up to the porch and set the food containers there anyway. Just as I stood up, Eddie opened the door.

"I saw you," he said. "I'll take that food, even if that girl is too simpleminded to accept it."

He wasn't drunk, but he wasn't sober either. He was wrapped in a midday robe, the scent of bacon, not liquor, surrounding him. The red-rimmed eyes told a tale of his drinking somewhere in the not-too-distant past, though.

"She isn't simpleminded," I countered. "Proud. Stubborn. Whip smart. She could use a little support, you know. Encouragement. Some direction."

Eddie reached inside and got something, then stepped out and pulled the door closed behind him. "I know what you think about me," he said, his gaze boring into me as if to frighten me. Inwardly, I chuckled. "And I don't give a damn. I done my best. It's always people with no kids that think they know how best to raise them."

There it was again. Judgment. If I didn't yet have children, it wasn't for lack of wanting, but nobody saw that. All they saw was some selfish choice. Ridiculous. "Is it too presumptuous of me, a woman without children, to expect that a father would encourage his daughter to think about her life, her future? That he would ensure she had good food, not that a fast-food joint or others would handle feeding his child?"

"Tyka is grown. And unmanageable. You don't know everything. I'm trying. Even made her breakfast this morning. And what did she do? Walk right past me like my food wasn't good enough for her." He was breathing hard when he finished.

Tyka was a wild card. But whose fault was that?

"She didn't exactly accept my food offering either." I gestured to the containers at Eddie's feet.

He shrugged. Then he handed me what was in his hand. It was the Southern University brochure, a little worse for wear, but it was the one I'd given to her months ago. It had survived the move. I grinned. She was at least thinking about it.

"You going to pay for her to go to this here school of yours?"

I didn't have that kind of cash, and I had to admit that Eddie didn't either. "We just need to get her to enroll. There's financial aid, grants. Once she signs up, we'll figure out the rest later."

I waited as Eddie regarded me with something on the verge of wariness. Weighing my words as if for truth or if there was, somehow, something in it for him.

"Why do you care so much?"

"Why don't you?"

CHAPTER FOURTEEN

While awaiting my next client, I sat on my little canary-yellow bench, devouring birdsong and the last dregs of a replenishing cup of red tea in equal measure. In bringing out that Southern University brochure, Eddie had doled out a dangerous thing—hope. Unmanaged, expectation could set you up for disappointment. But what was life without having a little something to look forward to? I'd broach the subject of college once Tyka got back to me about Arthur's whereabouts.

Between Tyka's future and Ms. Vangie's felonious husband, I was forgetting myself.

With a few deep breaths, my mind was cleared and centered back on the task at hand. I was a mambo, first and foremost, and attending to the needs of my clients, my community, was where my heart was.

A car door slammed. Footsteps on the path, clicking. The slender woman who emerged was an apparent expert in balancing herself on those four-inch heels.

"Melody Caldwell?" I stood and extended a hand.

"Call me Mel," she said, taking my hand between both of hers, an odd gesture for someone who looked a decade my junior. She wore a pantsuit the color of fall leaves with a matching gold necklace and bracelet. Mel's entire visage evoked the phrase "dressed to impress."

"Come on in." I preceded her into my peristil and closed the door behind her.

"Nice piece of metal," she said, indicating the machete. It sat back on the wall where it belonged. I thought back on my exchange with Kiah in the coffee shop and wished I could put it to use again.

"A gift," I said. "A little piece of home."

"And home is?"

In the early years after we'd arrived here, that question used to give me pause. More than that, it made me angry, as I thought it meant people wanted to mark me as an outsider. It took years, but the anger faded, and I chose instead to see it as nothing more than curiosity. My acceptance became the key that removed anyone else's ability to judge me either way. So it was with a smile that I answered, "Home is right here in New Orleans now, but I was born in Jacmel, Haiti."

"Ah," she said with a smile. "That's what the '1791' means on the sign out front. The slave revolt. No way they want to teach us that kind of history in school. Luckily my mom and dad filled in those blanks."

As had I.

"What can I do for you today?" I sat down and realized I'd forgotten my manners. "Forgive me, can I get you some water?"

"I hate water, but I know I need to drink it."

When I got up to get her a bottle and then came back to the table, she said, "Those are some freshly trimmed ends."

My aura of cool professionalism slipped, and I grinned like a kid. "Thank you," I said. "Just had them done." I took in her own smartly coiffed hair. "I have to say my ponytails never come out looking quite so put together."

Mel beamed. "Can't take credit for the hair or the style. Half the hair is from the beauty supply store, and the sleek style is courtesy of my stylist. I don't even have to go to the salon either. She works out of her home now."

Couldn't be, could it? "Does your stylist go by the name of Evangeline Stiles?"

Mel's eyebrows rose. "You know her?"

I pointed to my hairstyle. "This is her handiwork too."

"You know she used to cheat us, right?" Mel said. "When she worked at Coils and Curls for that hot minute?"

"Yes, that was something, wasn't it?" I'd totally forgotten. Especially since Ms. Vangie was quick to spout off how she'd always worked for herself. It had been a short stint, and I hadn't gone there enough before she left to notice any such thing, but I didn't tell Mel that. I was curious about where this was going.

"Charged whatever she wanted for the exact same service, depending on who was sitting in her chair. Counting people's money. Shady as all get-out."

"Huh," I said. Yet another surprise about Evangeline Stiles. I was beginning to feel like I didn't know her at all.

"She told everybody she left the shop because the booth rental got too high," Mel continued. "I talked to the owner, though, and she kicked her out when she found out what she was doing. Sad thing is, Vangie is good at what she does, so I keep going back like a fool."

"Guess I'm in the same boat," I said. Then I added, "I suppose we should get to it. What brings you in to see me today?"

"It's work," she said, leaning in and crossing her arms on the table in front of her. "It's about a promotion. I want it. I deserve it. And I need to make sure I get it."

"I take it there's someone else in line for this promotion?"

Melody looked away, and her voice lowered an octave when she said, "Yes."

"Are you both equally qualified for the position?" She might think this was none of my business, and for many practitioners it wouldn't matter. I, on the other hand, wouldn't take part in ruining someone else's chances without cause.

My new client sat back as if trying to put some distance between herself and a question that clearly made her uncomfortable. "I do public relations, but I started out in marketing," she said. "A lot of people think PR and marketing are the same, but they really aren't."

I nodded. "PR is more about brand reputation, and marketing is about sales, sales, sales."

"Right," she said, minus the earlier hesitation. She tapped her fingertips together playfully. "Somebody's been doing some reading."

"There's very little I remember from the marketing degree I did at Southern, but that's one of them."

A look passed across her face, as if she wanted to know more, but she forged ahead. "The other person is a friend. A really good friend. I kind of took him under my wing when he joined the company. I was still doing marketing back then. I've gone out for drinks with him and his wife a few times."

Now I understood. Friends were being pitted against each other. Competition. I thought of how I loved my peristil, but I still found cause to be envious of Lucien's practice. I was just as good a vodouisant as he was, yet he raked in the money, while my last few clients had barely paid anything at all.

This wasn't about me, though. "But you feel like you're more qualified?"

Mel blinked. "Yes, but I went back to school to get my MBA. The fact that I only had a bachelor's degree was called out in my performance review two years ago. As if somehow that meant I had no idea what I was doing, while I'm doing the job all along. Anyway, I put in the time, gave up any chance at a social life, let alone a love life. I probably operated on three hours of sleep a night for two years, but I got it done."

"That's great, right?"

"Yes, but Felipe—that's my coworker—he found this error in an ad campaign. A multimillion-dollar one. If that print had gone out, it would have potentially cost us big-time. He caught it, and the company was able to fix the error before launch."

Here, she paused, clearly uncomfortable with where things were going. Rushing at this point wasn't the thing to do, so I crossed my hands, set them on the table, plastered on the most patient look I could, and waited.

Mel pulled her ponytail over her shoulder and played at the ends. She sighed. Her lips parted, but still the words wouldn't come. Finally: "What he did was huge. It even got the notice of our department's senior vice president. The NBA is one of my firm's biggest clients. And they don't play. They can be pretty ruthless with people or companies that cross them."

I had no idea. But the NBA was a big business like all the rest. "But something's wrong?"

She looked down again and massaged the back of her neck. She fidgeted in the chair. "I heard that they're talking about promoting him . . ."

"And . . ."

"There's only one senior leadership position. *I'm* next in line for that role. They told me as soon as the current person retires, I'm in. He retires next month, and I'm supposed to just give up my spot? What they promised to me from all my hard work lost because of one lucky catch?"

Now I understood why Melody was so uncomfortable. I decided to ease her into it. "So you don't want your really good friend to get the promotion? Is that why you've come to see me?"

"He'll get his shot another time. He's smart. He just needs to wait his turn."

I explained how tricky the lwa could be. How sometimes they delivered what you wanted, but in a manner that you might not expect, or be happy about. I took the time to ask if, knowing this, she still wanted to go forward.

"I understand, Mambo Reina." She sat up straight in the chair and set her shoulders. "I have my future to think about. I'm really conflicted about it—I'm not going to lie. But I worked hard for this. I mean, what would you do?"

This was exactly what I despised about corporate America. Not only the long hours, having to beg for time off, asking permission like they employed a bunch of preschoolers instead of adults. It was the cutthroat competition. The constant striving. Sure, some of that existed among vodouisants, but not to the same degree. I, however, couldn't tell her what to do.

"I understand your plight, I really do. But this is your call," I said. "You sure you want to go forward?"

Mel said that she was. I got up to collect what I'd need. Wangas were probably the most popular of my works, covering the entire gamut of maladies and difficulties. And the good thing was, depending on the issue, they could be relatively simple to perform and earn me a minimum of a couple hundred dollars.

I was a little surprised—and frankly put off—by the fact that she would do this to a friend, but it wasn't my place to pass judgment.

I went to the back and got what I needed. A small metal bowl, matches, salt, a fallen piece of tree branch. I pulled the curtain closed and, palming Erzulie's vèvè, opened my pores and released some of my sangswe into the bowl. When about an inch of the bloodred liquid filled the bottom, I turned off the flow. I mumbled a payer to Erzulie and returned to my client.

"Here we are." I set everything on the table in front of Melody.

"Okay." She scooted up to the edge of her chair, whipped out a pair of lovely tortoiseshell glasses, and slid them on. "I'm ready."

I lit the branch and set it in the bowl. A small blue flame erupted at the tip. I pushed the salt container across the table. "Pour a handful into your palm and toss it into the flame."

She did.

"Now repeat after me: 'While Felipe's promotion burns, mine returns.'"

She chuckled.

My gaze was a menacing wintry blast. Vodou was nothing to laugh at.

Melody bit her lip and went rigid as a ruler. Then, in a flurry, a bit too fast for proper effect, she repeated the words. It was as if by racing through them, the weight of what she was doing to someone she'd described as a very good friend was somehow lessened. It wasn't.

"Tonight, take a bath with this." I handed her a paper bag with salts mixed just for this cleansing purpose.

All trace of mirth, along with the cool confidence, had fled my client. "I understand, Mambo Dumond."

I nodded and unpursed my lips. "Any questions?"

Melody shook her head, and I gestured with my chin toward the counter by the door, where my tablet waited for her to post her payment.

"That'll be $250," I said. "Without the tip."

CHAPTER FIFTEEN

The more I delved into Arthur Stiles's background, the more I realized how much I didn't know about his wife and my longtime client, Ms. Vangie. The prim, respectable lady with the black pillbox purse had another side.

Like my mother.

Like most kids, I grew up with one very narrow image of who Manman was. I was capable of seeing her only through one very flimsy veil: mother. It was only through maturity, snatches of overheard conversations, and words Papa spoke in spite that I learned that she was a real-life human being. One with needs and desires that didn't center on me.

Aside from the obvious things, like the height they shared and their predilection for all things proper, Manman and Ms. Vangie had a few things in common. What Ms. Vangie could do with hair was, in my eyes, the epitome of creativity. Manman was creative, too, but in a different way. She'd had a talent for painting and, as a teen, had studied under Levoy Exil, one of the pioneers of the Saint Soleil art movement. It was Levoy's paintings of the lwa that had connected her and Papa.

And she'd given it all up for me. For my father.

My appointment with Melody Caldwell made me think back to how happy my mother had been when I got my marketing degree and, soon after, my first job. I got everything she'd wanted for me: a stable salary, upward mobility, and medical benefits that I didn't need. And for a time, I convinced myself that I had wanted those things as well. If only to make her happy.

But in pleasing one parent, I'd angered the other, and with him, the lwa. They had a plan for me that didn't involve working for anyone other than them.

When I quit after far too short a time, Manman became sullen and withdrawn. Eventually the cold shoulder wore off, and in her way, she came to terms with my choice. Papa, of course, was thrilled.

Though she and my father were living mostly separate lives by then, we'd all fallen into something comfortable. Maybe it wasn't a complete family, but it worked for us. Until the storm wiped it all away.

The Manchac swamplands were untouched by the storm. Papa had begged my mother and me to come there to be with him to ride it out. But when she refused, not even wanting to come to my house but choosing to hunker down at home instead, I couldn't leave her.

I'd thought I could stop it. And we did. Erzulie and me, we faced that storm, channeled its filthy, wretched waters, and sent it back over the ocean and behind the levees that were supposed to be able to withstand a category 5 hurricane.

But they didn't. Whether through incompetence or malfeasance, who knew? It was a debate that still raged. And depending on what new bit of evidence you heard from one year to the next, your opinion could sway.

Like a game of hopscotch, the waters had decided which homes to flood. My street and several others both north and west, whether by Erzulie's grace or sheer luck, remained unharmed. So Papa came down to stay with me, and together, we searched. We combed all ten parishes, combined our magic, and did everything we could to find Manman. But she had vanished.

Traces of her essence were left behind, but every trail we embarked upon ended up a dead end. Each time, our hearts slammed against a wall and shattered a little more.

One night, when the disappointments had grown too much to bear, it all came to a head. Earlier that day, we'd chanced upon a man who had been ferrying water back and forth from Uptown to the Superdome, where thousands had crammed into that awful shelter. He looked at the picture I showed him and swore that he'd spotted Manman near the Jefferson Parish border.

We combed those streets, questioning everyone we could. But the search, of course, turned up nothing. Well after curfew, we dragged ourselves back home. Deflated and exhausted. Too destroyed to exchange even a cursory word between us. Papa retreated to the guest bedroom. I was in the bathroom. I came out, knocked on the door, and asked him if he was hungry. No response. I knocked again, and he grumbled something unintelligible. Back against the door, I slid down to the floor, covered my face in my hands, and for the first time since the storm, allowed the tears to flow. I cried a river. A torrent so strong that it threatened to drain every critical fluid in my body.

My father never let me in. I lay there, curled in on myself, as if my home had become a makeshift womb.

Finally, I composed myself and opened the door.

Papa was sitting there on the edge of the bed, head down. He looked up at me with murder in his eyes.

"*She* did this," he spat. "That woman is not dead. She has always hated what we are, our traditions. She tried to run away before. Now she finally got her chance. She left us. On purpose, I tell you!"

"She would never do that." I had rounded on him, incredulous. "How dare you say such a thing!"

My father jumped up and kicked at the nightstand, toppling the lamp. He pounded the bed, crying out with every ineffectual punch.

I watched, feeling conflicting emotions of anger and sadness. Each time I took a tentative step toward him, his rage sent me backward. Once that rage was expended, he turned his glare in my direction.

Then he collapsed. I had never seen my father cry before. It was if he were releasing everything he'd pent up ever since we left Haiti. It all came out right there, and I held him and rocked him and agonized over our shared pain.

An hour later, he rose. We silently went about cleaning up the mess of the room. He took a shower, and as everyone was low on food at the time, we shared an apple in silence.

We went to the altar, made an offering, and never spoke of that night again.

—

I propped my phone up against a bunch of bananas on the kitchen table, right next to my cup of tea, and called my father on Skype. "Hey, Papa," I said.

"Bonjou, kijan ou ye?" He gave the traditional greeting with a smile. He narrowed his eyes, then added, "What is dragging that face of yours down so?"

"Nothing," I said. Then I added, "Later. How are you doing?"

"Why do you even ask? You know I am well."

He was right; I had always expected my father to outlive me. So far, whatever had ailed him, he'd been able to address without doctors or hospitals. I prayed to our dear god Bondye that his streak would continue.

"Any news from home?" It was an expected question, the polite one. But over the years, the answers held less and less meaning for me.

He went on to tell me about people I no longer knew and places that were as forgotten as a childhood secret. But I listened anyway. Asked clarifying questions at the appropriate pauses. Those stories were like the last fraying edges of a blanket. The flimsy, deteriorating thing that tethered me to my place of birth. Whether because of politics, storms, or both, I hadn't returned. Neither of us had. And that unspoken guilt about it hovered between us unspoken.

At a natural lull in the conversation, I gently turned us to the reasons for my call.

"One of my clients," I slid in. "A good one. She's a little worried about her husband. Wondering how he came into some cash."

I got the sigh and a string of Haitian words or curses that I didn't have the linguistic memory to decipher. The look on his face told the tale of his annoyance well enough.

"You have one job to do," he said, switching back to English. *"Sèvi lwa!"*

"And I'm doing just that," I said. "If I'm doing something for a client, a paying client, then I'm sorry if that doesn't fit your narrow interpretation of what service is, but I don't see anyone else complaining."

"Is this lady, this client you speak of, going to care when you wind up half-dead again?"

"That's overstating it, and you know it," I said. "What amounted to a splinter in the chest. If you'd bothered to come to the hospital, you could have seen for yourself."

Papa's face went stony. "You think I want to see my only daughter laid up in that place?"

He hated hospitals almost as much as I did, and for the same reasons.

"I've been thinking," I said. "How was Rashad able to even do what he did? I mean, he warped everything. Used the lwa in a way he shouldn't have been able to."

Papa considered a few moments before answering. "Don't you think I have wondered the same thing? This is why I want you to keep your head down. Stick to your practice."

"Look," I said, trying to calm us both. "I'm just asking some questions. It's nothing serious, and . . . and I've been practicing the Sphere of Protection spell."

He narrowed his eyes, clearly conflicted. He'd wanted to know all about my progress, but he also wasn't happy about me even needing it. "You have *been* practicing. Tell me something I do not know. *Èske ou fini?*"

Now I was sorry I'd even mentioned it. No, I wasn't finished. "Still working on it, but I'm close."

We watched each other for a few seconds, nostrils flaring, breathing slowing. Papa tilted his head to the side, eyes gazing upward. He was digesting and thinking.

"You are just like your mother," he said finally. "You need my help. Do you think your tongue would fall out of your mouth if you just asked?"

It always came back to Manman. He'd find some way to tear her down. "She didn't ask for your help because everything always has to be your way. You want to rule like a dictator? Sooner or later somebody's going to stage a coup."

"You can take that disrespectful tone of yours and go on back to whatever you were doing."

And the call ended on that note.

—

My phone still sat propped against the bananas. The debate about whether to call him back and apologize was interrupted by a message from Roman.

On my way, bringing dinner, he texted.

Grateful for the distraction, and after the disaster that was Darryl's dirty rice recipe, I thanked him and jumped up to fluff my new hairdo and spritz on some of my homemade perfume.

After yet another tempestuous spat with Papa, we would need some time for our tempers to settle.

At the bathroom sink, loving my reflection in the mirror, I applied some berry-colored gloss and pressed my lips together to smooth it out. Amber spray bottle in hand, one pump of my lavender-vanilla blend at each wrist, and the backs of my knees. Another over my hair.

Then Kiah and his not-so-subtly-dropped bombshell about where Roman was spending his free time clawed its way out of the box I'd tried to lock it in. *Let it go,* said the part of me that just wanted to enjoy a meal with the man I loved. That side was invested, convinced even, that Kiah had only been trying to stir up trouble.

The other side of me, the side that sniffed out trouble like a bloodhound, that knew beneath even the craftiest lie lay an element of truth, knew I could never do that. If it was even a possibility, I needed to know.

Roman pulled up about an hour later. I heard his car horn from where I sat on the sofa. I looked out and saw that all the parking spots were taken. I went out to grab the food while he circled the block.

Ms. Lucy stepped out on her porch, pulling her robe closed. At dinnertime, her hair was still in pink curlers. "Now, I know that man been raised better than to go laying on that horn like that while I'm trying to watch my show."

"I'm sorry, Ms. Lucy," I said. "There was no parking; I needed to run out—" I stopped talking. She had planted a fist on her hip. "I'll make sure it doesn't happen again."

"I know you betta." Ms. Lucy turned on her heel, went back inside, and slammed her door. Just to make sure I wasn't glaring at her back, she peeped out the window near her door. It was my turn to head back inside.

Eventually Roman found a spot a few doors down and came on inside. I heard the front door close, the lock slide into place. The sound of his shoes hitting the wall as he kicked them off. By the time I looked up and saw him in the doorway, the table was set.

The shirt, the color of coffee creamer, was new and fit him as if tailor made. He didn't buy new clothes often; I wondered who he'd made the effort for. His skin shone like polished brass. His gaze settled on me, and my stomach fluttered. Still, I greeted him an inch over civility.

"Tough day?" he said, spooning food onto the plates while I filled our glasses with water.

"Something like that," I said as we sat down. He said grace.

"Your hair," he said, gesturing with his fork. "It's different. Who did it?"

Roman was a detective. He noticed things other people didn't. That he had noticed my hair was a good thing.

"Evangeline Stiles." If he read the angst on my face, he didn't say. "I don't think you know her."

"Don't know her, but I do know her husband, Arthur." Roman shoveled food in his mouth at a rate that would have been alarming to some. But having seen him take two bites of his dinner or breakfast, receive a call, and have to run out, I knew he did so out of necessity. "Didn't see it for myself, of course, but heard he was one heck of a basketball player. You know, in high school, he scored fifty-seven points in one game. Last I heard, he turned into some petty criminal."

There was an opening. This was the time when, if we were a normal couple, I'd share what Ms. Vangie had told me about Arthur and the money. But he'd just lecture me about my place, so I kept my business to myself. It wasn't like he ever told me anything about his work, supposedly for my own protection, as if I needed it.

"What?" Roman asked before pausing. I'd hesitated a blink too long. He regarded me with that look that said he knew I was holding back.

"Nothing." Taking a sip of water, I came up with something. "I was just thinking how much of a shame it is when people can't figure out another way."

Roman cut a piece of meat and swam it around in gravy. "What? No questions? 'What did he do? When did he do it?' That's not like you."

"I'm turning over a new leaf," I said. "Learning to mind my own business." Now that part was not a complete lie. In some ways, I had, just not in this case.

We ate in a companionable silence, the only sound the occasional smack. Somehow we made it through dinner without Roman getting a call. He rose, grabbed both our plates, and dumped the scraps in the trash.

"My kitchen is bigger," Roman said, moving over to the sink before turning on the faucet. I barely suppressed a groan. We were going to have *that* conversation again. "I have three bedrooms to your two. And I have a driveway. We could squeeze both cars in, so I won't have to be circling the block for an hour just trying to come home."

He had not asked my ring size. If I preferred a traditional, destination, or justice of the peace wedding. We had not talked about how we would raise children by respecting both our religions.

"Your bathroom is smaller," I countered. "That driveway of yours is a dirt patch that gets muddy every time the humidity is over sixty percent. And it's in Bywater, not Tremé."

"Ten minutes." Roman turned as he rinsed the dishes in the sink. "You want Tremé? If you just gotta see your old friend across the street, you can be here in ten measly minutes."

I could have mentioned the traffic but decided to let that matter drop.

"Why won't you at least consider moving in here with me? It would be too hard to find another place to put my—"

"I know, your *hounfor*."

"Or *peristil*," I added, impressed that he'd even pronounced it correctly.

Roman's expression was one of a man whose patience was on dangerously low supply. "Other women would jump at what I'm handing you on a platter."

You mean like some stripper? "Don't let me stand in their way."

We glowered at each other for a full minute.

"Here's what we're going to do." Roman reached for a paper towel to dry his hands. "Hand over this so-called rent-to-own agreement. I'll look it over and make sure it's legit. Then I'm going to find another place to set up your business. You must agree to at least look at it and really consider it. Deal?"

I would do no such thing, but I nodded anyway. "Deal."

Roman and I spent the night together. It was full of love, a gentle but fierce mingling of breaths and bodies. Without trouble, without either of our work lives messing things up.

But I hadn't told him about looking into Arthur Stiles's latest exploits, and I knew there were things he kept from me. And I could never tell him about my relationship with Erzulie. That was a part of my initiation, a pact with the lwa and the practice I would not compromise on. Was that really the way marriage was supposed to work? Certainly not something I could ask my father about, or any of my closest friends, really. Everyone I knew had relationships that were in some state of disarray.

These things were as complicated as Sunday's crossword. I hadn't raised the issue of where Roman spent his free time, and while he noticed my hair was different, he never said that he liked it.

CHAPTER SIXTEEN

Long after Roman had gone, his scent curled around every corner like a party streamer, rippling in the wind. Usually, I relished this lingering, but now it was as if the smell of him were a spoon, stirring up a nasty stew of doubt and fear.

All because of that nugget of gossipy dirt Kiah had dropped in my lap.

The closed blinds in the front parlor were Roman's touch. I preferred to let at least some light in, while he thought it provided thieves a restaurant-style menu of items ripe for theft. Aside from the now-fading aroma, it was the only sign of him he left at my place. Nothing of me, not even a pair of slippers, was at his.

Not yet.

Kiah's accusation still rattled around my brain, along with the self-satisfied smirk on his face when he'd delivered the blow. I could have pretended otherwise and tried to dismiss his words, but the nerve he'd struck crackled like a live wire.

And the fact that I hadn't confronted Roman and demanded the truth as soon as he walked through the door told me that at least some part of me suspected it was true.

The answer might mean the end of a dream already tethered between us with the most delicate strings of silk.

Ring.

I didn't recognize the number. There was a risk that it could be a robocall, but I was so accustomed to Tyka changing her phone number that I answered anyway. But in case a recording popped on, I didn't speak right away.

"You just gonna hold the phone?" Tyka said.

This girl. "If you would keep a phone number longer than a week, I wouldn't have to worry about whether or not you were some telemarketer."

"I can respect that," she said, surprising me. "Anyway, I know where we can find old boy. Pick me up at the spot." With that, she hung up, leaving me on the other end thinking, *"The spot"?*

With Tyka, things were never laid out simply. After some internal back-and-forth, I concluded that "the spot" had to mean the latest in the string of places she and her father called home.

Now that I thought about it, she had all the makings of a great police detective. Resourceful, smart, connections in the right places. She seemed to operate on top alert with minutes of sleep.

While I often pondered the idea of criminal justice as a college major for her, those words would never escape my lips for fear of the backlash of suggesting such a thing.

A quick shower, then I dressed and rearranged my new hairdo. After a stop at my altar for a much-needed prayer, I was out the door.

~

The day was easing into a warm October morning. It was that time of year before the cool, when each day could be summer or fall. The sun was on a low simmer, working its way up to what I suspected would be a full boil by late afternoon.

I was glad to have missed the rush hour traffic, and I navigated the empty streets easily enough. Aside from a couple being pulled down the street by a large, muscular dog and a few older folks warming their bones on porch swings and sofas, things were relatively quiet.

I turned down a one-way street and nearly ran headlong into another car, facing the wrong way.

The man waved a hand outside his window apologetically, then backed up and tore off in the opposite direction.

Tourists. New drivers in this city couldn't seem to get the hang of our admittedly confusing layout.

I made my way to Tyka's house a few minutes later. She jogged outside as soon as I pulled up. Instead of getting into the passenger seat, she came around to the driver's side and said, "Let me drive."

"What?" I waved her off. "No."

With the look of a wounded puppy, she took her time going around the front of the car before planting her behind in the passenger seat where she belonged. She had effortlessly perfect eyebrows, while mine thinned to nothing at the ends, and she raised one at me, pursing her lips. "It's not like I don't have a driver's license."

"Let me see it."

Tyka made a show of patting at her sweatpants pockets. "It's inside somewhere."

"You should always have identification with you." There I went again, sounding like somebody's mother.

"My pockets are big enough for my keys," Tyka said. "And ain't no way I'm carrying around something like that duffel bag you call a purse."

I checked the rearview mirror and pulled onto the road. "Where are we headed?"

"Art has been going in and out of a house in the Seventh Ward, Touro Street. You know it?"

Tremé was the Sixth; our drive over to the Seventh would be a short one, but I didn't know this particular street. I shook my head. "I don't."

"Which is why you should have let me drive."

"I can take direction as well as the next person," I said, navigating the heavy traffic.

"No, you can't," Tyka said, crossing her arms.

"I'm curious," I said. "What exactly is it about seat belts that bothers you so much?"

Click. She put it on without argument. Miracles were indeed a thing.

True to her word, Tyka had somehow installed a Bluetooth stereo system when she returned my car the last time she'd *borrowed* it. I turned on the music, the sound of a trumpet accompanied by drums and winds erupting from the speakers.

I could feel her watching me. At a stoplight, I turned to her. "What?"

Her hair had a curved part on the side and was smoothed back into a ponytail. She pulled it over her shoulder, pursed her lips again, and looked out the passenger window. "You and that cop getting back together?"

I held my breath. Why did things have to be so complicated? "We might. Does that bother you?"

"Why would you even ask me that?" She faced me again. I couldn't see the look on her face, as I was a driver who preferred to keep her eyes focused on the road ahead, but I felt her glare all the same.

"You don't even introduce me to your friends," I said. "Aside from Darryl and Eddie, I don't know who you pass your time with. Or where."

"I don't need to tell you everything," she said. Then she softened. "Sometimes, it's for your own good."

"That just means—" I stopped. I didn't want to have this argument again. It seemed all we did lately was battle about her future or her present. Neither was where I wanted her to be, but as Tyka frequently reminded me, it was her life, not mine. "Let's not do this. Roman and

I are back together. But we're taking it slow. And yes, get mad at me if you want, but I want the two of you to be civil, at least."

We were traveling east on North Galvez Street, nearing where it intersected with Saint Bernard, when Tyka announced a change in plans. "I need to make a quick stop."

I cocked my head at her. "You made me an accessory to your little heist the other day; I'm not getting into—"

"You worry too much," she said. "I just want to pick up something to eat. Hang a left, and Rally's is right there."

I eyed her, unconvinced. "I could have brought you something."

"Could have," Tyka said.

Despite my better judgment, I hung a left at Saint Bernard, and a few minutes later, the burger joint came into view.

I pulled into a parking spot. I had food at home and no funds for fast food. Still, I dug around in my purse and pulled out a five-dollar bill. "Get something for yourself. I'm fine."

Tyka sneered at my money and left without another word. I was ashamed at how grateful I was to put that bill back in my wallet.

My friend soon reemerged with a paper bag. "Got you one too." She pulled out a burger wrapped in foil, set one aside for me, and bit into the other. The smell of grease and bacon soon permeated the car.

I quickly swallowed the burger, right along with the guilt I felt for eating such a thing, then doubled back down the street to our destination.

"8421, 8423—there. That's it," Tyka said. "Pull over a little down the street."

If Touro Street was as long and narrow as a bowling alley, the house was about the width of a couple of lanes. The front facade had only enough room for the door and one long window, blue tape around the edge as if in preparation for a fresh coat of paint. Right atop the curb, a twelve-inch-wide patch of spotty brown and green grass. Two large trash cans filled to overflowing sat beneath the window.

Was this one of the ill-gotten houses that Arthur Stiles was helping to flip?

"Do you even know what Arthur looks like?" Tyka asked.

"I've seen him a few times," I said. "But it's been a while."

"I don't." She tapped in a few characters on her phone and pulled up a picture of Arthur in a basketball uniform. "This." She showed it to me. "Probably about twenty years and thirty pounds ago."

"You know," I said in as light a manner as I could muster, "I was thinking about how well you put puzzles together. How many people you know. The rapport you've built up in the community. I know this is going to sound crazy, but hear me out. Have you ever thought about becoming a cop?"

She looked at me as if I'd suggested she become a preschool teacher. Then her face broke into a grin. She snorted. She slapped her knee and mine. Hunched over, laughing. Tears oozed out of the corners of her eyes.

I didn't see the slightest thing I'd said that was funny. "You could be one of the good ones," I said, charging ahead. "And with a degree, you'd be on your way to detective in no time."

"You know," she said once she'd composed herself, "I'm not gonna lie. I looked through that Southern brochure you brought me. I thought about a lot of things I could do. I'd have to study criminal justice to do what I'd really be good at, hit woman for the CIA or, better yet, the NSA. But the last thing somebody like me should do is become a cop. The people in the neighborhood wouldn't look at me the same."

It was a long shot, but I was willing to try anything at this point. My heart latched on to the fact that she'd looked at the brochure. That she'd considered doing something, anything, other than her current form of employment, if you could call it that.

Of course, it made me think about how well we'd worked together during the French Quarter murder investigation. We were a pretty good team. The times when I didn't have her with me, I'd wished I had. She knew people I didn't. Frequented haunts and parts of the city I hadn't and wouldn't venture into. If not police detective, private detective could be the thing for her.

I'd even considered it for myself. I was a mambo, and at no point in my life would my dedication to that calling waver, but the idea of supplementing my income in a way that was fun, interesting, and could help fill those empty hours was tempting. And to do so with Tyka, even more so.

A matter to think about another time, perhaps.

I checked my purse for all the herbs and implements I needed. Vetiver, snakeroot, powders, potions. Making sure everything in the sewn-in pouches was easily accessible. I didn't know what to expect, but with the humidity unnervingly low at this time of year, I'd use the other tools of my trade. Anything south of 80 percent made it more difficult to draw from the air. We wouldn't be relying solely on Tyka's wrestling abilities in case things went south.

"Look." I followed Tyka's finger to the opposite side of the street. A man, tall as he was wide, was pacing back and forth on the sidewalk, gesturing wildly with his hands as if he were talking to someone. Baggy jeans, an overlarge T-shirt. His lips moved as if in a heated conversation. Only it was with himself. No phone or earbuds visible.

And then he cocked his head and stretched his neck forward, peering at us in the car. He became even more irate, his shouts about people messing with him clear now. His massive fists were balled up, spittle flying from his mouth. He stomped over and stopped right in front of my car.

Tyka and I exchanged questioning glances. Normally, someone might consider calling the cops at this point, but I couldn't. This man was troubled. NOPD wouldn't take the time to figure out why.

He slammed his fists down on the hood. Tyka's hand flew to the door handle. "Stop." I grabbed her by the arm.

Just as quickly, his expression went blank. He turned and walked away. He stopped by a small pickup truck that, upon closer inspection, looked to be crammed full.

"He's living in that truck." I sighed. Homelessness after the storm was still an issue, mental illness an afterthought in a town where we'd suffered so much. There was an expectation that one could always just shake it off and go on with life. It was a foolish assumption that had broken families and cost lives.

Tyka sighed. "Me and Eddie are one step off being just like him."

"I would never, ever, let that happen."

Tyka didn't say anything. The tension that had choked the air eased. The man, much younger than I'd originally thought, got in his truck and drove off.

We sat there for several hours, hoping to spot some activity at the house, any sign at all of Arthur. We talked about our mutual friend Darryl, about her new home in Tremé. We alternated naps. Because the sun set at a ridiculously early time in the fall, we soon decided to pack it in for the day.

On the way home, I twisted Tyka's arm into letting me get something for dinner for her and her father. We thought about stopping by to see Darryl but decided to do that another time. We were both bushed.

Our tentative plan was to come back the next day. Stake out a little earlier, even ask around to see if others in the neighborhood had seen Arthur. But that was tricky. Never knew who might tip him off before we got close. But we'd come back the next day, and even if we didn't see him, which I hoped we would, we'd check the house.

I dropped a frustrated Tyka off at home and then drove the few short blocks to my own place, where I fell asleep, fully clothed, on the sofa, thoughts of the huge young homeless man we'd seen still on my mind.

CHAPTER SEVENTEEN

The next morning, before dawn, I took a long spiritual bath with a few sprigs of rosemary, three cinnamon sticks, two palms full of pink rose petals, and a dollop of coconut oil. Called a "road opener," it could help sort out all kinds of obstacles. I lit a white candle and set it on the vanity. One thing I had to always remind my clients of was that the bath called for warm water, not hot.

I blessed the water and slipped into the tub with an exhausted exhale. Strictly speaking, I should have poured a bit of the water over my head, but I'd just gotten my hair done for the first time in years, so that was out of the question. Instead, I splashed a bit on my face.

Rather than focusing on anything related to this case, I soaked in silence, meditating on my breath for about twenty minutes. Sometimes the answers revealed themselves when you didn't attack the question head-on. After a good soak, I got out, toweled off, and cleaned the tub with a bit of salt water I kept in a jug beneath the sink.

Dressed in fresh, clean clothes, I sat cross-legged on the bed thinking, trying to plan out the day. My bedroom was already stuffy. I got up and cracked the window to let in some fresh air. The curtains fluttered like the sail of a ship. Leaning back against the pillows, I couldn't stop thinking about the homeless kid—and that's exactly what I thought he was, probably late teens at best—whom Tyka and I had seen yesterday. He had even troubled my dreams.

He needed help, but I had been so intent on my pursuit of some petty criminal that I'd sat there and let him drive off without a word. I always liked to think of myself as an optimist, my thoughts tuned to the positive. That, however, was only part of my identity. Like everyone, I could be overcome with a nasty case of cynicism. That skeptical part of my brain worried that the teen's situation would end in one of two ways: either an encounter with the NOPD, in which he would come out on the losing end, or, in a turn of the tables, he would be on the delivering side of an unfortunate clash with someone else.

A feeling in the pit of my stomach told me that his story hadn't ended when he'd driven away. Maybe when this was over, I would try to find him.

I glanced over at the clock on my nightstand. Tyka would bite my head off if I dared call her before what she deemed a respectable hour. Problem was, that changed, depending on how late of a night she'd had.

Luckily, I was already dressed. Perhaps I could slip in a cup of tea before we headed back to the house in the Seventh. I got up, fluffed my pillows again, and went to the kitchen. I had the kettle in my hand, standing at the sink, when it occurred to me that we might be spending hours holed up in the car. No bathroom. Uncomfortable memories of having to relieve myself on the side of the road or in a nest of weeds stopped me in my tracks.

I was going to put the empty kettle back on the stove when I heard a thud. I turned, set it down lightly, and waited. Had the sound come from outside or inside?

Thump.

It was clear now, footsteps. I padded forward, spinning a ball of water between my palms, seeping in a bit of my sangswe as I prepared to unleash. But the dining room was empty. And as I looked through the parlor, I saw that it was also clear. The only thing I couldn't see was the corner to the right—the front door, and my altar.

I almost—*almost*—called out Roman's name.

I was making my way toward the front when I heard another muffled sound. I froze, then spun around. I rounded the corner to the hallway leading to the bedrooms.

"What did I tell you about leaving your window open!" Tyka said, sliding out of my bedroom.

I cursed under my breath but quickly let my defenses evaporate. "What are you doing?" I wanted to slap her, but I gave her shoulder a good poke instead.

"What if it wasn't me?" Tyka chided. "Anybody could have snuck up on you."

"You didn't even know I was home," I said, heading back to the kitchen.

"Saw your janky ride parked out front. And more importantly, I didn't see Detective Frosty's car."

"Ever thought of a phone call? A simple knock on the front door maybe?"

"Lost my phone." Tyka pushed past me and went straight for the refrigerator. "I'll get another one later. You need to go to the grocery store," she added, pushing around the few containers of food I had.

I glared at her when she looked at me over the open door. "And what would you have done if Roman was here?" I asked.

"I don't know," she said, taking out the last of my sliced ham and cheese. "Probably set off his car alarm or something. Or maybe had a tow truck hike it up and haul it off. Would be funny to see him chasing his ride down the street in them pointy-toe shoes of his."

She probably would have done that. In my mind, if not outwardly, I laughed. I also stopped to wonder at why she was okay with raiding my refrigerator but scoffed if I brought her food. I settled on the fact that she operated under a set of rules all her own, and it was up to the rest of us to figure them out and fall in line.

Tyka grabbed a steak knife, but before she could dip it into the jar of mayonnaise, I took it from her, got a butter knife, and made the sandwich myself.

"Make that to go," she said, then got up and left the room. Before I heard the bathroom door close, she called back, "Our timing was off. A friend of mine said Art is always at that house at noon. That should give us plenty of time. We wanna get there before him."

I finished up the sandwich, then made another one for myself, too, just in case things went longer than expected.

Tyka came out of the bathroom and looked at me from head to toe, her expression doubtful. "Is that what you're wearing?"

Momentarily unsure, I had to look down at myself. I had on one of my long skirts and a snazzy red T-shirt. "What's wrong with what I have on?"

Tyka gave me a side-eye. "What do you hate so much about thirty that you itching so bad to be fifty?"

Both she and Darryl were always calling me an "old soul." And so what if I was? I didn't follow anyone's fashion guidebook but my own. My friend had, however, shaved a few years off my age. A fact that made me senselessly happy. "Don't blame me if I learned a little early that comfort is queen."

We left shortly after, stopping only to grab lemonade and chips on the way.

CHAPTER EIGHTEEN

"What is your boy doing?" Tyka pointed to a half-full dumpster in the driveway. "Making some side money in construction?"

From what I knew of the man, that didn't fit: a former athlete, petty criminal, and, at least according to the state of Louisiana, disabled. I doubted that construction was one of his talents. His end of the scam had to be something else. Whoever had been doing the work at the house was a little lax with the cleanup. Half the junk that was supposed to be in the dumpster never made it. The trail leading from the door through the grass gave the impression that someone had stood there and hurled the scrap and other detritus. If this was the way things were handled outside, I didn't want to think about what things looked like inside.

"It wouldn't be the first time somebody swindled the disability administration." I checked my watch. "Twenty minutes to spare."

By one o'clock, the only activity on the street had been somebody speeding past on a bike and a city employee half working on a power line. Even with the windows down, the car was becoming unbearably stuffy. Our nerves and patience were running on fumes. At half past one, we decided to eat.

We were a few delicious bites into our ham sandwiches when a late-model SUV rolled to a stop in front of the little white house.

After a few pitiful attempts at parallel parking, the driver gave up and wedged the SUV in at an angle. The engine died with a shudder, and three figures emerged. One I immediately recognized as the impossible-to-find-until-now Arthur Stiles.

The other two I didn't recognize. I squinted, taking them in. Both were taller than even Arthur, who looked to be at least six feet. They were younger, though, shoulders muscular but with the narrowness of youth.

"You know them?" I asked Tyka.

She leaned forward to get a closer look. "No. But that's our boy Art right there."

We waited. It was something in the way his head jerked up at every sound. The stilted manner in which he moved. Ms. Vangie's husband was shaken.

After milling around a moment, checking out their surroundings, they went to the trunk and took out a couple of bags. The boys followed Arthur to the front door. Their glances were different from their host's. Wary, yes, but if my eyes didn't deceive me, they held a touch of wonder. A newness you usually felt wafting off tourists or recent transplants.

As he already had a home with his wife over in Bywater, I expected Arthur to knock. Instead, he whipped a key out of his pocket. In a blink, they piled inside and shut the door behind them.

I turned to Tyka. "I think we should—"

She already had one foot out of the car. I grabbed my bag and, much to my irritation, had to hasten my step to keep up with her. "You don't think before you act. I'm rethinking my choice of careers for you."

My friend only spared me her berry-stained smirk. "This is your show, Mambo. I'm just here to see how it all plays out. Call me anxious, but I can never wait through all those previews before the movie starts. You feel me?"

"Let me do the talking." Erzulie wasn't always available. And sometimes, even drawing on my own defenses wasn't instantaneous. Tyka was the wild card, my backup. Part street brawler, part wrestler, all intimidation. She was unpredictable, but I always felt better when I had her by my side.

We made it to the front door, which, on closer inspection, looked to be barely hanging on by the hinges. Quality craftmanship if I'd ever seen it. Indistinct voices were climbing all over each other; they quieted as soon as I knocked. Were more people inside? Workers maybe? There was no peephole, and the lone window was covered from the inside with what looked like a piece of cardboard. After a full minute, a husky male voice barked, "Who is it?"

"You best open the door and find out," Tyka answered before I could silence her with a glare. She shrugged.

More muffled talk and a light chuckle. I knew what they were thinking. No matter how sure or stern, they'd heard a female voice on the other side of the door. We, in their already-uninformed opinion, were of no threat. Good.

The door swung open, nearly falling off in the process.

I was what you'd call vertically challenged, and Tyka wasn't much taller than me. I had seen Arthur in a picture and from a considerable distance in the car. When my gaze landed on his stomach, I realized how seriously I had misjudged his height. I had to crane my neck back to look up at his face. Traces of the high school kid he had been were still there, beneath a week's worth of salt-and-pepper stubble, a slackening chin, and deeply carved smile lines on either side of his mouth.

"Arthur Stiles?" I said, just to confirm what I already knew. "Evangeline Stiles's husband?"

His eyes narrowed as he gave us both the once-over. "Who's asking?" Apparently, he didn't recognize me. He had opened the door more fully, and I noticed that despite the years, Arthur was in great shape. His chiseled bulk filled the doorway so completely that it barely let me have a peek behind him into the house.

Surprised that Tyka hadn't said anything, I actually glanced over at her before I gathered my senses and spoke. "Mambo Reina Dumond," I said. "Vangie is a customer of mine. Why don't you let us in so we can talk without so many ears around?"

Recognition flickered in his gaze. He glanced behind us. A few people milled on the porch across the street. He was still a bit skittish, and I couldn't help but wonder why. I suspected something more than the house-flipping scam Juju mentioned was going on.

He nodded, then stepped aside to let us in. "I remember now," he said, before concern warped his features. "Is Vang all right? Has something happened? What's wrong?"

Interesting. At least he was worried about his wife. A point in his favor. The fresh-paint smell and the few splatters on a drop cloth told me the room had been painted recently. A workbench had been set up beneath a bank of windows along one wall. It held a few tools, brushes, and rollers. And the source of the shoddy work: a collection of empty beer bottles. Aside from a couple of mismatched chairs, the room was empty of furniture.

"As far as I know, she's fine," I said after he'd closed the door. I warred with whether to let him know that his wife had asked me to look into his affairs. I could spin this. I didn't have to let on how much she had shared with me. Best to leave the money part out. "But she is worried about you. I know she's living with her sister now, and I think she wants to make sure you're on the straight and narrow before she comes back home."

His posture changed; wide-eyed jitters gave way to a frown. And in response, everyone in the room, including my friend and the other two men in the room, tensed as well.

In the moment when Arthur shifted, I got a closer look at the other two men. They were younger than I'd thought, maybe Tyka's age. Either late teens or early twenties. One mirrored Arthur's every move as if he were a younger, thinner replica. His arms were at his sides, but he seemed poised to jump if Arthur bade him to do so. The other kid watched us with more curiosity. In him, I sensed—

"And so what? You and"—Art waved a hand dismissively at Tyka—"you're out here tailing me? You been following me around?" he snarled.

At that point, I heard a charged exchange between the two boys. It wasn't in English or the slang that sometimes sounded like a foreign language to me. French maybe? In any dialect, menace. If things got ugly, I would take out Arthur first. Let Tyka handle the boys.

"I'm the person that's going to report whatever you're doing with these kids to the authorities if you don't change your tone."

"Getting ahead of yourself, ain't you? Who said you going to leave here in good enough shape to tell anybody anything?" Arthur advanced on me.

"She don't need to worry about that," Tyka said, taking a step forward.

Arthur turned his attention fully on her. "I know you," he said, his eyebrows knit tight as a belt two sizes small. "That wrestler from Jefferson. 'Grip.' Thought you'd be taller."

Height mattered. Weight too—in a fair fight. Neither Tyka nor I would fight fair.

"And your wife thought you would be smarter," I said.

"Best listen to the lady," Tyka piped in. "Last I heard, you short on strikes. Next time you get sent up, it's gonna be for a minute."

That last little addition took the tiniest bit of the wind out of his sails. Arthur shook his head and plopped down in one of the stained armchairs. The angrier of the two boys took a step toward the other chair at just the time I did, and Tyka streaked ahead and planted her palm on his chest.

"I know you weren't planning on taking that lady's seat, now were you?" she said. "Come on now, and join me over here."

The boy bristled and swiped Tyka's hand away. "You do not touch me," he said in heavily accented English.

The other kid looked unbothered. From where he stood, we regarded each other with something akin to recognition. But that couldn't be; I was sure I'd never seen him before. There was an essence that surrounded him. Spiritual, without a doubt, but . . . different. Whatever he carried seemed to knock at a door he either couldn't or didn't want to open.

He turned away and gestured for Tyka to lead. Both boys followed her to the corner of the room behind us, where no doubt Tyka wanted to keep an eye on me, the door, and Arthur.

"Why don't you tell me what's going on?" I pulled the other chair around so I could face him and then sat down.

He leaned forward, forearms on his knees. "They're brothers," Arthur said and then paused. He studied his hands, then continued: "Parents are junkies. I knew their old man from a stint in county. They can't take care of no kids, but I dish on them, and everybody loses."

Another pause here, then: "Look at 'em. They're too old to go to some foster care. And who's willing to adopt a teenager? You? This place was empty, and a man I know was fixing it up to sell. He said they could use it for a while, till we figure something else out."

A plausible story. But unless this man he referred to thought thousands of dollars was a suitable babysitter fee, that didn't explain the money. And did this man think I was simpleminded? I'd heard that accent clear as the day was long. No way they were New Orleans natives. Another thread to unravel.

"Sounds like they were very lucky to have you step in," I said.

"I see the way you looking at me. I get it," Art said. "You don't believe a word I said." He turned to the angry boy. "Can you tell the lady I'm speaking the truth?"

Angry Boy nodded. "Yes," he said. "Mr. Stiles is helping us."

I was unconvinced and did little to hide the fact.

Arthur must have sensed it. "You can go talk to the owner of the house yourself."

That was a surprise. "You have a name?"

"Brad," he said. "Brad Wolf. He's working on another one of his spots now. Let me write down his address."

Arthur got up, told the kids not to worry, and disappeared into the back of the house. The one kid, the unusual one, was watching me. An unmistakable current there that I couldn't place.

"You know, I was a pretty good ballplayer," Arthur said when he returned. "A point guard. Point guards go through the game racking up assists. Their job is to help. To facilitate."

He handed me a slip of paper with a name and address. I motioned for Tyka to join me, and we were out the door a moment later. Outside, Arthur scanned the street again and, before he closed the door, said, "Consider this the best assist a point guard can dish. A no-look pass."

CHAPTER NINETEEN

I had never been a sports expert. I'd seen a snippet of a game or two that Roman was watching. He was patient enough to explain the entire game to me, but that lesson had evaporated as soon as the game ended and he planted a toe-curling kiss on my lips. So the whole no-look-pass thing had me stumped. What mattered was that I had an address. On a good day, the address Arthur provided was less than five minutes away.

"What do you think of what Arthur said?" Tyka asked as we drove.

"Who knows?" I admitted. "I have a really hard time believing a former petty criminal has now taken up the child-welfare charge."

"And what about those boys?" she said. "That skinny one said they weren't from here, but the other one, Mr. Mean-Mug, stopped him before he could say where."

I raised an eyebrow. "You mean, like, from another state or another country?"

"Your guess is as good as mine," Tyka said.

That confirmed what I already knew. Arthur had lied. At least once. If they were from elsewhere, that would explain what Juju had said about someone spotting him at the airport. But why and how would he and this Brad Wolf be trying to rescue kids from another country? Had they gone over to do a drop, developed a sudden interest in these kids, and just snatched them up and plopped them on a plane? This whole thing was making less and less sense by the minute.

That voice in the back of my head, the one I was prone to ignore sometimes, said that perhaps now might have been a good time to turn my nose back to my own business. To get back to my healing practice and my work as a duly initiated Vodou priestess. I was certain I had a client or two I could call to check in with. Cold-call to pick up some new work.

And I would do just that after this next stop.

Tyka counted off the addresses, and we found the house at the end of the street, near the intersection with North Dorgenois Street.

It was about the time that school let out, and a trail of uniformed kids marched down the street laughing and talking. A couple of people stood outside talking at a house across the street.

Judging by the dumpster crammed full of debris, the story about Brad being a real estate developer of some sort panned out. Aside from that, no workers were outside, but that didn't mean someone couldn't be working on the interior. Maybe Mr. Wolf did some of the work himself.

We went up and knocked on the door. It creaked open. "Mr. Wolf?" I called, stepping over the threshold.

The front room of the house was a construction zone somewhere between teardown and rebuild. Absolutely no furniture, only wooden planks and tools, paint, and yet more beer cans. The uncovered windows were small enough that only weak light illuminated the space. No sounds of work. No voices. "Mr. Wolf—"

As we stepped closer to the next room, the smell that wafted out hit us with a force that threatened to empty my stomach. The scent of death had implanted itself on all of us who'd survived the storm. It was a gaseous miasma of rotting flesh and human excrement. But there was something else underneath.

We advanced, choking and sputtering. Tyka buried her face in the crook of her elbow. I scrambled to get a few balled-up tissues from my purse and shoved them under my nose.

We followed the stench to what should have been the dining room. A workbench, more construction materials. In the center of the room, strapped to a chair and hunched over, sat the man who was likely Brad Wolf—if that was even his real name.

"What the hell?" Tyka muttered.

"Is he . . . is he breathing?" I knew he wasn't but inched closer. I reached out with my water sense and felt no stirring of blood flowing through the body. He was gone. Probably not more than a day or two at most. His eyes were wide open, as was his mouth, the inside hosting only charred remains and a few white teeth. No blood. Skin looked unblemished. No outward bruises or other injury that I could see. I gagged again as I breathed in. Now I understood the source of the other scent. Burns. And magic. Inexperienced but unmistakable.

Tyka reached out, as though she were going to touch his wrist, but pulled back. "We should get the hell outta here—"

"—and right now," I finished.

As we turned to leave, I spotted a small vial on the workbench. A syringe next to it. Instinct told me that these were useful clues, and I considered taking them with me.

The sounds of a police siren, too close, silenced that thought. Tyka and I froze, instantly ruling out the front door. We sprinted toward the back.

A couple of nailed planks covered the back door. Tyka ran back to the other room, returned with a hammer, and started smashing. I joined her, yanking and clawing away the remaining pieces. Once we'd cleared a path, she waved for me to go ahead. I pushed her through the opening instead and then followed close on her heels.

She took a running start and leaped up to the top of the fence in the backyard. Straddling the edge, she thrust a hand down to help haul me up. I jumped once, then another two times before my hand was in hers. I was scrambling for purchase when I heard, "Stop. Police!"

For a few seconds that felt like a millennium, I climbed.

"I said, stop!"

I had wept and raged over too many videos. I would not risk Tyka. I released her hand and dropped back to the grass.

"What are you doing?" The look on her face melted my insides.

"Go," I hissed at her. The police probably couldn't see her. The top of the fence was shielded by trees and foliage. I couldn't stomach the battle being waged on her face. I begged her once again: "Go. Now!"

She dropped down on the other side of the fence. The blessed sounds of her retreating footsteps were all I had to console me as I was cuffed and marched out front. It wasn't until I was in the back of the police car that I thought about how quickly Arthur had changed his tune and given me this name and address.

He'd known all along and had set me and Tyka up. Wanted us to take the fall for a murder that either he, or someone he knew, had committed.

I'd been so concerned about him underestimating me that I'd turned around and done the same to him.

Roman was going to blow his stack.

CHAPTER TWENTY

It had only taken a trumped-up story about a gas leak for Top Dog to warn his men off the house in the Seventh Ward. The one where the Snowman, the former Mr. Beau Winters, inexplicably still sat decomposing. The whole lot of them had sketchy backgrounds, but just two of the men had known enough to make any noise about him, and now one of them was dead. Certain that the other hustler might crack under questioning, maybe try to cut a deal to save his own ass, the man preferred that the NOPD learn of his crime more organically.

Top Dog had returned to the house a couple of times before, anxious about a nosy neighbor or one of the little shits who sometimes stole pipes stumbling on the body and making a stink about it. He chuckled to himself, relishing every bit of that pun. Anything or anyone to draw attention to the body so the authorities could clear it out, and his team could get back to work. But so far, he hadn't heard a peep.

He was driving down the street for another look when his whole body tingled with an adrenaline rush. Walking up to the house like she owned the place was none other than that short, cocky priestess he'd seen at the Voodoo shop in the Quarter. Her and a butch-looking buddy. What were they doing here?

The man's gaze lingered on the sidekick. Younger than her friend. A loose-limbed stroll. The baggy sweats didn't hide the compact but powerful build. He nodded, the tiniest fragment of a smile forming. She was an athlete—no doubt. Now or in the recent past. She had a definitive swagger to her, one that he recognized. That one had skirted the law. It was all in the way she scanned everything around her while looking like she didn't have a care in the world. And she strutted slightly ahead of the priestess; she wanted to protect her, then.

A formidable pair.

Top Dog drove past them, keeping his head forward, eyes plastered to the rearview mirror. When they slipped inside, he made an abrupt U-turn and crept back down the street. He pulled over a safe distance away. He flexed the fingers of his right hand, open closed, open closed, and waited.

The man figured the smell should hit them before they even found the body. And then, they would either cut and run or turn concerned citizen and notify the cops.

"Come on," he whispered to himself. What were they doing in there? Inspecting the body?

The man was wondering what had led them here in the first place when he heard the sirens. He slumped down in the car and watched as two squad cars screeched to a halt at the curb in front of the house. By the time the officers had piled out and rushed toward the front door, a small crowd had already gathered.

Top Dog's heart was thumping. Hand on the door handle, he was about to get out of his car for a closer look when an officer emerged from the side yard with the priestess in tow. Cuffed. The other one, the athlete, was nowhere in sight.

He settled back in his seat and had a good chuckle as the squad car sped past him, the great lady wide eyed in the back seat. One potential opponent vanquished. He'd hoped for a fall guy and gotten a fall girl instead.

Luck, he thought. *Luck isn't some random "maybe I'll hit the lottery or maybe I'll bring the house down in Vegas" bullshit. That's chance, and an altogether different thing.*

No, luck was being born in the right place, to the right parents. Parents with money were best, but parents with vision worked too. Unless you were a total screwup, that combo all but guaranteed a certain path in life. Not trouble-free, but one blessed with the ability to sidestep trouble and pummel it into submission when the need arose.

That was part of what had earned him the nickname "Top Dog." The man was many things: smart, handsome in a 1950s-movie-star way. But most importantly, he was one lucky bastard.

CHAPTER TWENTY-ONE

The officer who had cuffed me fixed his overly firm grasp on my bicep and led me around the side and back to the front of the house. A gaggle of neighborhood onlookers cast piteous glances at me, filled with shame on my behalf or empathy or both.

I averted my gaze. I was planted beside the police car and left there on display like the day's fresh catch, while my captor and the other officer chatted it up about where they wanted to get dinner later on.

I felt like I was a streetcar hurtling down a broken track that had dropped off into a ravine. I was plunging, sinking, my mind empty, my limbs weak. I teetered there, hoping my life wasn't about to be buried beneath a landslide.

How could I have been so stupid?

The daggers I tried to shoot at the officers held the sharpness of worn stones. Both wore the standard uniforms, minus the hats. From her thick neck to the calves that bulged in her pant legs, the female officer was a rippling mass of muscle. Indeterminate race, but the hair pulled back into the requisite bun had fuzz at the hairline that suggested at least some African ancestry. While her conversation was light, those amber-colored eyes were severe.

The male officer dwarfed her by a few inches and was no less muscular, but he had a lean, hard edge to him. Consciously or subconsciously, his hand kept checking the gun at his hip.

The female officer eyed me with a look on the precipice of hostility, then stepped away a few paces before lowering her voice and speaking into the radio at her shoulder. She cast a glance or two back over at me while she spoke. When she finished, she mumbled something to the male officer, who opened the sedan door and guided me into the back seat. I'd never thought about how hard it would be to maintain your balance with your hands cuffed behind you.

Before I got in, I looked down the street and noticed that my car was gone. Either Tyka or a thief—I wasn't sure which was responsible—but at least Tyka seemed to have gotten away.

To his credit, the officer gently dipped my head to avoid banging it. Nothing could be done, however, for the unsettling fact that I now sat on a seat where untold bodily fluids and other germs had festered. A foul odor clung to the inside, along with whatever commercial concoction had been used to try to quash the stench.

The finality of the doors slamming jarred me to my core. I was entombed inside a plastic clamshell. The floor beneath my feet, the seat, even the plexiglass partition separating front from back, were all hard plastic. No door handles with which to make a daring escape. I would break an arm trying to lean back and kick out a window. I couldn't help but think back about Salimah, similarly accused of something she didn't do.

I was not going to be locked up. That was a given. I'd return home to Haiti, flee to Cuba, run anywhere before I let that happen. My purse was in the front seat with the cops, so my potions and powders were out of reach. Reason. Yes, I'd try reason first.

The male officer got in the driver's seat, buckled his seat belt, and pulled away. Curiously, the other cop remained behind, but before long, I heard the sounds of another siren. Another police car whizzed past us just as we turned the corner. I struggled to remain upright, unable to stretch my legs out for balance. No way did I want my face to touch the seat.

"Officer," I said when I straightened. "You're making a mistake." I stopped. He probably heard that line all day, every day. I cleared my throat of the indignation and tried again. "What I'm trying to say is my name is Reina Dumond. I'm a local mambo. A man named Arthur Stiles sent me to that house. It's him that you want. In fact, it's not far from here, and I bet if you drove there, you might be able to find him and ask him about who really murdered that man."

"You didn't do it, huh?" the officer said. "You get that line off the TV? You a *Law and Order* fan?"

I wanted to scream. Before I resorted to other methods, there was another card I could play.

Roman.

No, I thought to myself. *He'd be furious.* With luck, I could get this all sorted out and be home before he even found out.

"What evidence do you have?" I sputtered. "You haven't even told me why I'm under arrest. What was my crime? Standing in a backyard?"

Come to think of it, neither officer had read me my rights.

"That's grade A murder back there," the officer said. "You'll get your phone call. Now sit on back and shut your trap."

My shoulder and arms were cramped and sore from being pulled back. My wrists chafed at the too-tight cuffs. My skin crawled wherever it touched a free surface.

With the officer's obstinance, it was clear there'd be no reasoning with him. The nearest precinct was probably the one on North Rampart. But as I looked around, I noticed the cop veer off and take an unexpected turn.

"Aren't you taking me to"—I paused, trying to remember the name—"the First District?"

Silence.

"I said, Where are you taking me?"

A steely glance in the rearview mirror was the only response.

Alarm bells went off in my head: it was time to play my last card. First the cuffs. I drew in what moisture I could from the stuffy air inside the car. It wasn't enough. That meant I'd have to use some of my own reserves.

I started with a trickle and willed a bead of moisture into the small keyhole in the lock. After a few minutes, a soft click, and the cuffs gave way. Behind my back, I rubbed my wrists. If the officer heard, he didn't make any indication.

I felt the depletion just at the edges, creeping in. But I wasn't exhausted yet.

Slowly, I freed my hands and rolled my shoulders, easing out the kinks that had already set in. I surreptitiously pulled my hands into my lap.

I didn't recognize where we were. The car had turned off onto a bumpy deserted road with grass high on either side. A cluster of abandoned buildings towered in the distance. My heartbeat felt and sounded like a bomb had gone off in my chest. I would have to do it when we stopped—the one thing I shouldn't. I would siphon the water from his body. It was self-defense, I said to myself, and to Erzulie if she was listening.

I closed my eyes, gathering my strength as the car rolled to a stop. His car door opened and closed. He opened mine. My magic was there, just at the edge of release, when I froze.

There, sitting on the hood of his police sedan, with that look in his eye that said I was in big trouble, was none other than Roman Frost.

It hit me then. They hadn't read me my rights because they never intended to take me to jail.

The male officer reached in to help guide me out and took in the cuffs now sitting on the seat next to me. He raised an eyebrow. "What the . . . ?"

I got out of the car by myself and tossed him the cuffs. Anger swelled within me like a thundercloud. That officer speaking into her radio had somehow recognized me and called him. Roman had set this whole thing up. It was a classic move for him. It was meant to send a message. To teach me a lesson.

I hated it. It was one of the ways in which he treated me like a child. Why not just talk like a grown-up? Why all the theatrics?

Because he could.

I stormed over to Roman's car and stood there with my arms crossed while he and the officer moved away and exchanged whispers, their glances occasionally flittering over to me. Roman handed the officer something, and with a two-fingered salute, he got back in his car and drove away.

Roman and I stood there glaring at each other.

"Why all of"—I waved a hand—"this?"

"*Thank you,*" he said. "You would think the first words out of your mouth would be thanking me for saving your behind from a trip to the chair. But no, I get lip from a woman who looked me in the eye and held back when I asked you, not two days ago, what was going on."

"We don't even talk about your work," I countered. "You don't let me in at all. Where is it written that I have to?"

He cocked his head. "So you being at the scene of a murder has something to do with your work? Were you going to *heal* the dude? Bring him back from the dead maybe?"

"Don't make fun." I stood my ground in front of him.

Roman leaned against the hood of the car, legs crossed before him. That little vein that slashed to the side of his forehead throbbed. "First you're going to tell me what the hell you were doing there."

I fumbled with my skirt. Scratched my scalp.

"You're thinking," he said. "Bad sign. Don't think. Talk."

"My mother always warned me that as soon as someone tells me not to think, I should run the other way."

Roman stood. "Really, Reina?" He began pacing. "That's not going to throw me off of this."

Fine.

"Vangie Stiles—"

"I knew it! I knew you were holding back the other day."

"She said her husband, Arthur, had come into some cash. A lot of it. She asked me to look into it." There. I'd crafted as much of the story as was needed, leaving out the further incriminating details.

"How much cash?" Roman said, stroking his chin.

"An infusion into their bank account to the tune of five thousand dollars." I didn't mention that I suspected it was a larger sum than that. I was tired of standing as if I were under an interrogation lamp, so I went to sit on the hood of the car.

"Why you?" he asked.

I hated to bring this up again. Talking about the events surrounding the French Quarter murder was like ripping barely healed skin from a scar. The only good thing that had come out of that was that Roman and I had found our way back to each other. The other was that certain people knew I'd helped Salimah in some way, if not all the details, and that brought me business. But I didn't want to dredge up that history.

"She figured that some of the people I know might have a line on what her husband was into. Nothing more. All I intended to do was to ask around. I learned that he was seen at that house, and I went to ask him directly. She's worried about him."

Roman didn't take his eyes off me the whole time I was speaking. I held my face neutral and didn't turn away. Didn't flinch, or pick, or swallow.

He gave me a curt nod. "You know what position you put me in? You're lucky Officer Daly recognized you and called me first."

I hated myself for caring, but Roman had at least told someone about our relationship. That this made me happy made me furious at the same time. To be so beholden to one person made me almost physically ill.

"I didn't intend—" I started and then corrected myself: "I appreciate it."

Roman sauntered over and leaned down to face me. I almost puckered up, expecting a kiss.

"And?" he said. His breath was warm, smelling of coffee.

I shifted. "And what?"

"She was with you, wasn't she?"

"She?"

"Don't play with me."

"If you knew, why did you ask me?"

"Why did you leave Tyka out?" he asked. "I don't understand your choice in friends. Never will. But the fact that you left her out of your little story makes me wonder what else you're not telling."

"You know everything I do," I said, then added, "now."

"Arthur Stiles is small potatoes," Roman explained. "Nobody's going to care that he's got a little extra cash. There's a patrolman I know that can keep an eye out for him. But you"—he went around to the side of his sedan and opened the passenger door—"you're going to stay out of it."

I got in the car and allowed Roman to drop me off at home. We didn't talk much, both of us lost in our own thoughts. Halfway home, Roman reached over and rested his hand on top of mine, and I didn't move it away. The warmth traveled through my entire body. He had stepped in to help me, even after I'd lied to him.

As if I already knew my thoughts were traitorous, I turned to look out the window, plotting to get to the bottom of this. Ms. Vangie's husband wasn't the "innocent" petty criminal everyone had painted him to be. He'd caused me to be handcuffed and trotted out like a common criminal. He had put me back in the crosshairs with Roman. Tried to frame Tyka and me for a murder he was likely involved in.

Erzulie sent a rippling wave of ice-cold spikes through my veins. It was time to find another killer.

Arthur Stiles had no idea of the storm that was heading his way.

CHAPTER TWENTY-TWO

Tyka was fine.

After hot-wiring my car, she had trailed me as far as the field where Roman was waiting. Once she saw him, she hightailed it out of there and dropped my car at home. Judging by the state of my gas tank, she had made a few stops along the way. The expletive-laden text she sent along with her new phone number proclaimed what was awaiting Arthur after she finished what she referred to as "some business" with her sometimes coconspirator Bounce.

I had been set up. Played and discarded like a broken instrument.

After Roman left, I drove back over to the house on Touro Street. Surprise, surprise. The SUV was gone. Nobody answered the door. My restored good sense confirmed what I was seeing with my own eyes. The place was empty, taking on that abandoned look once more.

Arthur Stiles was in the wind, and he'd taken those kids with him. I wondered if the dead man's name really was Brad Wolf, and how the two were connected. It was painfully obvious that this was much more than a house-flipping scam. While Roman and the police were looking for the murderer, so would I. My way.

Back home, I got in the shower and scoured myself until the feel and stench of that police car were gone. I threw on some sweats.

Scrying was an ages-old piece of magic. Wars had been waged over who invented it, but that didn't matter. Vodouisants adopted it and molded it to fit our own unique needs. For our purposes, the mirror was used to glimpse the immediate past.

I went out to my peristil and set the lights on dim. I lit a single white candle and, from the bottom cupboard in the back of the room, removed the mirror.

It was a simple affair. More oval than round, about a foot and a half tall and the width of my shoulders. The frame was polished brass with a leafy pattern woven around the edges. I cleaned the mirror with a combination of water and vinegar and set it on the table, in the stand made just for it.

The scrying mirror was a looking glass that showed no reflection. That wasn't its purpose. The surface featured what I could only call an emptiness. Like many tools of the Vodou trade, the mirror should serve only a single function.

Unlike the water-gazing bowl that cost me precious memories of my mother, scrying had other limitations. If you were granted sight, some called the messages unclear, others deceiving. And if too much time had passed, you'd get nothing at all. After thousands of years of experimentation, that range could still only be pinned down to between a day and a few weeks. Beyond that you were out of luck.

I brought the white candle to sit on the table. I bit my lip. I also needed a floral offering. I popped outside and snipped a few flowers from the bougainvillea vines and the other pots I had beside the little canary-yellow bench.

Back inside, I put them in a glass vase and set the arrangement on the table.

The white candle served to drive away negativity and open up the space to the lwa. I watched my breath, not changing, just observing.

Once my heart rate was even and slow, I said a prayer to the lwa: *I will look up mine eyes unto the void, from whence cometh the sight.*

As I uttered the last words, the mirror filled with a fine mist that matured into full, dense pale fog. It was impenetrable. The fog pulsed and swirled, mini tornadoes spinning into existence and then dissipating. Minutes passed. A full half hour.

"Come on," I pleaded. "I have got to see what happened at that house."

Scant details of the scene remained fresh in my mind. Tyka and I had run out so fast that much of it was just a blur. A chair. Electrical wire. The state of the body.

I'd closed my eyes in concentration, and when I opened them, the fog was beginning to disperse. My spirits sank. But as soon as I stood, images began appearing.

I sat back down and leaned in. One figure materialized, face obscured. Then another, this one all shadow. An image on the wall facing the man, vague. Next, a barrage of pictures that raced by so quickly I could barely retain one before another appeared. The tide slowed and an image materialized: a round swath with an indistinctly lettered outline around the fringe, the colors muted. Some kind of insignia? A logo? But of what?

Daring not to disturb the mirror, I turned my head this way and that, studying the image. A fog surged in from the corner and in one swoop blotted everything out. The reveal was over. It was now up to me to take those disjointed pieces and arrange them together into a cohesive story.

I thanked the spirits, cleaned the surface, and put the mirror away until next time.

It was clear to me that the person who had committed the murder was one of considerable strength—and given the state of the body, maybe someone with access to some sort of magic. That meant it was likely anyone but Arthur Stiles. Probably another person who had yet to surface. Someone, like in the mirror, lurking in the shadows.

CHAPTER
TWENTY-THREE

Trouble was coming, sure as a Mardi Gras parade. And it wasn't like the scrying mirror would print it out in bold letters for me. But if you were tuned to the right channels, news traveled quickly in the Crescent City. There was no place more likely than the Lemon Drop to have at least some of the details.

But my practice called—more important work to do first.

Any other time, a client appointment and the potential for much-needed cash would be reason to celebrate. But with everything Ms. Vangie had gotten me involved in, the interruption felt more like an inconvenience.

Unacceptable. Neither I nor the lwa would tolerate that kind of insolence. My subconscious could go to work on this patchwork of clues while I got back to my real job.

I was visiting a client over in Mid-City whom I hadn't seen in more than a year, Nicholas Crown. He was a real estate broker, wheeling and dealing with the swarm of locusts who had descended on the city after the storm. For Nick, the money poured in as if from a broken pipe. The tricked-out car, the imported furnishings for his home, and the closetful of tailored designer suits soon followed.

As investors turned their attention to other areas ripe for razing, Nick's cash flow slowed, and he'd been forced to turn back to selling small properties again. But through his work with those developers, he'd amassed a number of enemies. Namely, people who'd lost generational homes to greed. I wasn't surprised he'd scheduled a money ritual with a general wellness tincture chaser.

With everything I needed for the ritual packed in a satchel, I walked out front and hopped in the car.

Just a few miles north of Nick's house was Mid-City's crown jewel, City Park. Given its thirteen hundred acres, nobody ever really saw the whole thing. Even from the street, so much had changed. Thousands of oak trees had been lost during the storm, drowned beneath several feet of water, but the city had replanted at least half of them. Damaged buildings repaired. The botanical garden was arguably better than before.

A trip that should have taken twenty minutes took nearly an hour. The traffic in this city was well past the epidemic level, and the mayor, the council, nobody seemed interested in doing anything about it except complaining.

Nick opened the door before I even got halfway up the walk. "Mambo Dumond," he said, extending his left hand. The skin on his ring finger was a paler brown where his wedding band had been a permanent fixture. Cheeks that were once plump and fleshy were now gaunt.

"It's been a long time, Nick." I came in and, as I always did, asked if he'd like me to remove my shoes. He declined as usual.

"My cleaning lady didn't show up this week," he said, rolling his eyes in a move I suspected was for show. "You'll have to excuse the place."

The real estate mogul's home was a North Star grown faint, a lustrous gem obscured by neglect. Every surface was covered in a fine layer of dust. The overstuffed silk pillows on the sofa were now flat and limp. On each of my previous visits, a virtual forest had thrived beneath the south-facing front window. Now, their numbers had thinned to two pots, both in need of last rites. I could tell by the lingering smell that he'd smoked recently—something his wife forbade him to do in the house.

"How is Amanda?" I asked.

Nick looked away. "I wouldn't know."

He didn't speak in past tense, which I took to mean that she was alive and well, just someplace other than with him. I didn't press him further; his expression confirmed my suspicions.

A television the size of a small barn teetered on a stand crowded with papers. It was tuned to a sports channel. A perky blonde announcer gazed up at some new official as if he were her personal god. The man wore a striking red tie and matching handkerchief and droned on vaguely about the community and sports youth.

"You probably want to turn that off," I told Nick. Rituals of any kind were best conducted with as quiet and calm a setting as possible. Which was why I preferred to work out of Le Petit Temple Vodoun. Plus, I hated driving. If the client was paying, though, I'd make every effort to accommodate.

"Right, right." He rushed over and grabbed a remote off the sofa, then silenced the noise. "It's great news, though. There's a new recruit coming to LSU next fall. It'll be a big help to the team. We're talking championship material."

I mumbled a feeble attempt to match his enthusiasm while Nick led me into a dining area. Here he had made an effort to straighten up. The glass table, though empty of any decoration, had been cleaned recently. The streaks on the surface told me he had only used water.

Nick and I sat across from each other at the table. He must have noticed how rigid his posture was because he scooted back his chair and crossed a leg over his knee. He flashed a smile, the one that had graced billboards across the city. I hated to admit it, but though I was here, my mind was still traipsing around, looking for Arthur Stiles.

"Why don't you tell me more about why I'm here?"

"The deal was sound." He emphasized the statement by tapping an index finger on the table. "Gather a group of like-minded investors. Pool your considerable resources and pursue real investments. The kind of stuff elites invest in, not what they offer the average 401(k)."

"I've heard of these kinds of stock categories." It didn't exactly matter how he'd lost money, but I was as interested in a good story as the next person, so I simply inclined my head. In doing so, I gave him the stage to spin the tale.

"This was no buy-and-hold scheme. None of us wanted to be on that forty-year road to retirement. This man presented himself well. Had a track record of success to go along with the Ivy League degree. He was a former member of a hedge fund and knew how to spot the up-and-comers. The early Microsoft- and Google-type companies. We were going to all be millionaires inside a year."

At this point, he stopped. I wondered if this was what had sent Amanda packing. "It's okay if you don't want to go on."

His gaze had been fixed out the window behind me, but when I spoke, he snapped back. "You're judging me," he said. "I can hear it in your voice."

Incredible. "You're judging yourself," I said. "And you're probably angry that Amanda judged you, so you're projecting. Don't do that. Not to me."

Nick swallowed and uncrossed his leg, then continued his story.

"We were supposed to meet once a week at the broker's office to go over how our investments were doing. First meeting went fine. Charts, figures. Even a catered lunch. But we show up the next week and the place is abandoned. Desks, chairs, phones. All of it. Gone."

The lure of easy money was a trap. One that snared people in capitalistic societies around the world. The narrative was a familiar one. *Hate your job? Want to have more time to yourself and with your family? You, too, can escape the rat race. With my course and just [insert outrageous fee], you, too, can have financial freedom.* I decided not to ask Nick how much he'd lost. But since I was here, it had to have been significant.

"That had to be tough. Did you involve the police?"

He made a small, incredulous sound and waved a hand. "Some of the other members said they were going to try, but I wasn't going to embarrass myself. They went right on down there, against my advice, and got laughed out of the damned station. Cops don't care about this kind of thing."

I knew him to be right. I could only guess at the horrors that consumed Roman's nights and some days. Our agreement not to discuss it, he said, was for my benefit.

"Let's get down to business," I said. "You have the things I told you to get?"

"Yes, right here." He reached over to grab a box sitting on the floor. He took out the items one at a time. Green and gold candles, a clean glass candleholder, and a glass dish.

From my purse, I removed my supplies:

- a swatch of kelly-green fabric
- sea salt and pyrite
- a hunk of charcoal
- matches
- the piece of paper where I'd written out the spell
- a small bottle of general wellness tincture

I instructed him to take three drops of the tincture morning and night for two weeks. Then I took the piece of fabric and laid it flat, one corner facing my client. In the middle, I placed the salt and pyrite. Finally I folded the corners into a small bundle and tied it closed with a piece of string.

"The charcoal?" Nick needed to pick it up and hand it to me.

I set that on the glass dish. I whipped the match alongside the edge of the box, and flame erupted. I lit the charcoal, then watched it catch and begin lightly smoking. "Now take the charm bag and pass it back and forth over the smoke. High enough so it doesn't catch the flame."

I handed him the paper, words written in clear blocks. "Repeat this nine times."

He took the paper and read: *Essence of light, earth, and fire, make me whole. Show me the way to recover what was lost; exact no price and no cost.*

After he completed the ritual saying, I doused the flame and told him to dump the charcoal in the trash. When he came back, I provided the final instruction: "Keep this charm bag with you at all times."

"Like in my pocket or something?" he asked.

"If you're home, it doesn't have to be on your person," I explained. "But if you leave, take it with you."

He nodded. "I can do that."

"Now, the lwa will determine how and when prosperity will grace you."

He looked deflated, and I understood why. This was the toughest part of the practice. People expected the lwa to be at their beck and call. They didn't work that way. There were matters of their own, things that we, the living, were not privy to. Time didn't even work the same way for them.

"It could be something you find, an inheritance—"

"I doubt that." He chuckled.

"Lottery winnings. Even a new job."

He perked up. "I'm not one for the lottery, but if I play it, I'm taking the charm bag with me, right?"

"You got it," I said as I stood and gathered my things. "There will be times when you'll expect something. If it doesn't come to you, understand that the lwa are sending you a sign that it isn't right for you. At least at that time."

"I can't say I don't wish I could have an idea of when I'm going to be out of this bind," he said. "I have bills that I'm not going to be able to pay this month. Well, after next month, at least."

And here it came.

"I appreciate you coming out here to help me. You've always done right by me, so I set your money aside."

Nick paid. In cash.

"But there's one more thing."

I stood there, table cleared, purse on my shoulder. Nick hadn't budged. I tensed.

"Nick," I said. "Something wrong?"

He glanced up at me with an expression that was troubling. He was struggling with whatever he was about to do or say next. He shook his head. Palmed his face with both hands. Rubbed at his skin. When he looked up at me again, his eyes had gone cold.

"I need to put a hex on a man."

I sat back down and waited patiently for Nick to compose himself.

"I guess I should tell you why I need the hex." He thrummed his fingers on the table. The nails, slightly browned from tobacco, sounded like rain pattering against a windowpane.

I clasped my hands together on the table. "That's as good a place as any to start."

He chuckled, more a nervous cackle than from mirth. "You can't trust anybody these days." He swallowed down what was probably a sizable lump in his throat a few times before he continued. "I lost a lot of money. I'm not talking chump change here. I had to get some of it back, and fast. And what do I get? Another con artist takes advantage of me. Cheats me."

It wasn't unusual for people to put one thing on the appointment and then ask for something altogether different. In this case, Nick had paid, then sprung the whole two-for-one thing on me. But depending on what type of spell he wanted, it was possible that I couldn't help him.

"Let's start at the beginning," I said.

"It sounded good at first," Nick began. "An investor wanted to buy a few homes in the Seventh Ward, of all places. You know that's not typically my area."

Nick fashioned himself an Uptown, Garden District type of broker. Perhaps he had been five years ago. Now, whether he wanted to admit it to himself or not, he'd sell a one-room shack in the swamp if he had to.

"And something went wrong," I coaxed.

He nodded. "This man asks me to keep an eye out for distressed properties. Cheap homes. If I helped him get them before they made it to the MLS, there would be a small finder's fee."

"Sorry, the what?" I asked.

"The multiple listing service. Anyway, these homes aren't advertised, you know. I spent hours driving around looking for those 'for sale by owner' signs. Canvassed neighbors, knocking on doors. Half the people slammed the door in my face; the other half sicced dogs on me. But I still delivered. Countless properties. Needless to say, I never saw one dime of money for my trouble."

In layman's terms, I thought to myself, a kickback. Nick had gotten cheated, and it was likely what he deserved.

"How did this man approach you?" I asked.

"We went to high school together," Nick said. "I didn't really deal with him much after that. He called me at my office."

"And what do you want done to him? Hexing can mean different things to different people."

"Don't get me wrong. I don't want him hurt. I just want him taught a lesson."

There were spells. "Hex the Perp," "Damnation," even one attributed to the great Marie Laveau. But I wouldn't use any of these things for Nick.

Sometimes people didn't understand that I was a healer first. Had I done things to protect myself that caused harm? Yes. Would I willingly cause harm for money? No. There were, however, spells that would take away an enemy's power to harm. I was thinking about a confusion spell.

"I don't have the things I'll need for the spell I have in mind," I told Nick. "You'll need to make another appointment." *And pay another fee.*

Nick looked disappointed but said that he understood.

It dawned on me then: How had this person even found him? "You said you didn't really see this man anymore. Why not?"

"He's a criminal, for one," Nick said, and when he saw the look on my face, he added, "I know, I should have seen it coming."

Something tickled at the back of my mind. "Does this criminal have a name?"

"He sure does, and I hope you curse it. Arthur freaking Stiles."

CHAPTER
TWENTY-FOUR

"Don't tell me," Darryl said as I dragged myself through the front door of the Lemon Drop and plopped down on a barstool right next to the bar's permanent fixture. "You finally finished season five of *Game of Thrones*."

"Chicken," I said to Darryl's other best friend.

He raised a glass. "Hey, *cher*."

The Lemon Drop was fairly empty at this time. The late crowd had yet to arrive for their evening festivities.

To my friend, I only shrugged. "Can I have some tea, please?"

"Chicken," Darryl said as he reached beneath the counter and pulled out my tea. "What's done gotten into this girl? Walk in here with her face dragging against the floor and don't even give me a proper how-de-do before making demands about tea."

"Downright disrespectful," Chicken said, nudging me in the ribs.

"I ought to slip her a bag of Lipton instead of this fancy jasmine mess she loves." Darryl slapped the tea bag on the counter and continued mumbling as he walked toward the kitchen and called out for Wes to boil the water and bring out a cup.

"All right," Darryl said when he returned. He slapped a towel over his shoulder, leaned back against the counter, and said, "May as well spit it out."

There was nobody near us, and the only other people in the bar were in the far corner near the stage.

I told him and Chicken about everything that had happened so far, from talking to Juju, to tracking Arthur, to being set up to be present at the scene of the murder. I capped it off with a not-too-overly-dramatic retelling of how I'd been unceremoniously cuffed and dumped in the back seat of a police car.

Darryl did something he rarely did during the day: poured himself a shot and tossed it back.

"Top me off too." Chicken signaled for another drink.

"Beau Winters," Darryl said. "That's your vic."

"Goes by a nickname. The 'Snowman,'" Chicken said. "Least he used to."

Beau Winters. That wasn't the name Arthur had given me, but it *was* the one that had Ms. Vangie all tied in knots. "Wait. Are we talking about the same person? Found at a house on Laharpe Street?"

Darryl nodded. "One 'n' the same."

Of course he'd know. If Roman knew, then so did his partner, Darby. It still annoyed me that Darryl had kept that friendship a secret.

"Why do they . . . I mean, why *did* they call him the 'Snowman'?"

"He was some big-time ballplayer," Darryl explained. "They said he had ice in his veins. That and his use of a certain white powder that cost him his career is how he got the nickname."

I had a name at least. But why? Why had Beau been killed?

"You obviously have this all figured out," I said with a little ice of my own in my words. "Why don't you go ahead and tell me."

"Chicken knows a thang or two," Darryl said and then gestured for Chicken to tell me.

"Seventh Ward, you say?" Chicken asked.

"Well, Chicken was working on a house in the Seventh Ward," Darryl said, charging in as usual. Chicken's mouthpiece. "Fast, sloppy work. High pay, though. The Snowman and Art were the ones directing the contractors on the work. Ain't that right, Chicken?"

"Sho' as the day is long," Chicken droned.

This played into what Nick had said about selling those homes to whoever Arthur's financier was.

"Huh." I thanked Wes as he set the cup of hot water on the counter in front of me. I dropped my tea bag in. "This doesn't make any sense. What are we talking about here? House flipping? Using kids for free labor?"

"What did Juju have to say?" Darryl asked.

"He's also leaning toward the house-flipping angle. But that still doesn't explain the kids."

Darryl, Chicken, and I considered that in silence for a few moments. I sipped my tea. Too hot. Just under boiling brought out the best flavor in the tea and prevented third-degree burns in the process.

The door opened, ushering in a few new customers just as Chicken stood. "Best be getting on home. You watch yourself now, you hear?" He held my gaze and only broke it off when I nodded. He waved to Darryl, who had gone to get his customers seated at a table, and left.

I blew on my tea, took one more too-hot sip, and gathered my things. Arthur thought he'd framed me, probably Tyka too. He wouldn't know that wasn't how it had turned out, and for as long as I could, I would use that to my advantage. He probably assumed that he and whatever scheme he was involved in were free and clear at this point.

Not a single chance.

I couldn't let Arthur get away with what he'd done. It was time to take another trip to the Seventh Ward.

A light rain had started falling as I left the Lemon Drop. I walk-sprinted down the block to my car.

The more I thought, the angrier I got. When I arrived at the house on Touro Street again, raised voices and the sound of music rode out through a partly open door.

I barged in, leaving the door cracked behind me. The three men standing there—one with a paintbrush, the other stirring, and a third beating out a rhythm on the bottom of a plastic pail—all stopped to gape at me. None of them were the two young men from the day before.

"Where is Arthur Stiles?" I craned my neck, trying to see in the back of the house. I bet he was here someplace. The house had gone silent.

One, the drummer, stood and walked slowly toward me. Swagger, confidence, even amusement painted his face. "I'm guessing if Arthur wanted you to know where he was, he would have told you. So why don't you turn around and you and your little skirt waltz back out the way you came."

The other two men had turned back to their tasks and, aside from glances over their shoulders, ignored me.

Men were always so sure of themselves. I gave the drummer my best side-eye and went to move around him. "You may as well come out and face me," I called to the man who'd tried to set me up. I wouldn't have been surprised if that coward was holed up in a closet somewhere.

The drummer stuck out his arm to stop me. "Where do you think you're going? You don't hear too well?"

"Get out of my way." I didn't even look at him. There was steel in my voice and my back.

I was certain he intended to grip my arm hard enough to make me cry out, but he only got halfway before Erzulie flared and I turned, my right hand extended, calling the water through the door and to me, unseen by my attackers. I drew it in, drunk on its fullness. Seconds stretched where the drummer and his cronies stood stock still.

When I was full, I opened my eyes and flashed the smile of a predator.

I shoved the drummer and drew my hands together, mixing in a bit of my sangswe wine. I splashed it on the drummer and watched as he stumbled backward, wrapped in a rainbow that held him tight.

He screamed out, and the other two took a step forward, but with a glance from me, they backed away.

"Mambo," I heard one whisper as I darted forward and checked the remainder of the house. No sign of Arthur or the boys. On the kitchen counter, I did find a small white business card, bearing the name of none other than Gwendolyn Guillory. An official-looking stamp and a website. New Light Charter School. I pocketed the card. The only other things I found were an open back door and footsteps leading away, indentations in the grass.

I followed the trail out front and glanced up and down the street. Empty. Arthur Stiles had been there, I was sure, but he'd escaped. No matter. In time, I, or Roman, would find him, and he would pay.

CHAPTER
TWENTY-FIVE

No rebuke had come from Erzulie. Quite the contrary, the absence of any sign from her meant that she thought I'd done what I had to do in defense of myself.

Now I wanted nothing more than to go home, take a bath, and crawl under the covers. Anytime you called to the lwa, invited them into your body, you were left exhausted afterward. That energy needed replenishing.

I turned the corner of my street with that thought in mind. So much so that I could almost feel the soothing water of the spiritual bath I'd prepare. But there, in my parking spot, was Lucien's car.

And there wasn't one other space available. I sighed, reached in my purse, and blew out a powdery concoction I saved for just these types of emergencies. In a few minutes, someone raced out of a house a few doors down, and just like that, a parking space opened up.

Kiah stood beside the car like a sentry guarding a gate, his back stiff, head lifted, gaze somewhere off in the distance. All that was missing was a uniform and a sword. But when the wind rustled that ridiculous long black coat of his, I saw the tip of his machete sticking out of an inside pocket. We exchanged sneers.

"I see you've been promoted to driver," I said.

Kiah took his time surveying my house and me, then said, "And I see you're still the second best, running your two-bit business out of your garage."

Lucien rolled down his window. "Get in."

Without a suitable retort, I walked around and got in on the other side of the car.

Snakeskin shoes on the plush, dark flooring. Dry cleaner–pressed navy slacks. Lucien had forgone his ubiquitous blazer in favor of a sweater, probably cashmere. How he managed to look twice his height and half his age could only be attributed to the lwa Agassou.

"That was a frivolous use of magic if I've ever seen one," Lucien announced, punctuating his judgment with a catlike purr. A sound that never ceased to raise goose bumps on my arms. He probably didn't even realize he did it. The leopard king to the end.

"If you'd kindly removed yourself from my parking spot, I could have saved the energy. You coming inside?" I hoped he wouldn't.

He looked around, and an unreadable expression crossed his face. "Can't," he said.

Thank the benevolent god Bondye.

Lucien rolled up his window. The man doled out trust as if it were on some endangered-resources list.

"Why the interest in Gwendolyn Guillory?"

I considered his question and decided it was none of his business. "If I tell you, would it change the information you have for me?"

Lucien's expression said that I'd scored a point with that one. "Privately, Gwendolyn Guillory has made some friends and some enemies. Publicly, she was fairly popular around the community. Liked kids and was pretty easy to talk to."

"So far, she sounds like Mother Teresa. What's the catch?" Despite my loss of energy, I was perking up.

"Her file reads like she was darn near a Rhodes Scholar, with a seven-figure law career before she gave it up and took to the bench to serve the people, albeit with a notably stern hand," Lucien said. "Officially? Her record is as clean as a whistle. Retired with full benefits."

"But there's more."

"That's the story they printed in the papers," Lucien said. "But some say she was forced into that retirement. About a decade early. The infraction that sent her out the door, unknown."

It was equally possible that Lucien did know and was just choosing not to tell me. I said, "Stands to reason that whatever she did was bad enough to cause her to lose her seat, but it was sanctioned by someone important enough to cover it up."

"So it would seem." Lucien reached into his pocket and consulted a notebook. "She lives over in Lakeview. Since you fancy yourself a detective nowadays, you'll have to find her address yourself."

I knew he had that address right there in his notebook. It crossed my mind to snatch it and run. But faster than I could blink, he'd slipped it back out of sight. I exhaled a tired breath. "I appreciate the information."

"I know you'll probably go talk to her, but keep my name out of it. If you don't, I'll deny it."

"I'd expect no less." I opened the car door and was about to head toward the sanctuary of that much-needed bath when Lucien's words caught me in a snare.

"There's just one thing I need in return."

I stopped and made a show of turning around. Favors came with a cost, yes, and I thought I'd already paid mine by agreeing to support his bid to lead the "Voodoo" council. I shouldn't have been surprised he was asking for more, but I was. "And what would that be?"

Lucien turned and leveled that unsettling feline gaze of his on me. "My practice is a prosperous one, and neither I, nor the lwa, are ashamed of the fact. But what that means is that I need to unload a certain segment of my clientele."

"Let me guess. The ones without deep-enough pockets to keep a driver on call?" I shook my head. "You see, that's the problem with you. You think money means everything."

"I knew you'd get emotional about this."

"I'm not emotional, I'm insulted."

Lucien sighed. "I've got two kids that have no interest in our practice and a cat that my wife loves almost more than me, but for obvious reasons, the creature can barely stand to be in the same room with me. My phone rings nonstop, everybody needing something. Including you. You don't know me or my life."

"And you don't know mine."

I got out of the car without another word.

CHAPTER

TWENTY-SIX

The fact that Gwendolyn Guillory, newly appointed charter school owner, lived in Lakeview told its own story. Named for its close proximity to Lake Pontchartrain, the area was a veritable postcard of picturesque cottages and homes. Aside from the Garden District, it was the neighborhood those who wanted to make a statement about all they had accomplished chose to call home.

Obstinance being his preferred state of existence, Lucien had refused to provide the address he surely had. I powered up the computer, and a few clicks and taps later, the New Orleans property-search website solved that puzzle. It really was concerning how much information was publicly available.

With luck, Arthur would be there.

Tyka in tow, I drove north and west of Tremé. Down Canal Boulevard and just past the always-buzzing Harrison Avenue. A few turns later, we found the address on Milne Avenue.

The home was an impressive two-story, partially brick-faced affair. The circular drive gave the effect of a mini mansion. The carefully carved shrubs and verdant grass, trimmed and edged to perfection, were the

work of a professional. A walkway was lined with potted chrysanthe-
mums and pansies and marigolds, all in lovely fall bloom, likely planted
by the owner. A pair of exceptionally creepy winged gargoyle statues
reigned over either side of the crowded flower beds.

"Let me do the talking," I told Tyka as she trotted up the freshly
swept steps. She rolled her eyes at me as I did the more sensible thing,
grabbing the railing and planting my foot firmly on each step.

"Not my strong suit anyway," Tyka chirped and then flashed me
her smile.

The porch spanned half the length of the house. A couple of
Adirondack chairs and a small table filled the space. At the end, a
wooden swing hung from thick metal chains attached to the ceiling. A
nearby camera was pointed in our direction.

That it was working and not there for show was confirmed when
the door swung open before I could push the ornately gilded doorbell,
and the five-foot-three menace that was likely Gwen Guillory glared at
us. She swung her massive head between Tyka and me, then glanced
over my shoulder, taking in my aging car before leveling her ire back
at us.

"What?" she barked at Tyka—not me.

Gwen wore a pink two-piece jogging suit and so much makeup I
wondered if she had to peel it off with a butter knife at night. She had
a face that, minus the scowl, may have been called pleasant. Something
had her wired up. Maybe whatever had gotten her ousted from the
bench.

Or a recent murder.

I opened my mouth, ready to deploy the cover story I'd cooked up,
but Tyka, who was never good at following instructions, snapped back,
"That ain't no kinda way to answer the door."

Gwen planted her hands on her hips and cocked her head. "Have
you been in my courtroom?" she asked Tyka, narrowing her eyes. "You
look familiar."

If I hadn't seen it myself, I wouldn't have believed it. Tyka . . . blanched. She blinked, mumbled under her breath, then looked away.

It was time to put a stop to this and right the course. "Excuse me, Gwen—"

"Judge Guillory," she said, turning her wrath back on me. "My name, which I guess you already know, is Justice Gwendolyn Guillory. People that I call friends only make the mistake of calling me Gwen once. And you aren't one of them. What you need to do right now is hop back in that piece of junk littering my drive and go on about your business."

"Ex-judge," Tyka corrected, apparently recovered.

"Justice Guillory," I said, trying again to wrestle back control. "I'm . . ." I faltered. The story I'd concocted didn't include a name, and no way was I giving her mine.

She saw the opening and charged in. "I'll give you thirty seconds to come up with whatever absurd alias you want," she said, tapping her foot. "Make it good."

Even Tyka remained silent. "Gwen" went to close the door.

"Beau Winters is dead." The door stopped closing. And almost instantly, I saw that the fact that she'd let us see her stumble irritated her. She knew the name, check. Time for another.

"Murdered," I said, charging on. "And whatever scam Arthur Stiles is running is behind it. I'm thinking that somehow, someone wanted to cheat someone else. And as always, these things end up in violence."

But what I didn't know was how a judge was involved.

"Sounds like a good story you need to tell to the police," the ex-judge said. Some of the wind had abandoned her sails. "I don't know what you think that has to do with me."

She was right. Gwen was now an owner of a school—career change for certain but, with her daughter's experience, not outside the realm of possibility. That would explain the kids: perhaps they were going to this school. Perhaps they were also being exploited for free labor.

I lifted my chin. "I was hoping you could tell us just that," I said. "I think that you are involved with Arthur Stiles. I know you've been seen with him. Your relationship could be both professional and personal."

It started as a smirk, then worked its way up to a chuckle; when she doubled over with a full-bellied laugh, my blood was boiling. Tyka and I exchanged uneasy glances. A sharp tongue, I could handle. Danger, Tyka's space and mine. But ridicule? Neither of us knew what to do with that.

"Me," she sputtered, "and that lowlife Arthur Stiles." Her laugh trailed off, and her face turned mean again. "Get the hell off my porch before I call the police. In fact," she said, "I'm going to call them right now."

Gwen slammed the door in our faces, and we made no attempt to stop her. After our last encounter over in the Seventh Ward, we did the only thing we could when we realized we'd been bested. We ran.

I got in the car and looked back to see Tyka wrenching one of the gargoyles from where it sat in front of a shrub. She hopped in the front seat clutching the monstrosity. I gave her a look before I tore out of the driveway.

I didn't even have to remind Tyka to put on her seat belt.

"That old lady is crazy," Tyka said and then laughed. I couldn't help myself and laughed along with her as I took Canal Boulevard on two wheels, right back the way we'd come. Luckily, I heard no sirens in the distance. That part, it seemed, had been a bluff.

Lucien's words—"easy to talk to"—rattled around in my brain, along with the wretched image of his mocking grin.

Without saying a word, Gwen had still confirmed a few things for me. However briefly, she had reacted to Beau Winters's name. She hadn't known he'd been murdered. That was clear in her eyes. So that ruled her out as a suspect. And she didn't exactly deny knowing Arthur either. My theory of a torrid affair, though, was dispelled.

I had already come to the conclusion that the stakes at play here were higher than a simple house-flipping scam. High enough that a man was dead. This was no longer about a petty criminal. Arthur had tried to frame me. I'd follow the money, and maybe that would lead me to the killer.

Beau's death had not been an easy one. The signs on his body, the smell of it emptying of its fluids, pointed to a slow, torturous end. I hadn't seen the likes of it since the storm. A nagging feeling had been pulling insistently at the fringe of my mind ever since we found Beau's body—a possibility that I could no longer, in good conscience, deny. Magic, of the vodouisant variety, was in play.

CHAPTER
TWENTY-SEVEN

Tout lapriyè gen amèn.

Another of my mother's favorite Haitian proverbs. Roughly translated, it meant all prayers have an amen. Break that down a little further, and what that really meant was that all beginnings have an end.

Because my mother loved proverbs, my father had to hate them. Nothing was ever easy between those two. "Platitude," overused and common, was what he called these treasured words of wisdom. Why bother, when any lesson worth teaching could be delivered with exacting efficiency by action—a swift kick to a shin, a bruised ego, a lighter pocket? "Trite," he called them on a good day, "nonsense" on others.

I supposed this was why Manman had used them so freely. This one especially. It was something she'd once used to console me when I'd lost a young friend to a forgotten illness.

Whenever I encountered death, her words came back to me. And this murder had stirred them again.

You would have thought that the hurricane a decade earlier would have been enough death for a lifetime.

In other parts of the country, people referred to the disaster that struck New Orleans on August 29, 2005, as Hurricane Katrina. But the folks who lived through it called it "the Water."

Now, water, in and of itself, isn't good or bad. It can take the shape of anything. Just enough causes things to grow; too much, and it can drown. Water is our lifeblood, but it is also apathetic.

The warnings had come, like others, so many years prior. I'd lived in New Orleans long enough to have learned from the natives. You get some supplies, you board up the windows, and you ride out the storm. There was no reason to leave and, often, nowhere to go.

It surprised everyone else that we felt that way, but only locals could understand it. So most of us didn't heed the early warnings, and by the time Mayor Nagin called for evacuation, for many, it was too late.

After the storm, my father and I combed the streets, searching for traces of my mother. She was as defiant as Gwen Guillory.

I could recall a blue-and-white newspaper box, still stuffed with waterlogged newspapers, a headline, dated a few days earlier, that read **Katrina Takes Aim.**

Weeks and months after, abandoned cars littered the city like left-over candy wrappers. Houses, some in my own neighborhood, marked with red *X*s—a sign that there was nobody left living on the premises.

My mother's house also had a red *X* on it, before Papa and I tore the place down.

Much of the police force had gone AWOL. Some were swept away; others had escaped with their families to one of the many places that offered New Orleans residents a welcome and a warm meal. Who could blame them?

Many of those who remained took up residence on one of two Carnival cruise ships, aptly named *Sensation* and *Ecstasy*.

Of all the things I could remember from that time, it was the smell that still haunted me the most. It was the scent of an ending. A turning point of sorts, one that told us that if and when the city recovered, it would never be the same. Streets and homes overrun with a gruesome pulp of trash and raw sewage. And those who didn't survive left their own mark. Human and animal bodies, decaying in attics, or in plain sight.

When the cleanup began, the cars, the torn roofs, and the shattered glass. When it all was removed and swept away, buried among the shame of a country that either could not or did not want to react quickly enough, the smell still remained.

Chirp. A text message from Roman snapped me from my reverie. We hadn't spoken since he'd rescued me from a trip to the local jail.

Hi

Hi yourself

Swung by a few minutes ago, check your porch

I grabbed a robe and went to the front door.
There was his overnight bag.

I've got it.

See you tonight.

A rare night off, then. Such was the depth and breadth of text messages from the man I was aching to love but still not allowing myself to fully commit to loving. As much as I wanted to see him, he was probably only doing this to keep an eye on me. To see if I had dropped the issue of the murder like he had demanded. No matter. Vodouisants knew how to keep their secrets and when it was important to do so.

I was in the kitchen, sitting at my table, lost in appreciation of how the morning sun streamed through the window and softened every surface in the room. Inhaling the lingering scent of sandalwood incense, exhaling the irritation.

My mind quieted, and beneath closed eyelids, the fragmented clues surfaced one by one: Ms. Vangie's unexpected financial windfall; two Seventh Ward homes, procured by Art through my client Nick; two former basketball players, one now dead; a former judge turned charter school owner; and those two kids from parts unknown.

My eyes sprang open, and I bolted out of the chair. Skin from my scalp to the soles of my feet prickled. The air trumpeted the unmistakable reverberation of—

Magic.

It was coming from . . .

I snatched open the back door and charged outside, calling on my mistress. But she didn't answer. I took one step, then two. The feel of it was slippery, something I couldn't quite latch on to. Knotty tendrils coiled around the backyard in fits and starts, then dissolved like smoke.

My pores yawned open and devoured air that was clammy and damp, ready to conjure.

A towering silhouette emerged from the shadowy cover of the holly trees.

I began to weave a water shield.

And then, he took a step forward. Misty sunlight fell upon the boyish face of one of the teens I'd seen at the house with Arthur: the contemplative one.

The same duffel bag that he had hauled from the SUV was at his feet. He held his hands up where I could see them, but I didn't drop my shield.

"You will want to know how I got here," he said. His manner was tense. He trusted me no more than I trusted him. "I do not know the answer to that question any more than you. Maybe you are just another American that wants to use me."

It was the timbre of his voice, not the accent, that made him difficult to hear. The feel of his magic was gone, but the unmistakable trail of the lwa was plain for those trained to see it. That did not mean I could let my guard down, though.

"How *did* you get here?"

"I walked."

I didn't respond right away, instead listening and reaching out to feel whether another person or any malevolent force lay in wait. He watched me with warm brown eyes the color of wheat toast, his expression curious.

"Arthur said you were from around here. That's not true, is it?" I asked finally.

"Far from it. My home is Cotonou."

Now the accent made sense. But how? *Impossible.* "Benin?"

"Tu le sais?" He dropped his hands, his smile showing every one of his teeth. "You know of it, then?"

Vodouisants believed in the unexplained. We held firm to the fact that the universe worked in ways all its own, but this coincidence had to mean something. "Have you been trained?" I asked. I stopped short of asking about initiation. Everything about him screamed "untapped."

He pondered a few moments and shook his head. "My parents would not allow it."

"But you know what you are?" I'd come a few steps closer now and invited him to sit on my bench.

He sighed. "It is a difficult thing to be different," he said, with more wisdom than I expected. "There was a big houngan out in the country that wanted to train me. My parents wanted nothing to do with the old ways."

Here, he stopped, getting a faraway look in his eye. "My father is not well. He has been ill for a very long time, and we know he will not get better. My mother busies herself with work so she does not have to face it. This, coming to play basketball, was the only way I could help out."

To play basketball? Arthur and Beau were former basketball players. "Are you registered for school, then?"

"There was a change. I'm going to—" He paused here, as if searching his memory. I held my breath. "George Washington Carver."

Not what I expected.

If he was brought here to go to Gwendolyn Guillory's bogus school, then why the change? Something to unpack later.

What was clear was that this kid had a very strong presence of the lwa around him. My task was to figure out which one. It hit me then: I was sitting here with a child from the birthplace of my tradition. A potential Beninite, untapped and untrained, had fallen right into my lap.

"There is someone else. Like us."

His face lit up. "I can feel it, you know," he said. "But I don't know what to do with it. Nothing is written down at home. The tradition is passed through apprenticeship."

The thought came to me: I had to hide him. I needed someone with the resources to do so, and as much as I hated to admit it, that was Lucien.

"Excuse me a moment." I took the phone out of my pocket and called Lucien directly.

"You need to get over here right away," I said. "I can't explain it, but there's a kid here; he's . . . he's probably a Beninite. He's involved somehow with Gwendolyn Guillory and Arthur Stiles, and I need to make sure they don't get him back in their clutches. You need to come get him and hide him."

Silence. "Did you say a Beninite?"

"I did. Straight from Benin."

I could sense Lucien perking up. "Is he trained?"

"That will be up to"—I paused because I knew this would be a battle, but one I'd have to fight later—"up to us."

"Give me twenty minutes." He hung up.

I turned back to the kid. "There's someone coming to help. A powerful houngan. We'll make sure you're taken care of." I was conflicted about handing him over, but there wasn't much I could do about it. "I don't even know your name."

"Odi," he said. "Odion Moussa."

"Reina Dumond, duly initiated mambo priestess."

Odi stood to take my hand but stopped midway, his gaze skyward. "Your mother," he said and then trailed off.

I blanched. "What do you mean?"

He tapped his temple. "You think she is lost to you."

Think? Interesting choice of words. "Ten years ago. A hurricane."

Odi's brow furrowed. He seemed on the verge of speaking, of probing further, but didn't. This happened to me all the time. My mother wasn't dead, but she wasn't exactly here either. People didn't know how to handle that.

"Have you started school yet?" I asked, letting him off the hook.

Odion fidgeted, obviously put off by the question. "Not yet. I expect there may be some problem with my visa."

"What kind of problem?"

"Well, because of the change—"

I wouldn't get the chance to hear his answer.

My back had been turned, but the fright on Odi's face preceded the warning Erzulie sent. Then a low rumble ratcheted up to a crackling boom, and a blistering pain seared my back.

I went down hard. I fought against the fuzziness creeping in at the edges of consciousness, but I felt myself slipping away. The last thing I saw was Odion's hand, stretched out toward me, before he was pulled out of sight.

⌒

I lay facedown.

Blinding spikes of agony jabbed the flesh between my shoulder blades. The smell of summer and earth and the lingering tang of gasoline.

Frantically, I rolled over and reached behind my back, groping for the source of the pain. Half expecting to dig my fingers into an open wound, I found only smooth, unblemished skin. Not even a scar.

I sat up, and my mind settled. By now the pain was subsiding, what little remained soon fading to a dull throb. It was replaced by a panic that gripped my heart. I crawled to my feet, breathing in short, convulsive breaths.

"Odion!"

The yard was small. A quick look around confirmed that he was gone, those traces of him overpowered by another. I raced to the back door and tore through the house, though I knew it was fruitless. I ran back outside, phone in my hand. Instead of Odion, Kiah stood there.

He took one look at me and my haggard condition. "You lost him."

And then Lucien was there.

"She couldn't hold on to him for ten minutes," Kiah sneered.

"I need you to listen to me," I said to Lucien, ignoring Kiah.

I went on to describe the nature of the attack, the feel of the fire. I let him examine my back, the scar that should have been there but wasn't.

"You know what this means?" he said.

I felt like my stomach was consuming itself. "A houngan," I said.

"Or mambo," Lucien said.

Kiah's mouth remained closed, but his stance went rigid, poised and ready like a poisoned dart.

"Does this have anything to do with Gwendolyn Guillory?" Lucien asked. "I think it's time you fill me in on what you've gotten us into."

"Us." There is no us.

"Kiah," Lucien said. "Ask around, quietly. See if you can find him your way, while we strategize ours."

Kiah threw up his hands. "I should be with you. I don't even know what I'm looking for."

Lucien's head went low, teeth bared. His growl sent both Kiah and me back a step.

I gave Kiah a description of the teen. We *had* to find him.

Kiah nodded like a soldier and set off.

I told Lucien as much of the story as I wanted, leaving out bits that were none of his business. He stalked slowly around the yard as I talked, pausing here and there, sniffing, toeing at spots in the grass. "Someone's masked the trail."

"His voice is distinctive," I put in. "Can you hear anything? Anything different?"

Lucien shook his head. "Not like this."

That meant he'd need the help of his lwa, Agassou. The spirit must have been otherwise engaged. If we couldn't find Odion soon, a ritual invitation might be called for.

"Who's the only new houngan around here?" I asked.

That statue I'd seen at Voodoo Real. Shango, the lwa of fire, thunder, and lightning. I'd suspected it was for the new houngan.

"Walters, you mean?" Lucien fingered his chin. "It's possible. Azaca-Tonnerre is his patron."

Maybe not Shango, then. Azaca-Tonnerre was also an lwa associated with thunder. Though what I felt had subsided, it could certainly be said that it felt like I'd been blasted by a bolt of lightning.

I nodded. "If that's true, it fits. But it doesn't make any sense. Why?"

"How could he be tied to whatever scam Arthur is running with these kids?"

We stood there thinking for a few moments, unable to make any of this make sense.

The sounds of the neighborhood nearing midday came to me then. A door slamming next door, voices. More traffic zooming by out front.

"I'll go feel him out," Lucien said, heading for his car.

"I'm going with you," I said. "Give me a minute to throw on something."

"I'm not waiting." Lucien was already walking toward the pavers at the side of the house. I didn't have time to argue with him. I'd have to catch up.

"There's something else," I called.

Lucien stopped.

"The kid," I started. "Odion. He brought up my mother. I can't explain it, but I got the sense that he felt . . . I don't know, something."

Lucien's expression turned oddly grave.

"Impossible," he whispered dismissively before gliding into his car and driving away.

CHAPTER
TWENTY-EIGHT

I was halfway out the door when it occurred to me I didn't know where I was going. Houngan Walters had evaded me when I'd asked him where he planned to set up shop. Had he told Lucien and not me?

My phone buzzed. Lucien. He said Houngan Walters's shop was closed—odd for the middle of the day. And he'd dispatched Kiah to intercept the houngan at his home, only he wasn't there either.

Like a labyrinth with no exit, the dead ends were piling up.

There was nothing left to do for now. I could only nurse a fragmented hope that, somehow, Odion would find his way back. On leaden legs, I plodded to the sidewalk, checking the street in both directions, even the neighbors' porches.

No sign of him.

I turned to head back inside and, at the top of the steps, noticed an envelope. It must have been wedged into my front door, fallen when I came outside.

An official letter from the City of New Orleans. I ripped it open and stood there on the porch reading. My hands were shaking by the time I finished, and I crumpled up the paper.

Now they were threatening my business. Some unknown official was saying that my occupational business license, the one that had taken half a year of calls and inspections to procure, was now somehow invalidated. No inspection had been performed, yet they had suddenly determined the structure of Le Petit Temple Vodoun to be unsound. Without significant (and costly) improvements, I would have to shutter my business in ninety days.

This couldn't be a coincidence.

I hustled through the door when I heard the phone ring. I snatched it up. "Odion," I said breathlessly.

"More like Chavonne," the cheery voice on the other end said. My longtime client had moved to Austin to pursue the education that would ultimately land her a career in technology. As soon as I heard her voice, I remembered.

"Chavonne, I totally forgot about our appointment today, and something urgent has come up," I explained.

Silence. Then a sigh. "I'm not trying to be difficult or anything, but I've been holding off going to one of these sketchy doctors before I talked to you."

"Is it urgent?" I said. "Life threatening? If so, I think you know what I would say anyway." This was also one of the reasons why I had resisted online appointments—it was hard to diagnose a malady that way. Video obscured much of what you could observe in person.

"I guess it isn't," Chavonne admitted. "We can reschedule."

I was about to thank her and hang up when I recalled the business card. "Can I ask a favor?" I said. The gall to ask her for help when I had blown off our time together wasn't lost on me. "If I gave you a website, could you find out who was behind it?"

"There are some limits," Chavonne told me. "But I'll see what I can do. What's the URL?"

"URL?"

She chuckled. "The website address: *www* dot something."

I gave her the address—the URL—and thanked her.

"Okay, I'll get back to you as soon as I find something," she said.

"While you're looking, can you see what you can find out about a man named Beau Winters?"

"What are you looking for?" she asked. "Criminal information or something else?"

"Anything you can find." She was much better at this stuff than I was, and I was glad to have her help.

"Check," Chavonne said.

"Oh, one more thing," I said. "I had a run-in with your cousin. I may have told him by accident that we were, you know, acquainted."

"Now it makes sense," my client said. "My mother said he was over there complaining about me. Don't worry about it. I'm surprised we kept it a secret as long as we did."

I wished her luck on her upcoming exams and hung up.

My thoughts swirled and then settled. Finding Odion in a city this size would be difficult, but what about who had taken him? If it was Houngan Walters, I'd try to look for traces of his lwa.

Back in my peristil, I rattled through drawers and shelves, pulling out what I would need. I had a spell in mind, one that could provide a trail, a spotty road map to follow.

On the bare table, I laid out a circle of cornmeal and dried rose petals. I placed a dressed pink candle for Erzulie at the center and sprinkled the remaining petals around it in a tight circle. I then set small votive candles, alternating yellow and white, at each of the cardinal points.

Invoking the four directions, starting with east, I lit each of the votives, reciting the prayer to the lwa. Finally, I lit the pink one. I wrote the name of the lwa, Azaca-Tonnerre, on a piece of paper and laid that in front of the setting.

Now the tricky part. This worked well in areas where you could walk, but I would need to drive. After burning the paper over the pink flame until there was nothing left, I blew out each of the votives, carefully lit a final one from the pink candle, and took that with me.

In theory, the flame would guide me in the right direction. I didn't need to cup a hand to protect it from the wind; this candle would burn until it led me to its quarry . . . or lost the trail.

I drove aimlessly, the flame rising and swaying in the direction it wanted me to turn. In this way, I navigated east of Tremé, toward Mid-City.

After a mile or two and a few more turns, the flame died in the middle of an intersection.

I pulled over, set the expended votive on the dashboard, and placed my forehead against the steering wheel, allowing my eyes to close. I was suddenly exhausted.

My phone rang again, and my energy spiked as if I'd been shot up with a gallon jug of adrenaline. I reached for my purse in the back seat and ripped it open, but by the time I'd reached my phone, it had stopped ringing. The call was from Ms. Vangie.

A moment later, the voice mail chime sounded.

Arthur's missing. Ms. Vangie's voice was like a blade dripping with blood. *He hasn't been home for two nights, he hasn't answered his phone, and . . . and something just feels off.*

She rattled off each point as if reading from a list. Something about it put me off, but I wasn't sure why.

Jason is swinging by with something I found when I searched Arthur's things, she said. *It's an old photograph. I don't know the men in it, but maybe it'll help you.*

She'd met Jason at my house more than a year ago, following an appointment. She'd taken in the state of him and, like the rest of us, appointed herself one of his unofficial guardians.

After a second or two, there was a sound, like a hand sliding over the receiver. Voices raised, but I couldn't make out the muffled but clearly agitated words. Abruptly, the voice mail ended.

I looked around. I was near Bayou Saint John. I searched every face and car. Odion wasn't here. Whatever existed of the trail was lost. At the nearest intersection, I made a U-turn and sped back home.

Inside, I paced, stopping only to peek out the window. Sure enough, a little while later, I spotted my young friend coming up the walkway to the door. Jason had seemingly grown three inches since the last time I'd seen him months earlier. Or perhaps he'd lost weight. His jeans were an inch above his ankles and hung loosely, a belt cinched tightly at his narrow waist.

He smiled when he saw me.

"Ms. Reina," he said. After much haggling, I'd finally convinced him to stop calling me Mambo. He still flat out refused to just call me by my first name. "Ms. Evangeline gave me this to give to you."

He handed me a photo. I gave it a quick glance before turning my attention back to him. "How are you doing, Jason?"

"Okay," he said. "I'm in a foster home."

He trailed off and looked away as if there were more to say. I could fill in the blanks for him. He had been in foster homes before, but his stays were never long ones. "You always have a bed here."

He regarded me with an expression I couldn't read. "I know," he said. "But I'm better on my own."

He said it with the weight and certainty of someone twice his age. I wondered at what kind of country we lived in where a boy of twelve, maybe thirteen, felt that way. And why he had chosen a foster home instead of the bed I had offered him on too many occasions.

"I charged Ms. Evangeline twenty bucks," he said, all business. "For you, I'll make it ten. That way I won't have to rob anybody for another week."

It was the smile he tacked on at the end that had me reach in my purse and pluck out a bill instead of lecturing him.

"Get something to eat," I said as I handed him the money. "And don't forget . . ." I raised an eyebrow and waited.

"A vegetable," he huffed. "I know."

But he didn't promise to do so. I was still learning to accept things that were out of my control. I thanked him, and as he turned to walk away, I looked at the picture.

In it were four men, one of whom I immediately recognized as a younger Beau Winters. One white man. The two other Black men I didn't know, but I'd find out. I could tell it had been snapped without them knowing. No posing, no smiles. I wondered how Arthur had come into possession of the photo. Maybe he, too, knew that one day, it might provide a means to solve a murder—or get himself out of trouble.

One of the men in this picture was connected to whatever Arthur had gotten himself tangled up in.

I still doubted that he had it in him to commit murder, though he was certainly the type to use any information he had to his advantage. But now, even he was missing. I'd find out why, but first, I had to find Odion. No way would I let any harm come to one of the few Beninites I had ever met.

He was untrained. And these things were tricky. His ability could manifest at any time, and without proper guidance, the results could be disastrous.

CHAPTER TWENTY-NINE

My spell had led me somewhere, yes, but I couldn't understand the significance of the spot where the candle's flame had extinguished. Sometimes the lwas' road maps were difficult to follow. I was standing with Arthur's photo in my hand, wondering what to do next, when my phone buzzed. A text from Chavonne: Check your email. I sat down at my computer and read with growing interest.

The website on the business card bearing Judge Guillory's name said the school was twenty years old. Yet, according to Chavonne, the website had only been established six months prior. Through a ruse that made me proud, Chavonne had found the web developer and gotten me a name. Marcel Rider.

One Marcel Rider lived in Baton Rouge and, judging by the obituary I found, had been dead for three years. The next lived right here in New Orleans but appeared to work in finance. *Maybe, but not likely.* With the next entry, I got the feeling I had found my man. A physical education teacher—one who also worked at the Sojourner Truth Neighborhood Center.

After searching the website, I found that he taught a computer class there, part-time. And if the dates and times were correct, not always a given with websites, he would be teaching a class soon.

I had no idea how involved Marcel Rider was in this whole thing. I knew that hopes of him leading me to Odion were slim, but it was the only thread of a trail I had at the moment, so I'd follow it. And I would go in with backup. I fired off a quick text, asking Tyka to meet me there. I was out the door again.

My stomach growled, reminding me that I'd had little to eat today. And precious little water. I drove down Canal Street and listened to a streetcar rumble past as I sat at the light, pondering who could be behind the murder. Was it one of the men in the photograph Ms. Vangie had produced? If it had been in Arthur's possession, then the answer was a likely yes. White vodouisants existed, yes, but they were extremely rare. So much so that if one had been initiated, word would have spread through the community like a rash. I decided then that the next thing I'd do was work on identifying the other two Black men. One of them might be my killer.

When the light changed, I gunned it but quickly slowed as a police car appeared at the intersection. The new houses built along the street barely registered as I navigated the streets that would lead me to the center.

Tyka got out of a car I didn't recognize and fell in step alongside me with a nod as we went to the door. "This is the last place I expected to see Marcel," she said.

"What do you mean?"

"This dude wasn't no joke," she said. "He could mix it up."

I cataloged that bit of intel and was glad I had called Tyka. With no time to call ahead, I could only hope the computer class was still going and that I could talk to the coder. We stopped at the front desk. The young woman there had hair that sat somewhere between a carrot and an overripe tomato on the color spectrum. Nails so long I wondered how she typed on the computer perched to her right, where she seemed to be in the middle of some kind of digital card game. "Can I help you?" Her gaze shifted between Tyka and me as if wondering which of us would speak first. Her features had softened when she looked at Tyka.

"You have a computer class here." I began to weave the lie as I spoke. "One led by Marcel Rider. She's interested in taking it." I tossed a thumb over at a surprised-looking Tyka.

The woman's eyebrows knit together. Had she sussed out my pathetic story-weaving skills?

"That class is for kids," she replied. "What you want is the adult class. Someone else teaches that one, and it's only on Saturday mornings." She leaned forward and handed Tyka a brochure with a smile.

Total lie fail.

"How old you talking?" Tyka also leaned forward, placing her forearms on the counter. Giving the woman her full attention. "For the kid class, I mean."

The woman blushed. "Eight to twelve."

I saw where Tyka was going. Saving the day.

"I got—" she started, then corrected herself when all of us at once realized she was far too young to have a child in that age range. "I mean, my friend here's got a kid. Maybe you want to check out this teacher for your daughter, then?"

My daughter.

If only.

One day.

I snapped out of my reverie when I noticed them both staring. "Y-yes," I stammered. "You're right, it would be good for me to talk to the instructor."

The woman gave us both a look and then turned to Tyka. "Your name is Grip, right?"

"To some people," Tyka said. "But for you, my name is Tyka."

Just then, a group of kids came laughing and running down the hallway. Parents and friends gathered them up and hustled them outside.

"There he is now," the receptionist said.

Tyka and I moved to intercept. We both stopped, blinked. We stood facing an incredibly buff man in a wheelchair. His biceps were the size of my thighs, and his chest muscles bulged in a shirt that could have stood to be a size or two larger.

"Mr. Rider," I said.

He eyed us warily. "Yeah."

Though the kids were still putting up a ruckus, I gestured for him to move with us out of earshot of the receptionist and the others gathered near the entrance.

I handed him the card. "Can we ask you some questions about this website?"

He glared, then mumbled something under his breath. "I knew it," he said and then spun his chair around. For a moment, I thought he was going to try to take off, but he said, "I don't have much to say, but I ain't saying nothing where Soraya can hear it. It'll be all over the city in an hour."

We followed him down a hallway covered with kids' decorations and pictures lining the brick-faced walls. After passing one door on the left and two on the right, we turned into the last one. The room was set up with rows of desks and computers. A large window on the opposite side of the door.

Marcel whirled around. "Whatever Art and Beau have done, I didn't have any part in it. They needed a website—not much more than a landing page. I needed the money and didn't ask any questions. That's all I got to say, and now you can *S-T-E-P*. Step!"

He put his hands back on the chair's wheels as if, after that measly confession, we were going to let him go on his merry way.

"How did you get paralyzed?" Tyka stepped up and blocked his exit. I thought it was rude to ask, and judging by the look on his face, so did he.

"None of your damn business."

"But I'm sure my friend here had a question or two," she said.

"In fact, I do," I said. "When did you build the website?"

"I'm outta here." Marcel spun down hard on the wheels but didn't get far before Tyka intercepted him. She grabbed his crotch and squeezed.

I winced, almost covered my eyes.

Marcel grinned. "Waist down," he said and then moved to shove her away, but she was quicker and soon was behind him and got him in one of her famous choke holds.

He clawed at her arm, and she released him, just enough to let him breathe.

"I'll ask again," I said. "When?"

"Had to be back in March or April," he sputtered.

That fit with what Chavonne had said. The first question was just to establish whether Marcel was going to tell me the truth.

I pulled out one of the chairs to sit in so it wouldn't look like I was towering over the man. I gestured at Tyka to release her hold on him. She did, but she stood like a sentinel behind him.

"Did Arthur approach you or Beau?"

"It was Beau," he said. "But Arthur is the one that paid me."

"Did either of them tell you anything about the school?"

For the first time, Marcel looked deflated. I gave Tyka a subtle head flick; he was talking, and I didn't want her crowding him. She went over to the classroom door, alternately peeking out in the hallway and then watching us as if she expected an attack at any moment.

Marcel shook his head. "It's what he didn't say. Like, why two old-time scammers that could barely spell their names had something to do with a school in the first place."

Two old scammers and an ex-judge, I thought to myself.

"And," he continued, "I've been texting Art. Beau told me that he was supposed to pay me out of his cut, ten percent. But he only paid me five hundred."

Math wasn't my subject. The sciences, soft and hard, were more my thing. But I did know that five hundred was indeed 10 percent of the five grand Ms. Vangie told me Arthur had put in their account. Unless.

"How much was Arthur's cut?"

"Twenty-five ducats." He looked indignant. "Tried to cheat me. Probably thinks because I'm in this chair that I can't handle him. He'd be wrong about that. Unless, of course, you're a girl that goes around sneaking up on people."

Tyka snorted.

Either Vangie was lying or he was. His chest was heaving, eyebrows knitted, lips slightly poked out. My guess? He was telling the truth. Ms. Vangie had promised me her husband's ill-gotten earnings as payment, and she was going to do exactly what her husband did: misrepresent the amount of money and keep the difference for herself.

Intuition, not the wheelchair, told me that Marcel probably wasn't the killer, but confirmation was in order. Time to drop the bomb. "Beau Winters is dead."

"What!" The man actually rolled back a few steps away from me. "Look, I didn't have anything to . . . Is that why you're here? You some kind of cop?" His wild eyes took me in and, from the looks of it, decided that was unlikely.

I kept silent, anxious to see where this would take him.

"Arthur probably did it," he said. That made me sit up. "I told Beau that fooling around with his boy's wife was going to get him in trouble."

I blinked. Stopped breathing. Beau and Ms. Vangie? They'd had a thing going on? It hit me then, the hushed words exchanged between Ms. Lucy and Vangie while I was at her house getting my hair done. Who else would know what was going on but your best girlfriend? This revelation floored me.

"I'm not here about a murder," I said, but I was extremely grateful for the information he'd given me. "Did you ever talk to this woman? Gwendolyn Guillory?"

He shook his head. "I put her name on that website because they told me to."

I took out the photo Vangie had given me and handed it to him. "Would you happen to know these two men?" I pointed to the two Black men in the photo with Beau.

He looked up at me quizzically. "Guess you don't watch a lot of sports?"

"No. I don't."

"This one here used to be a coach at New Orleans State. Can't remember his name. This one was a pretty good point guard. Did a year or two in the NBA before he bounced back home." He handed the photo back. "Don't know the white dude."

Basketball. The college insignia on the cap the man was wearing at the house in the Seventh Ward.

"That's it. That's all I know. Now can I go? I got someplace to be."

I stood. "I'm not holding you here."

He pointed at Tyka. "Is she?"

Tyka looked at me, and when I shook my head, she moved aside. "Roll out, my man," she said with a flourish of her hand.

Marcel wheeled through the door as if he were in a race. But he'd been most helpful. I'd learned, once again, that people never showed you all sides of themselves. Ms. Vangie, prim and proper, had been having an affair with her husband's good friend. That put her firmly at the top of the list of potential suspects in his murder. A fact that, at least for now, I'd keep from Roman.

CHAPTER THIRTY

Marcel Rider's revelations were rattling around in my mind like dice all the way home. That Arthur Stiles was a con man was the certainty with which I'd begun this case. That his wife was just as scammy as he was—that burned. This was a treasured client who'd reminded me of my mother. To think that I'd known her and really not *known* her all these years had me questioning my supposedly fine-tuned powers of perception.

And whether she was capable of murder.

Under the right circumstances—defense of self or loved one, or through blind rage—anyone was.

Had Ms. Vangie given me the photo to point me in the right direction, or to throw me off her trail?

Marcel had said that one of the men was a former coach at New Orleans State. I'd start there. I booted up my computer, and after a quick search of New Orleans college coaches over the last several years, I found him.

The paper had covered a local fundraiser that benefited a children's charity. There he was, Francis Cole, in an image with the white man from the photo, apparently an NCAA official.

Mr. Cole wasn't a Crescent City native but had relocated here to take what was a ridiculously lucrative job offer. He was a former athlete himself, one who, like my new client, Mel Caldwell, also had an MBA from Rice University. He'd started as a position coach, risen up the ranks to head coach. His tenure had been a short one. After a third losing season, he'd been promoted to some position in the front office. Special assistant, whatever that meant.

Vodou practitioners weren't confined to the city limits. Our tradition was thriving. Believers and initiates spanned the country and world. But my gut suggested that the person I was looking for was a native. Someone familiar with our neighborhoods, comfortable existing in places where tourists, even some transplants, rarely ventured.

I plunged into my research, combing through articles and photos on the college website until I found an image of Mr. Cole with the other Black man in Arthur's photo. The other man was indeed a basketball player with a short-lived career, Kareem Nelson. There were several photos of him and Mayor Martin Richard. Apparently the two had been childhood friends. Also a native, then. With political connections. One who might have a friend or two who could cook up trouble with a certain business license.

Scrolling through, I found a story that pointed to Kareem's recent trip to none other than the African continent—Nigeria.

That led me down a rabbit hole, where I eventually stumbled upon an article about a young Nigerian man who had been tased and arrested by the police after refusing to leave a local library. He'd said he was cold. But what chilled my bones was the fact that I recognized him. That face. He was the man Tyka and I had seen over in the Seventh Ward. The one who looked like he was living out of that pickup truck.

The piece went on to say that he had been a basketball standout in his native Lagos and had originally entered the country to attend high school. There was no mention of Kareem in the article, basketball the only commonality.

I was putting the pieces together, but I still had to find a murderer. A murderer connected to a powerful lwa. He would most likely be a native, so I would focus my attention on Kareem. A spell was in order. One that might tell me which of the two men held an aura or trace of the spirits.

I headed back to my peristil. Near where the row of trees met the building, I checked to make sure no spiders were lurking around, then plucked a few of the delicate webs and cradled them in my palm. Inside, I grabbed a dark-navy fabric swatch and carefully laid the spiderwebs on top. I snapped out a clean white tablecloth and set the photo and swatch down.

From my cupboards, I pulled out oils of rosemary and angelica, along with a bit of shaved mandrake root. I dressed a Seventh Day candle with the oils and carefully applied the spiderwebs. When I finished, it looked like the candle was covered in a fine lace.

A strike of a match and the candle was lit. I sprinkled a pinch of the mandrake root over the flame.

Next, I positioned the picture directly in front of the candle, then recited the spell:

North, south, east, and west
The spider's web shall snare him best
West, east, south, and north
Reveal his true nature, and I will follow the course

The flame grew and expanded to nearly the length of the slender candle. It flickered and danced, licks of fire curling down to caress and lift the photo. Though it lay on the bed of flame, the photo shouldn't burn. I tensed when a flutter of sparks crawled over the surface. Hmm, that wasn't supposed to happen.

Suddenly, the edges of the photo caught fire.

"No," I hissed, wondering what I'd done wrong.

I hated to ruin my tablecloth, but I snatched up an edge and used it to beat out the flames. In the end, the picture was ruined, singed beyond recognition. All that remained was a speck of white, likely from the wall, of all things.

The lwa were sometimes unavailable, often cryptic.

They communicated in the way of the heavens, and it wasn't always clear what they were trying to tell me. It was time, then, to turn to some good old-fashioned detective work. I blew out the candle and cleaned up the space quickly.

Temporarily thwarted, but undeterred, I knew it was time to take this search to the streets.

CHAPTER

THIRTY-ONE

The suspects were stacking up. Ms. Vangie and her husband—acting either together or individually. Same for one or both of the men in the photo. As my brain ran through the possibilities, it snagged on something unexpected. The other teen, the one at the house with Arthur and Odion. He'd carried an air that suggested more than simple wariness; there was more of an edge, a coldness.

Someone had attempted to frame me, my livelihood threatened. I had faced down oddly agitated construction workers and been attacked in my own backyard. Intimidation as clear as a saint's conscience. I was getting close.

Whoever had bested me would not have the chance to do so again. And there was only one way to make sure. An often-surly houngan who could help me with the spell that thus far had been failing to come together.

The last phone call with my father had ended badly. That didn't stop me from barreling down I-10 for an impromptu visit. The tranquil scenery, which normally soothed frayed nerves and diminished the troubles left behind in the city with every mile traversed, went by unnoticed.

I didn't have to call ahead; Papa rarely left home. His isolation had begun as an escape from memories of Haiti and had only worsened after Manman's disappearance.

I took the Pass Manchac exit off I-55, and within a few minutes, I was turning into my father's unmarked, unpaved driveway. My car churned up dust and gravel as I sped down the path, his patron's butterflies scattering ahead of me as if by escort.

By the time I came to a stop in front of the house, Papa was outside on the porch, walking stick in hand and a grave expression on his face. Giant swallowtails, orange sulphurs, monarchs, a few common buckeyes. Growing up as I had with a follower of Atisou, every variety of butterfly had visited our homes at one time or another, and I had learned them all by sight. A stunning medley of colorful, quavering wings cracking and clicking, the mass blanketed the porch and the better part of Papa's body.

"Sa k genyen?"

He asked me what was wrong as soon as I got out of the car. A parent's sixth sense was the most impressive magic I had ever seen. With two taps of his staff, the butterflies scattered.

"I need your help," I said, coming onto the porch, then rising on tiptoe to brush a kiss against his cheek, the gray stubble like sap-coated stickpins.

He turned to walk inside the house but held up a hand when I followed. "Pluck some goatweed and elderberry first," he said, gesturing off toward his massive yard.

I huffed. There would be no arguing with him. I snatched the basket that he kept in the far corner of the porch and stomped down to collect the herbs.

When I came inside, the scent of boiled plantain reminded me that I couldn't recall the last time I had eaten. My father went to the stove and turned off the burner and filled two bowls. As usual, the dining room table was like an apothecary filling station. Fragrant herbs and gnarly roots. Bottles of all shapes, sizes, and colors stood alongside his amber-hued glass vials. Pestle and mortar. Instead of the peristil out back, reclaimed by the swamp long ago, this was where Papa operated his covert but thriving healing practice. Other houngans peppered this and other remote parts of the state, but my father was the best.

I was clearing a place for us to eat when I noticed the candy wrappers. Papa didn't eat candy. "What's this?"

"See that?" He gestured at a small bottle with a handwritten label that read STUTTER. "A nice family on the other side of the swamp. That is for the youngest. He comes in here, stuffs his little trap with the sugar, and leaves the mess on my table."

We sat down to eat. The starchy sweetness quickly filled my empty stomach. Between bites, I filled Papa in on everything that had happened since we last spoke.

He rubbed his chin. "A Beninite. *Ou sèten?*"

He asked if I was certain.

I bit my lip, considering. "I'm almost positive."

"Ours is a noble tradition. A healing tradition. Everything good can be twisted to something ugly in the wrong hands. Last time it landed you in the hospital." At the mention of the hospital, he dropped his fork and pushed his bowl away. "You said you were done with this kind of thing. Already you have invited trouble to your doorstep again."

I wanted to tell him that this would be the last time. I wanted it to be the last, but I also knew that if someone came to me in need, it would be hard for me to turn them away.

"Helping someone means sometimes you put yourself in danger. Vodouisants can't walk away from trouble if one of our clients needs us."

A thoughtful silence filled the span of the next minute before I thought to ask him about what had happened with the photo.

"Shango," Papa said with a nod. "Someone is using him. Misusing. One piece of the photo remained, you say?"

I thought back to the statue, the state of the body. And Houngan Walters.

"Yes, but I couldn't make out anything useful."

"Seek what you do not expect," Papa said. "It is in the tiniest details that your answer lies. Use that thick head of yours. Think. And now, we will make sure that you can protect yourself."

I popped the last thick slice of plantain in my mouth and considered his words. I was looking at the New Orleans native, when maybe, just maybe, it was the other man.

I went on to tell him about the spell I'd been working on. The Sphere of Protection.

"Obsidian is nothing to play around with." It grated when he told me things I already knew as if I were some novice. "Not only is it expensive, but that negative energy it is supposed to absorb can funnel right back into the wielder of the spell if you are not careful."

My previous tests had been failures, but I hadn't done any real-world testing. "That's why I'm here."

"What are you using to charge it?" he asked.

"John the Conqueror root," I explained.

Papa thumbed his chin. "That is likely best."

He got up and started opening and closing cupboard drawers, pulling out even more bottles and roots and herbs. He set a Guardian Angel candle on the table to help strengthen and protect our practice. "Up, up," he said, gesturing for me to take the bowls to the kitchen.

"We don't have a lot of time." I trotted over to the refrigerator and downed a glass of water, then got the last of the obsidian stones from my purse.

"You do not rush the spell," Papa warned. "That was always your problem. You want everything quick, quick!"

I was tired of being chastised like a child, and he must have seen the fact written on my face because he added, "Do not worry—whoever has taken your boy wants him alive. Of that I am sure."

I hoped he was right.

"What makes you think the boy is a Beninite?"

"It's not only that he's from Benin, but that certainly doesn't hurt. The feel of the lwa is all around him, and his parents knew it too. They didn't want him to apprentice. He's untapped, but it's there. And . . . and he said he sensed something about Manman."

Papa's mouth opened and closed. "Your mother?" His eyes narrowed. "What could he have to say about her?"

"Just that he had some kind of feeling about her," I explained. "I got the sense he thinks she's alive, but he didn't get a chance to tell me before he was taken."

"Did those words come from him?" Instead of expressing excitement, even curiosity, Papa was getting angry. "I doubt it. You heard what you wanted to hear."

I seethed but kept my thoughts on the matter to myself. "Let's just concentrate on finding him before you dismiss anything."

My father gave me a look that, as a child, would have sent me running for the safety of my mother's arms, but with even the slimmest possibility that we might find her, I was emboldened. I crossed my arms, and while I didn't utter a word, it was clear that on this, I wasn't prepared to back down.

"Now," Papa said after kissing his teeth. He motioned at everything laid out on the cleared half of the table. "What is the first ingredient?"

Everything I had tried with my other attempts had failed. It was time to change things up. "My sangswe," I answered with a certain confidence.

He shook his head. "That we will save for last."

"But," I protested, "I've wasted three stones doing it the same way; I think I need to change the order."

"Yet you drove all the way out here for what?" he said. "For me to watch you mess up again?"

When I didn't say anything, Papa continued, "Like I said, we will do it my way."

"Fine," I conceded. "First thing is the war water."

"Right." Papa set a silver bowl down and handed me an unlabeled bottle. I didn't need to ask if he was sure he had the right one. He always was.

He gestured at the bowl. "Two generous splashes."

I raised an eyebrow. "Generous?"

He folded his arms. "No measuring. You don't need it."

Why was it that all the confidence I felt at home evaporated as soon as I was near my father? I added the two splashes, and when Papa moved to get the next ingredient, I took that to mean I'd added the correct amount.

Next in went a pinch of ground alligator teeth. And the obsidian stone.

"A bit more," my father said, leaning over my shoulder. "Just enough to fit in the crook of your pinkie fingernail."

I sighed. I could have studied with him every day for the next five years and not come up with that one.

"And this." The vial was no bigger than my thumb. Glass, with a cork topper. Papa plucked out the cork and handed it to me. "It's not easy to get, but I think this is just the thing we need. Tell me what it is."

I took the bottle from him and examined it more closely. The granules were sandy colored and finely ground. One sniff, then another. Pungent like manure. Rotten eggs or old cabbage. My eyebrows shot up. "Devil's dung?"

"You asking me or telling me?"

I took another sniff and nodded. "Asafetida," I said, using its medicinal name. "Devil's dung. I'm sure of it."

Papa patted my shoulder, and I leaned into it like a lapdog. "And what is it used for?"

I combed the memories of our lessons and soon settled on the answer: "It's not one thing, but two. Both to protect and to attack."

A smile quirked at the right corner of Papa's mouth. He tapped the bowl. "No more than a quarter teaspoon."

We combined all the ingredients, and when done, Papa turned to me and said, "Now, add yours."

I urged my pores open; the lines of my palms bled my sangswe wine as it flowed into the mixture. I held my hands aloft, draining myself for a good five minutes before my father patted my back.

"It is enough."

And it was. I wobbled and sank down into the chair as I watched him put on the finishing touches. He used a wooden spoon to combine the ingredients into a kind of paste. Then he went into the kitchen and turned on the gas burner. He held the bowl over the fire, moving it back and forth like he was cooking up a batch of popcorn.

After a few minutes, he was back at the table. He dumped the dried contents into the mortar and then ground them into what became a dark-red powder. He held the contents close to his mouth and whispered, *"Pwoteje li."*

It was so simple; if circumstances weren't so dire, I would have laughed.

I grabbed the funnel that was on the table and handed it to him. As I was reaching for my purse, he picked up one of his glass vials.

"I'd rather use one of my satchels," I said. "They're silk lined and much easier to stash wherever I need to." Namely a bra or pants pocket. I handed him the pouch, and when he was done filling it, I stuffed it in my pocket.

"Now go," he said.

I hesitated. This opponent scared me more than I cared to admit to Lucien, but to my father, I was an open book. I gathered up my things and then stopped with my hand on the door handle. "Come with me," I said.

His gaze floated out the window beside the door. A great weariness creased his features. A lone monarch butterfly came in through an open window in the kitchen and alighted on his shoulder. Papa brushed a finger at its wings.

"A child is like a caterpillar," he said. "Once she grows into a beautiful butterfly, becomes all that she was meant to be, you must let her fly."

I didn't have time to argue. I hopped in my car. The hour-long drive back to New Orleans took me forty-two minutes.

CHAPTER
THIRTY-TWO

It was in the clash between summer and winter, the distillation of little things, that autumn always cleared the path for change. The biggest change I had made in my life was leaving Haiti. When we'd first arrived in the US, one of the things I recalled most was my mother's exasperated phone calls to the immigration offices. Flustered snatches of words and conversations that, in my own way, I understood were of vital importance. Even then, I realized that moving country was no simple process.

Juju had mentioned seeing Arthur at the airport. I couldn't figure how to connect that to the flipping scam, but I now realized that he must have been there for another scheme altogether. And before Odion was taken, he had expressed concern about his visa. I got an idea.

A few keystrokes later, I found the number to the New Orleans Immigration Court.

A recording. One telling me that hold times could be extensive. As soft jazz played over the line, I paced. I went to the kitchen and chugged a glass of water. Twirled the drying ends of my hair around my index finger. Between the kitchen and the table where my computer sat, I must have trudged the length of the Nile River and back before, finally, a voice came on the line.

"Can I help you?" the man's voice droned with all the solemnity of a funeral director. He hadn't named the agency either.

"Is this the immigration office?" I asked.

He rattled off the phone number I had just dialed. "If that's the number you dialed, then you know you called immigration. Is it really necessary for me to repeat it a thousand times a day?"

To keep the acidic retort I had ready from coming out of my mouth, I clamped down so hard on my teeth that pain spiked in my jaw. I had been on hold for a lifetime already; all I needed was for this man to hang up on me.

"My name is Judge Gwendolyn Guillory," I said with all the bite I could. "What is your name?"

"Oh," came the response. "I apologize. You wouldn't believe how many ass—I mean, how rude people are to us."

I believed him. I had witnessed the way people treated retail or other public service workers, and it was vile. Still, that thing about two wrongs meant that you didn't take it out on the next person.

"I need to check on the status of the I-20/F1 visa application for one of my students," I said to the now-recalcitrant person on the other line.

"Name of the school and the student?" he asked, suddenly reenergized.

I provided the requested information and agreed to the short hold. I hadn't even started pacing again when he came back on the line. "Judge Guillory, your first two visas were already approved. Looks like the last one, for Odion Moussa, should be coming through this week."

I thanked the man and hung up.

Gwen Guillory used her fake school to provide I-20/F1 visas to get students from Africa into the country. A ruse that probably paid her very well to file these false applications.

The fact that she was now an ex-judge told me that someone had uncovered just what I had. That she was allowed to retire with full benefits and a sealed file told me that this went much higher than Arthur and his dead friend Beau.

Someone who had ties to the mayor. I thought back to what my new client, Melody, had told me about the NBA, and suddenly, I understood it all.

The homeless man-child may or may not have been the first, but for whatever reason, things hadn't worked out for him. Odion and his friend were also caught up in this scam. The motivation, as always in these things, was money. The scammers either had swindled money from the kids' parents to get their children into the country in the hopes of a better life, or they'd had them sign contracts guaranteeing their benefactors a piece of any future NBA earnings.

The mayor, the athletic director of one of the city's biggest colleges, and the body that governed it—they were all involved.

Ms. Vangie, me, Roman. Every one of us had underestimated Arthur Stiles. While "petty criminal" had defined his past, he envisioned his future to be much more elevated. He and whichever of the men in the photo he was working with. And with these kinds of players involved, I imagined large sums of money were at stake. Enough to kidnap, enough to murder. Both kids and I were in more danger than I had thought.

CHAPTER THIRTY-THREE

Whoever had attacked me may have thought they'd killed me. And that was a good thing. It meant their guard would be down.

My client Nick had said that Arthur had tapped him to search for distressed homes in the Seventh Ward. And each time Tyka and I had run afoul of the man, it had been in that very same neighborhood.

It was a long shot, but with help, I could quickly traverse the mile-long ward that stretched between the Mississippi River and Lake Pontchartrain. As I was about to call Tyka, a better solution came to me.

"Mambo Dumond?" Nick answered.

"You have access to your sales records at home?"

"I do," he said. "What do you need?"

"You sold Arthur or whoever he was working with homes in the Seventh. Can you get me a list?"

"Give me five minutes," he said.

My heart and stomach were twin storms spinning with anticipation. Soon, Nick came back on. He rattled off four addresses. With this many houses, my guess was that they intended to funnel more kids through this pipeline and use the homes for lodging, even if temporarily. Not if I could help it.

I recognized all the addresses except one, and I wrote it down.

"Is this about my request?" Nick asked.

"I'm working on it," I lied, then thanked him and hung up. Not much of a lie, really: if things worked out the way I hoped, Nick wouldn't have to worry about Arthur Stiles getting what was coming to him.

My next call was to Tyka. I gave her the address. "Meet me there as soon as you can."

"Arthur, right?" she said.

"That's what I'm hoping."

I grabbed my purse and locked up, and in a flash I was on my way.

I arrived at the house just as Tyka opened the door and waved me in. Of course she had beaten me there. "Why didn't you call when you got here?" I asked, coming up the path.

"Old boy busted up my phone," she said.

I came inside to a home that had the look of being once loved but newly abandoned. I could still see holes in the walls where portraits had been displayed. Scuff marks lined the floor where perhaps a sofa had been moved. Blinds hung slightly askew. The scent of an artificial air freshener still lingered in the air. What I didn't see was the man we were looking for.

"Where's Arthur?"

Tyka got that shifty look in her eye. "He's back here."

I followed her to the next room. And there, in the center of an empty room, was "old boy," a.k.a. one Arthur Stiles. He was trussed up like a hog at a state fair. His eyes were wild, muscles bulging at the ropes secured around his limbs. One shoe was off. Expletives spewed out of his mouth like molten lava.

I could only shake my head at Tyka, exasperated. You didn't get the best information from people by hurting them.

"What?" She shrugged, a look of innocence painting her delicate features. "This dude sent us to a house with a dead body and then dropped a dime on us. What do I care if he gets a few rope burns? Besides," she said, folding her arms, "wasn't like he was going to wait patiently and talk about the state of the neighborhood until you got here."

She had a way of making something wholly unacceptable acceptable. I was trying to teach her something about violence. But if I was, why did I continue to drag her into these things?

"I had him in an arm bar, but I couldn't hold him forever," she said, explaining her wrestling moves like she was going over a new recipe. "You want to be mad at somebody, it's Bounce. It was his idea to tie him up before he left. Not mine."

"No way she get the best of me without Bounce," Arthur put in.

"Untie his legs," I said. When Tyka's shoulders slumped, I added, "Thank you."

She whipped out an implement that was much more than a pocketknife but short of a switchblade. Arthur stilled his squirming.

"You gonna just let this girl cut me?"

"She'll do no such thing." I didn't have full confidence of the fact, but why tell him that?

Tyka went over and patted him down, perhaps looking for weapons. She pulled out his wallet and started counting money. I gave her a look, and she tossed the wallet back on the floor—minus the money—before she cut the ropes on his legs.

Arthur rolled over and kicked out, but Tyka was faster and leaped backward.

"Sit down," I said, coming forward as I built my defenses.

Arthur had sense enough to take in my stance and back down.

"Mr. Stiles." I pulled over an upended chair and sat down. "You're in big trouble. Whether or not you make it out of this without going to prison for the rest of your life depends on what you say next."

Arthur shifted and sat up, his hands still tied behind him. Tyka waited. "Jail is better than dead."

"I hesitate to call what you're doing a scam because, unlike your other little hustles, a lot of money is involved." I went on to tell him the pieces of the puzzle I'd put together and then asked him to fill in the blanks. "Why bring the kids over here?"

"Everybody here swears everybody in Africa is broke," Arthur said. "That's bull. Beau . . ." His voice broke at the mention of his former friend's name. "He said he saw more Black millionaires over there than you could imagine."

A fact that I also knew. The American campaign to malign our past and thwart our present included consistent narratives about our lack both here and abroad. Those who cared to look uncovered the lies.

"Basketball in this country is a big-money game," he continued. "And everybody is looking for the next star. And many of them are in the motherland. Some of the parents pay good money to have their kids come over here and play for the chance to earn millions in the NBA."

"And the others?"

"The rest?" He shrugged. "It's kind of like consignment. We pay to get them over here. Put them up with a family or a caretaker like me. Sign them up for a big-time high school program. And they sign a contract that guarantees they fork over a part of their earnings if they make it to the NBA."

"Or," Tyka put in, "they make it to the NCAA and take some of that under-the-table money that isn't supposed to exist but everyone knows it does."

Arthur nodded. "Smarter than she look."

"Where are the kids you had at the house in the Seventh Ward?"

"I don't know."

I wasn't sure whether I believed him.

"And what part does Gwendolyn Guillory play?" I asked. I'd already figured this part out, but I wanted to see if there was something I'd missed. "You said you try to get them into a local high school. So what's the point?"

"It's all about I-20 visas," Arthur explained. "She agreed to set up the school, agreed to apply for the visas to get the kids over here, and then we take over, move them to another school."

This so-called scam went all the way from high schools to the NCAA and NBA. A local judge, a friend of the mayor's. I shuddered, thinking about what I'd unwittingly stepped into. "I found your photo. Two Black men, one white, and Beau Winters between them. You know the one?"

Arthur frowned. "How did you . . . I wondered how you got onto me in the first place. It was Vangie, right?"

He would have to settle with his wife without me. "Which of those two Black men in the picture is at the top of your little food chain?"

He looked at me and Tyka, then laughed. "Lady, you got it all wrong. It's not either one of them brothers you looking for."

"What?" I demanded. "What are you talking about?"

Arthur's nostrils flared and then he chuckled, deep in his throat. "You don't know shit. And he's going to do to both your asses what he did to Beau. It's the white dude, the 'Top Dog.' Solomon Rise."

Everything crashed down on me then. How could I have missed the signs? My heart sank to my stomach with a thud. The statue Salimah had been holding for a special customer. The man on the newscast at Nick's house in the bright-red tie and handkerchief. The spot of white left from my photo ritual. The lwa had been trying to tell me, but I had been too blind in my belief that a white man couldn't be a practitioner.

I got up and grabbed Tyka by the arm. We left Arthur Stiles tied up where he was.

"Let's get out of here."

CHAPTER THIRTY-FOUR

There are three kinds of lies: ones you tell to hurt someone, those you tell to save someone's feelings, and those you tell to save yourself. I was a poor liar. To pull this off would require drawing from the well of fear bubbling in my gut.

"This isn't worth our time," I told Tyka as soon as we were in the car.

"How do you figure?" she asked, head cocked.

"I didn't tell Arthur this, but Lucien's already found the boys." The lie had the taint of something foul, like fermented food. I swallowed it down nonetheless and kept my face impassive, my manner loose.

She shook her head in protest. "And what about this dude, Top Dog? Is he gonna take the fall for that murder? There was still a body in a house, remember?"

"That's a matter for the police," I said, partially believing that to be the case myself. "I'm going to tell Roman everything I know and let him handle the rest."

Tyka digested all this in silence, picking at the mole beneath her eye. She seemed skeptical but was probably weighing things out for herself.

I affected an air of nonchalance. The goose bumps, though, may have given me away. I had to face a man, an outsider, trying to practice Vodou, with no training. And I struggled to contain my mistress, my body raging between heat and ice cold.

"If that's the way you want it," she said. She unzipped her sweat-pants pocket and produced a cell phone.

"I thought you said Arthur smashed your phone?"

"He did, so I took his."

I thought back to when she'd patted him down. I wanted to chastise her, but I needed that phone.

"You don't want to be caught with this," I said. "Trust me. I'll get rid of it."

Left hand on the steering wheel, right hand held out.

"Aw, man," Tyka said, but she gave me the phone.

With night pressing in, I dropped her off at home and doubled back the few blocks to my own.

If things went badly, it would only be me at risk. Not Tyka. And not the police. I didn't know how he was doing it, but somehow, Solomon Rise was twisting the practice. Turning Vodou into something alto-gether different from what it was supposed to be.

Just like Rashad.

I followed the blue-and-white paving stones straight back to my peristil. Inside, I glanced at the machete on the wall, fitful memories bubbling back to the surface. Trouble had once again found me. I thought about taking the weapon but instead grabbed the potion Papa and I had perfected.

My guess was that my opponent wouldn't hurt the kids. To him, they were a commodity, something to be bought and sold like human stocks. Beau and Arthur? They were expendable. With the kind of money likely involved, they were replaceable cogs in the wheel.

The first question was how to find him and get a message to him.

For that, I took out the phone that Tyka had boosted from Arthur Stiles. No password, typical. His stupidity saved me the last bit of detective work. Contacts listed plain as day. I scrolled down to look for the name Solomon Rise, but nothing matched.

He'd called him Top Dog. I scrolled back up, and there was the entry.

He'd been to my home, soiled the place with his twisted use of the practice, and taken a child under my protection right from me. Erzulie roiled her outrage. The thought that she had not been there to warn me crossed my mind, and a blitzing cold blast through my veins reminded me that neither she, nor any of the lwa, were available at my beck and call. It worked the other way around.

My mistress flooded my system. I could feel her swirling around, ready to unleash her fury and outrage. I dialed the phone, and on the third ring, he answered.

"You had better have a good reason for disappearing on me." The sound of Solomon Rise's voice was formidable. Deep and booming. The timbre of a bass or tuba.

I still struggled to believe that Solomon, a white man, was playing at being a priest and follower of the lwa Shango. Was it possible? Sure. I supposed it was also possible that I could become the next pope. This magic was an ancient, sacred tradition, brought to the colonies by enslaved Africans hundreds of years ago and handed down from generation to generation since. This was no white man's game. It couldn't be. No, it was more likely that Arthur was up to something again, trying to throw me off the trail and send me in the wrong direction. Could he be protecting one of the other men in the photo? My mind turned back to Kareem Nelson. Maybe this Top Dog had gotten tangled up in another man's untrained ventures into Vodou. But I still needed to test him to make sure.

"You have no idea what you're messing with, do you?" I said.

"Who is this?" There was the tiniest note of hesitation.

"Mambo Reina Dumond," I said. "I believe you know who I am."

"I'm sorry, lady, but I don't. And how did you get Arthur's phone? Have you and Kareem killed him too? Oh God."

Wait a second; he *was* implicating the other man in the photo. "Hold on," I said.

"You must think me a fool. I'm going with my first mind. I'm calling the police."

"Don't hang up," I said. "If you're talking about Kareem Nelson, I'm not working with him at all. I'm looking for him."

All I heard in the silence that descended while I thought about how I shouldn't have given this man my name was heavy, exasperated breaths. I took a chance.

"I know about the school, Africa, everything. I just want those kids back."

"They forced my hand, you know. The NBA commissioner is behind it all. Africa is a gold mine of talent and new fans to them."

"You mentioned Kareem," I said. "Has he contacted you?"

That pause again. "He has the kids," he said. "But it also won't be too long before the police pin Beau's murder to him, so he wants to disappear. I give him some cash, he gives me the kids, and if I'm lucky, he gets picked up somewhere far away from here."

Arthur had done it again. I hated being tricked. "Where does he want you to meet him?"

"Audubon Park. Newman Bandstand. After closing."

CHAPTER THIRTY-FIVE

It took a little more coaxing, but I got Solomon to agree to let me join him at the park—without involving the cops.

I ransacked my purse until I found the Sphere of Protection powder I'd worked on with Papa. I shoved it in my pocket, left my purse where it was, and bolted out the door.

Every nerve ending in my body crackled like a live wire. Known for his powerful axe, Shango was one of our tradition's most powerful lwa. Indeed, he was said to have a voice like thunder and a mouth that spewed fire when he spoke. Thunder and fire were his talismans. Shango was the epitome of all things hypermasculine.

This spirit could be unpredictable even in the most practiced of hands. What had been done to Beau Winters proved that whoever killed him couldn't control the spirit's power, a fact that could work to my favor or detriment. Unless, of course, he had intended to kill him all along.

I made it to Audubon Park about ten minutes past closing. The driveway that led to the parking lot was blocked off. I circled twice before I found a parking spot on Saint Charles Street, right in front of

Tulane University's Thomas Hall. I scanned the other cars. Empty, as far as I could tell.

I got out of the car and watched a trio of backpacked students walking toward the inner campus, their laughter trailing off moments later. After a streetcar rumbled past, I darted across the street.

I skirted the entrance and slipped into the park down the street. The night held other dangers besides a person toying with spirits he didn't understand, so I kept my head on a swivel. It took a few moments for my vision to adjust to the dark.

A fat yellow moon provided enough illumination for me to make my way to the two-mile path that would lead to the bandstand. Ancient, towering oaks blotted out some of the moonlight. Spanish moss dripped almost to the ground.

Avoiding the paved pathway, I darted between the cover of the trees, pausing to listen.

Insects chirping. A bird screeched. A soft rustle in the grass. The thump of a bass-heavy song, willowed and softened by distance. And there, not too far away now, the waters of Olmsted Lake lapped at the edges of its confines, calling to me. A song of water and wet.

Audubon Park had been a huge plantation and, ironically, alternated as both the site of a Confederate camp and a military hospital for Union soldiers during the Civil War. I had glimpsed their ghosts once before, emerging as they did at dusk. Those poor souls stuck in their never-ending war, bound to play out their historic roles in the park's ceaseless nocturnal dream. They were out tonight, some bandaged and bloodied, others administering aid with practiced efficiency.

I greeted them by inclining my head and left them to their eternal work, all the while calling to Erzulie in my mind. I urged her to emerge from the land of the spirits.

The polished white stone of the bandstand gleamed in the night. I tasted the air. Dry. Much too dry for my liking, the humidity hovering near 70 percent. I urged my senses further, deeper underground.

A rainfall, perhaps a week earlier, had left some moisture beneath the surface, but the top six inches held nothing for me.

Timing was critical. I couldn't hold water forever, but I didn't want to be caught unprepared either. I siphoned what I could from the parched air and earth and pressed on, the bandstand and the lake in sight.

Twenty paces short, a shadow peeled itself away from the cover of an oak.

I saw the eyes first. Irises of tiny flames that looked almost disembodied in the night. The figure stepped into a pool of moonlight, and I realized I had been duped again.

"I've asked around about you." Solomon shook his head and shrugged. "And I gotta admit—I'm a little disappointed. You're supposed to be this big deal, and I took you out before you could even raise a hand."

My mind raced. This wasn't possible. No way was he initiated. That process was as severe and grueling as it was for a reason. If you didn't learn control, the fact that you could hurt someone else was a given, but you could also harm yourself. "You talk big for someone who did something akin to shooting their opponent in the back."

"A smart man takes every advantage."

"Where are those kids?" I demanded.

"They're fine," Solomon cooed, caressing an ebony-colored beaded necklace. "As long as they do what they were brought over here to do, they'll stay that way."

So the boys were safe—for now. "You're nothing but a wannabe, toying with something you can't possibly understand."

"Is that a hint of prejudice I hear?" His tone was playful, disrespectful. "You think Black people have some sort of monopoly on Voodoo? You don't."

"Prejudice has nothing to do with it. Where did you train? Apprentice? When were you initiated?"

"I realize a person from your meager beginnings probably had to learn in a dirt-packed hovel, but there's these modern inventions. You should check them out. Books. The internet. And any blanks I needed filling in only required an online consultation or two."

The man was so uninformed he was dangerous. "Prove it." This time when I called to Erzulie, she responded. It began as a tepid flutter at the soles of my feet. Traveling through my legs, stomach, chest, the cold raged through my body and manifested like an iceberg breaking me apart and chipping its way through my veins.

I brought my hands up and shot the water I'd gathered from my palms, channeling in my sangswe and sending the temperature below freezing.

The barrage slammed into Solomon. I wound the frigid water around his wrists and ankles. Manacles of inches-thick ice froze his movements. He roared his frustration.

"Stop," I said, coming a few steps closer. "You have a chance to end this all now. Tell me where the boys are and get out of this city."

Solomon's struggling continued.

"Are you doing this for Evangeline?" he eked out through gritted teeth. "She's a troublemaker, that one. Why do you think she married Arthur? And had a thing with his friend? She's no better than they are. You point a finger at me, but all they care about is money. Not even their own people."

"So you killed a man why? Because he was going to expose you?"

He regarded me with a strange curiosity. "Beau was practice. A necessary casualty. It's a matter of influence. Control. If anybody gets out of line—players, employees, even the mayor—with one touch, they know who's in charge. You're right. I couldn't control Shango at first. But I did eventually, with the help of a little substance."

I recalled the vial and syringe I'd spotted near Beau's body. I had wondered how Solomon was able to do what he did. Our practice didn't, shouldn't, work this way.

"Who do you think is going to help those people, the Red Cross?" he spat, his voice full of indignation. "What chance would those kids have otherwise? Sure, I make some money off it, but everyone benefits. All you Black Americans have is lip service. You wear your little African medallions, sport a little kente cloth at Juneteenth, but I rarely see any of you go over there and lift a finger. You don't get to judge me because I do."

As Solomon spoke, his voice rose until it thundered. A sound that made me take a step back. I scrambled in my pocket for the protection powder as Solomon threw his head back and raised his cuffed hands to the air.

Solomon's wail ripped open the sky and rained down three lightning bolts. Before I could even release my own scream, one bolt snapped the protections on his wrists, another the ones on his ankles; then everything exploded in a vaporous mist.

The third came straight for me.

I backpedaled, then turned and ran, pulling in the meager mist that he'd released and all that I had reserved and then summoning an icy shield. I dived to the ground, banging my knee. I rolled over as the bolt shattered the shield. Shards of ice rained down, lodging painfully in my face and exposed hands.

While I swatted and yanked at the stinging, spiked fragments, Solomon was using a needle to draw liquid from a small vial. The same kind that Tyka and I had seen left behind at the scene of Beau's murder.

"A little boost," he said with a vile grin.

I could only gawk. Solomon began to shudder. His entire body glowed as he ripped off his shirt. His chest erupted with the image of Shango's vèvè, alight.

I was dehydrated and sluggish. I needed to make it to the bandstand, to the lake. My knee ached, but I limped to my feet and ran.

"You think because I'm white you have a leg up on me?" Solomon called after me. "You don't."

Solomon's footsteps sounded too close. A wall of fire sprang up directly in front of me. It was only with great effort that I didn't crash right into it.

Olmsted Lake roiled at my call. A great wave arched upward, spiraled toward where my fingers directed it, and then doused the flame.

But I'd miscalculated. It was a diversion.

I spun around and Solomon was there. He laid both his palms on my chest.

My insides constricted, as if it were me caught in the fire. I clamped my lips together but still couldn't stop the howl that escaped from my throat. I squeezed my eyes shut as the pain blurred the edges of my consciousness.

The sliver of my mind that wasn't dissolving in the fire called to the lake once more. A tendril crept up over the edge, all that I could muster. It squirmed through the grass and eased up my feet, ankles, thighs. Sinking into my skin.

First a sliver of a crack, and then the hold Solomon had on me shattered.

I tore away from his grasp.

"Ah," Solomon hissed. "You need the water."

He turned and raced toward the lake.

I pursued.

He snatched off his beaded necklace and tossed it out over the water, infusing it with his fire. I watched in horror as the beads hit the lake and flames erupted. They ripped across the surface and spread so fast that it was like the lake had been coated with an invisible layer of oil.

The lake shrieked.

I doubled over, covering my ears from the horrific keening that mingled with the rough croaks of Solomon's laughter.

He came back toward me, his eyes blazing like embers. Time to finish it.

I took my eyes off him for just a moment, fumbling for the pouch in my pocket. When I looked up, Solomon had disappeared. I cursed under my breath and scanned the area. He was nowhere in sight.

I could barely think over the lake's wails. I couldn't draw from the water; I had to give back to it. So I did the only thing I could think of.

A rustle of footsteps on the grass. From my periphery, I spotted a flicker of movement. Solomon.

As he reached out to grab me, I sidestepped, staggered forward, and dropped the satchel in the grass. With him so close on my heels, I couldn't turn back. I prayed he didn't see it. Then I dived into the lake.

A ring of fire enveloped me, but Erzulie wrapped me in her protective cocoon.

And then I was beneath the surface. Sinking into unnaturally warm depths. My pores released. Every single one of them. All my life I had taken, made myself near-drunk on this city's air and water. It was time to give it all back. I opened myself and let the lake take its replenishing, healing fill, draining the sangswe wine from my body until there was nothing left. I fed the lake as it had fed me.

The suffusion acted as a barrier between Solomon's tainted fuel and oxygen, and the flames died, consumed by a magically infused influx of the three atoms that made up good old-fashioned H_2O. The lake cooled back to its normal temperature.

And then I heard a splash. Through the murky dark, I could make out the figure that was likely Solomon cutting through the water like a knife, headed straight for me. I dived deeper and propelled myself in the other direction.

I kicked and clawed my way back to the water's edge, the lake coated in a thick fog. Erzulie worked her wonders inside me, the only thing keeping me on my feet. When it was ready again, the water came to my aid.

I groped around on the ground for the pouch and, when I found it, ripped it open. Solomon had resurfaced about ten feet away and was marching toward me. I released the powder, watched as it sparkled and floated out across the lake. The water took over as I collapsed. On my side, chest heaving, body spent, I guided the mixture like a cannon blast at Solomon.

I knew fire needed three things: fuel, oxygen, and heat. Block any one of these, and the fire couldn't burn. For Solomon, the Sphere of Protection powder snuffed out his fuel, whatever was in that vial. In a clash of ancient and modern, he had found the amplifier, and now I'd extinguished it.

The foamy mixture settled over him, clinging to his skin. His body sizzled and popped as if carbonated. When he opened his mouth to scream, it was choked off as the frothy brew poured down his throat. He bloated until I thought he would burst into a million tiny bits of flesh; then the mixture sloughed off like shed skin.

Solomon fell onto all fours, and this time, the poisonous liquid, and seemingly everything he'd eaten for a year, poured from his mouth in great racking waves.

His flame was doused.

When he was empty, he fell to the ground. I gaped as I felt, then saw, an ethereal Shango float away from Solomon. He turned and fixed me with a glance full of gratitude, and then he disappeared. I felt Erzulie retreat with him.

I crawled over to Solomon. He had a pulse, but it was erratic and slow. I made sure the vial and needle were by his body, then made my way to my car. When a man getting into his own car tried to come to my aid, I simply begged him to call 911, report that the Seventh Ward murderer was near the bandstand, and forget he ever saw me.

I had watched Solomon Rise twist my practice. He had tried to kill me, more than once. Used kids like they were high-priced commodities. But I still didn't wish death on him.

I climbed into my car and waited until I heard sirens in the distance before pulling away.

CHAPTER
THIRTY-SIX

I awoke to an insistent tapping, the sound of a fingernail or a coin on glass. The fatigue registered next. Damp clothes clung to my skin. Opening my eyelids was an impossibility, shifting my torso an avalanche of woe.

It all came back to me. I'd dragged myself back to my car after getting someone to call the police. Driven. Not more than a few blocks. Pulled over, locked the doors. Killed the engine and slept.

I inhaled a ragged breath and willed my body to respond, to move. Bright light seared my corneas when I opened my eyes. Midday? I turned to find a woman peering at me through the driver's-side window. I needed food, but that would have to come later. I pulled some of the damp from my clothes and greedily sucked that into my pores, but it wasn't enough. There was water in the trunk; I just needed to get to it. Sad as it was, if this woman broke the window and tried to rob me, there was little I could do to stop her now. That didn't mean I couldn't give her my strongest mean-mug.

"Hey," she said, pushing her face closer. "You alive in there?"

"Last I checked." Speaking felt like my vocal cords were on fire. I needed that water.

"Ain't safe to be out here all night like you was," she said. "But I watched over you."

Huh. I got a good look at the woman for the first time. Her face lined, grime coating her hair. She smiled, the teeth she showed me with reckless abandon browning. I glanced over her shoulder and saw a large cardboard-box cutout, a kind of shelter. A grocery cart. A large wrench and a pole. My mistress had guided me to a safe place. I motioned for the woman to move back and opened the car door.

"Thank you," I said. "A bit of a rough night." The air was frustratingly lacking in humidity. I'd have to replenish the old-fashioned way. I reached out and assessed what moisture ran through my benefactor's veins. A reflex I wasn't proud of. Hydrated, but not overly so. I resisted the very strong urge to pull water from her.

"You one of them special ones," she said, and when I raised an eyebrow, she added, "You don't have to explain anything to old Melba. She knows what she knows, Mambo."

Melba turned to shuffle off back to her makeshift home. "Wait!" I stretched, worked out the kinks knotting every muscle in my body. I took a step toward the back of the car and stumbled. Lightning quick, Melba was there. One hand grabbed my forearm; the other snaked around my waist.

"The trunk," I said, leaning into her for support. She guided me there, and I propped myself up on the hood and asked her to get the keys from the ignition. I opened the trunk and grabbed three bottles of water. One I handed to Melba; the other I downed in two sloppy gulps.

Every life-giving sip gave me back an ounce of strength. Almost immediately, my body temperature regulated. My eyes went from feeling like tiny rocks coated their surface to moist as tapioca pearls. I downed a second bottle as I watched Melba recap hers, waddle over to her cart, and stuff it into the folds before she came back.

There was only one of my reserves left, but I took it out and handed it to her. "Take this one too."

She eyed me. "I get the feeling you need it more than me."

I shook my head. "I'm fine." And I flexed my arms and legs to work the blood back into my limbs. "And come on," I said. "I'm taking you to get something to eat."

Melba held up her hands. "I don't need any charity. Besides, I can't just leave my cart."

There was certainly no way for me to get it into my car, and I sensed she'd turn me down even if I offered. Instead, I went to my purse and pulled out the lone twenty-dollar bill sitting in my wallet.

"From the looks of you, I'm guessing you know about the shelter on Rampart, but if you would allow me to pay you for your services, I'd feel much better about forcing you to stay up all night and keep an eye out for me like you did."

Melba smiled. This, she could accept. There was a delicate balance with people on the street. Many of us painted a static picture on what was fluid. Some people, at least for a time of their choosing, were exactly where they wanted to be. It was a thoughtless thing, shortsighted, to assume that they all wanted or needed handouts.

"My fee for such services is usually double this." She plucked the bill from my hand and stuffed it in an unseen pocket. "But for a lady such as yourself, I'll make an exception."

She turned to go back to her home and then paused and faced me again. "Put in a good word for me with"—she stopped, looked up and around, then said—"them?"

I told her that I would, and I meant it. I wanted nothing more than to torch these clothes and take a long hot bath. Would have settled for a ten-minute shower, but now it was time to assess the fallout and to find two kids from Benin who needed me.

Three unanswered calls on my phone. Two from Lucien, one from Roman. Neither would be easy conversations. I'd call Lucien first and deal with Roman later.

I spotted the car that tensed my shoulders up again, sitting right behind my parking spot. There he was, leaning against the car, arms folded, an impressive scowl on his face. Had Roman been staking out my place?

He stalked over before I even had both feet out of the car. "Where were you?"

I got out of the car and scanned the street. A few cars passed. A door somewhere down the street slammed. And there, across the street, Ms. Lucy had cracked her door.

"Good morning to you too," I said, buying time.

Roman looked at me slowly, for effect, from head to toe. Hands on his waist. Head cocked. "Why do you look like you spent the night in the back seat of your car?"

He was wrong. I'd folded myself up in the front seat. I busied myself by leaning in to get my purse while I ran through and discarded a myriad of lies that he'd see right through. The truth? Not a chance! An errant client? Melba? A midnight ritual? None of these!

My friends. Which of them to throw under the bus, and how would I free them later?

I coughed first. Then cleared my throat. I looked over at Ms. Lucy's house, willing the old busybody to come out and complain about something, anything. She watched us for a minute and disappeared. Her door stubbornly closed.

I shook my head. "You're not going to be happy about it, but it's Tyka." I spun the tale as I walked toward my front door, Roman close behind on my heels. I could practically feel his eyes boring into the back of my head, his sweet breath on my neck.

"What about her?" His voice was even, probing.

I opened the door and kicked off my shoes. Quickly touched Erzulie's altar as I passed by. Roman came in, laid his jacket across the sofa in that familiar way of his, and followed me to the kitchen.

"You having tea or coffee?" I asked, grabbing the kettle and then filling it at the sink.

After a moment of silence in which I refused to turn around and meet his gaze, he finally said, "Coffee."

The sound of the chair skidding across the floor as he pulled it out and sat down settled my nerves some. I'd had a few more moments to concoct my story.

"It's that father of hers." I set the kettle on the stove and turned it on. I took out cups and instant coffee, then joined Roman at the table. When I looked at him, skepticism was written all over his face. "He'd gotten himself into some sort of trouble."

"And she called you? For what? To help comb the neighborhood bars?" Roman snatched his mug, dumped in two scoops of sugar and a tablespoon of those unsettling brown granules he called coffee.

"Yes." I happily followed the trail he was laying out. "I helped her search for him. Most of the night. He'd gotten into some kind of brawl, and somebody called her. We found him slumped on the ground outside a bar near Preservation Hall. I helped her bring him home. It was so late, I just fell asleep in the car rather than risking the drive home."

There—that sounded reasonable, even to me.

Roman watched me, and I affected the most natural expression I could. Luckily, a few seconds into this silent war of wills, the kettle screeched. I moved to get up, and Roman commanded, "Sit."

He splashed water into both our cups, and we sat brooding silently, staring into the depths in order to avoid anything more uncomfortable. There was a point in most couples' lives—many points, in fact—where you had to make a decision. Press on and ask questions that could lead to uncomfortable revelations, an argument, even a breakup. Or choice two, more difficult than it would seem, was to consider the words (or lies) you'd just heard and accept them to keep the peace. I didn't know which way Roman would go, but I had my hopes. A thing in the arsenal to try for the person waiting for the ball to drop: distraction.

"And why are you here so early?" I risked a sip of tea. "Did you have to pull another all-nighter?"

"I'm here because when I dropped off my overnight bag, I told you I would be. And you didn't return my phone calls."

Wrong question. "I forgot, okay? And you know when I don't want to carry my purse, I put it in the trunk. We were running from bar to bar. Why risk it?"

Silence.

"Look," I continued. "I'm sorry. I know you like me to check my phone. I didn't mean to worry you, and I'll make sure I don't do that again." Whenever he pulled this, I got nervous and kept talking long after I shouldn't. Time to clamp my mouth shut.

"You know what's interesting to me?" Roman said. "You look like you've been dragged through the mud and back. You barely gave that altar of yours a second glance when you came in. And I didn't catch the case, but some big-time NCAA official got arrested last night. Suspect in that murder."

When I raised my eyes, he was staring right at me. "Are you interrogating me?"

"Do I need to?"

"Waste of your time, but this murder—"

"Yeah, the man murdered at that house where the cops picked you up."

"Who?" I asked with as much genuine curiosity as I could. "And do they know why?"

Roman took a blessed sip of his coffee. He'd accepted my story . . . for now. "Some tip called in. Get this—dude shoots up with some drug. A weird blend. Guess all the athletes are taking it now. Only this stuff does

233

something to the brain. Anyway. I heard something weird was found at one of those abandoned houses."

Weird, I thought. *As in, signs of two teenage boys?*

Roman went on to tell me the scant details he would share about the case before we moved on to other things. For the first time, I lamented each second he took to share his life with me. I was desperate to talk to Lucien and find out if he or Kiah had found Odion and the other boy.

But for now, I would sit, listen to the man I found it so hard to be honest with venture to share his life with me, and hate myself just a little for having to lie to him.

CHAPTER THIRTY-SEVEN

Roman had spent more than an hour at my house—plenty of time for him to pepper in a few more questions to determine the extent of my involvement. When the probe ended, in that final conflicted glance he leveled at me was an unspoken agreement to never raise the issue again.

As soon as I saw him pull away, I whipped out my phone.

"Did you find him?" Lucien and I blurted out in unison.

Over that line flowed a feeling. Familiar to me, but nothing I had ever sensed in Lucien before. Panic. "Meet me at the warehouse," he said, steeling his voice. "You don't need to bring anything."

There could only be one warehouse. The one where I'd first met him, more than fifteen years prior. It was the place where I had come to know that he was a true leopard king in human form. His lwa, Agassou, the priest king and magician. The product of a divine mating between a princess mother and a leopard. His was the lwa of home, family, and lineage.

It was there at that warehouse that I'd seen him transform into the leopard king. It had taken years to stop having nightmares about it. I hadn't been back since.

Until now.

I changed out of my damp clothes and headed out to New Orleans East, a part of the city devastated by the storm. It had rebounded slowly, the middle- to upper-class residents from Baton Rouge, Houston, and other parts of the country where they'd fled eventually returning en masse.

The vacant lot where weeds and discarded bits of human life had thrived was now a paved concrete splendor, yellow lines marking the parking spaces. Even a little guard shack, empty now, sat waiting for a new employee.

Lucien's car was there, but the merry-go-round of drivers he employed was not. He was ever cognizant of making an entrance, so the fact that he had beaten me here and had come alone said something about what we'd attempt.

I pulled into the spot beside him and jogged toward the entrance on the left side of the building.

Gone was the rusted metal door, replaced by what could only be described as mahogany artistry, the ribbonlike grain visible beneath a shine so clear that I could almost see my reflection.

Round bronze knockers decorated both doors, and an antique metal grate covered a slat, which slid back at my knock and closed just as quickly.

The right door opened without a sound, and I joined Lucien inside. He closed and bolted the door behind me.

The houngan was clad in unusually pedestrian clothing. Not sneakers and jeans like normal people, but slacks bordering on khakis, a light sweater that, under better lighting, might have been identified as cashmere, and shoes that weren't hard bottomed but were cushioned so much that I didn't hear his steps against a wooden floor still in the midst of renovation.

Inside, the space was large without being cavernous. It was empty, save for a raised stage and a long, rectangular table. His altar to Agassou was painstakingly arranged. Candles, his *asson*. And from a rafter, which I remembered, still hung Agassou's *vèvè*.

"So what do you have in mind?" I asked.

"Some people, determined not to be found, require other methods," Lucien said. "Our kind of methods."

Lucien and I were the only Beninites we knew, at least in the city. If my instincts were right, Odion could be the third. By nature and necessity, we were secretive. I had only vague notions of the gifts granted to Lucien by his connection to Agassou. And he likely had the same general thoughts about me and Erzulie. I wanted to keep it that way. In order to find Odion, we'd have to work together, but I'd only show him the barest sliver of what I could do.

I'd never worked with anyone outside of my father before, and the thought of working with Lucien was abhorrent. Erzulie agreed, but she wanted Odion more. We were running out of time, and other methods had proven unsuccessful thus far.

I had an idea.

"We'll need to use your hearing," I said. Leopards by nature had excellent hearing, and if I was right, I could use it for the spell I had in mind.

Lucien's whole body tensed. We stood there staring at each other like two ships on a collision course, trying to decide if one would concede and turn away or if each was determined to proceed on a course that couldn't be reversed. We would be laid open, revealing more, if not the full extent, of our abilities.

"Tell me what you're thinking," Lucien said.

I swallowed the lump in my throat. "I know Odion's voice, the accent. My guess could be off, but I'm willing to bet that besides the other kid with him, there isn't anyone else from Benin in New Orleans at the moment. We use your hearing, and I . . ." I paused, finding it difficult to speak suddenly. "I can amplify it."

A compromise. It was clear *what* I could do but not *how* I could do it. What I had in mind was to use the Evolution realm of my magic. Evolution takes raw material—in this case, Lucien's hearing—and adapts and expands it. In effect, I can turn it into a kind of homing beacon. And if—*if*—we caught Odion speaking at the right moment, we would have him.

"Follow me." Lucien's manner was that of a man resigned. Gone were the smart-aleck quips and the expression of someone who always felt they were ten steps ahead of you. He was afraid that I might prove more up to the task than he was.

We walked to a door that I hadn't noticed in the far corner of the room. Instead of a regular lock and key, the door was secured with an electronic keypad. As if he thought I was plotting to come back and break into the place, he positioned his body in front of the keypad, blocking my view. In a few seconds, a beep sounded.

The door swung inward, and a gust of cold air flooded out. Lucien flipped a switch, and I walked into a place with the footprint of a small bedroom and the opulence of a palace. Warm light cascaded from strips along the floorboards and the backsides of the wooden shelves lining the walls. A buttery-rich love seat atop a thickly padded rug. A desk and an unimaginative leopard-print chair tucked in front of it. There was even a crystalline chandelier hanging from the ceiling. Bottles and vials and wooden containers labeled with every manner of ingredient that I could think of. "This is quite the stash," I murmured as I followed him inside.

"Grab some of those candles, third shelf from the bottom, behind the vetiver. You know the colors."

I did so, while the houngan opened a wardrobe in the corner and grabbed a cushion, his asson, and a change of clothes. Back in the warehouse, I set the candles on the table, and he laid the other things nearby.

"This . . . ," Lucien said, waving a hand. "This working together like this. Neither of us is happy about it. But there's another potential Beninite out there, and we have to find him."

"And it's clear that neither of us were successful in doing so alone," I said.

"First and last?" he said.

I inclined my head. "First and last."

With that, Lucien dimmed the lights. We lit candles. Pink and blue and yellow for Erzulie. Gold and brown and white for Agassou.

Lucien sighed. "Guess you've seen this before, but I'll still ask you to turn away."

He grabbed the cushion he'd brought out from the back room and placed it in front of his altar. He knelt and began chanting. Softly at first. Words that sounded familiar, accompanied by a series of growls and grunts, then a sound like a wood plank being cut with a saw.

I backed away and turned around. At the same time, I concentrated on the candles and whispered prayers to my mistress. Called out to her from the land of the lwa, hoping that for Odion, she would respond. She was a spirit who cared deeply for children, after all.

She responded: this time, a burble in the palms of my hands that spread throughout my limbs.

The warehouse throbbed under the weight of Lucien's baritone. I couldn't help myself; I glanced over my shoulder and saw Agassou's vèvè writhing, and soon the paw reached out from the center, claws extracted. With a swipe, Lucien's chest began the peeling.

And I willed myself to look away, but my eyes stayed fixed, as if by unnatural force, to the scene before me. But he turned.

With his back to me, I couldn't see the pain that must have contracted Lucien's features, but I could see his body go rigid, then jerk. Then the flaying began. The skin loosened, crawled over his shoulders and torso, and collected around his ankles.

His body bucked and popped, reshaping itself into the leopard king. In his new form, Lucien stalked away from his skin, his shiny black coat glistening in the candlelight. He narrowed those yellow eyes at me, then growled and hissed. And I understood. It was my turn.

I allowed my body to go slack, my head tilted back. Erzulie rode in to claim my body, a watery rush that turned my solid form pellucid. I raised my watery hands, went over to the leopard king, and plucked a whisker from his face. He snarled and bared his sizable teeth, more for effect than harm.

Leopard whiskers were powerful talismans.

My sangswe formed a swirling, frothy rapid in my left palm. When a small bloodred storm erupted, I dropped the leopard whisker into its midst.

Time slowed. The warehouse's surroundings blurred and faded away. The city sprang up in its place, rushing by us as if we were on a fast-moving train. I nearly buckled under the pressure of the sounds that crashed in on us from all sides—car horns, barking dogs, a plane shooting across the horizon.

With a swipe of my hand, one by one, I cast them all aside. And there, beneath it all, voices. What sounded like a million of them.

The leopard's ears perked up and pointed forward.

Erzulie held me up as I combed through it all, like sifting flour. Checking, then discarding everything I didn't need. To find one voice in the middle of all this was a near-impossible task.

The leopard began pacing back and forth. When a voice sifted through that caught his attention, he stopped, raised a paw. Once his assessment was done, he'd start the pacing again.

I continued to channel my sangswe into the storm, feeding it my vital lifeblood. We continued in this way until well past dark, past the time when I'd sunk to my knees, past the time when my head lolled forward.

The storm was weakening. What had been the size of a tennis ball was now a marble.

I felt my body begin to fail. My heart was beating too slowly, and I felt as if I'd shed half my body weight in sweat. Just as I'd pulled on what I was certain was the last bit of strength I had, Lucien's leopard stopped pacing. His ears fluttered.

And I heard it. Odion's accent.

I released it all.

Spent, I dropped to the floor and watched in horror as Lucien turned back to human form. Bones and flesh shifting and melding like a building being demolished and rebuilt. The whole thing concluded by a sickening pop.

He was breathing heavy, curled in on himself, naked as the day he was born. If someone, anyone, had chosen this moment to burst in and accost us, the two most powerful vodouisants in New Orleans would have been powerless to stop them.

"Did you . . ." I struggled to speak. "Find him?"

It took a long time for Lucien to speak, and when he did, his voice was different. "I . . . know where he is."

I crawled over to my purse and got out the water bottle and energy bar I'd stashed just for this occasion. I took a swig and then offered Lucien the bottle. He shook his head.

"Not yet," he whispered. "He's at an abandoned house."

"Where?"

Lucien lifted his head, wrinkled his nose, then sniffed. "Near the high school. Saint Augustine."

Upon hearing this, Erzulie infused me with a brushstroke of strength before she took most of herself and departed.

I got to my feet. "Eat this," I said, shoving the energy bar at him. "When you can."

"No," he muttered. "Wait for—"

I stumbled out of the warehouse, the sound of Lucien's hoarse roar of outrage clawing at my back.

CHAPTER
THIRTY-EIGHT

I was parked across the street from Saint Augustine's, thinking of how to begin my search. It was the Seventh Ward: no surprise there. The other houses had been in the same area. I'd run out of the warehouse instead of waiting to see if Lucien could narrow things down. Nothing to do now but drive around and see what caught my eye.

I navigated up and down the narrow one-way streets and stopped to check every house that appeared to be abandoned or had a FOR SALE sign. It was slow going, and all the while, I prayed that Odion wasn't hurt.

Halfway down Law Street, my gaze was drawn to a weathered pink shotgun. It wasn't just the trash piled on the sidewalk, nor the dilapidated look of the place, but instinct that caused me to slam on the brakes.

I was out of the car a second later. Two steps from the gated front door, the taint of twisted magic reached out to greet me. "Odion!" I called, fumbling with the door, which arrogance had caused Solomon to leave unlocked.

Inside, a wave of heat slammed into me. I blinked at the impossibility in front of me.

"You came." Odion scrambled to his feet. He had been seated, cross-legged, on the floor, surrounded by a towering wall of flames.

I skirted around the edges of the circle and ran to the kitchen. I turned on the faucet, hoping to draw on the water, but the spout was stubbornly dry. I ran back to the front and past Odion, right through the front door. I needed to find water some other way.

The house next door was in pristine shape. I unscrewed the hose connected to the spigot in the side yard and turned the lever. Water gushed out. Back inside with Odion, I called to the water and channeled in my sangswe, raining it down on the flames.

But they resisted.

I drew more; at the same time, I could hear someone outside ranting about who had turned on the tap.

I pulled and channeled, the flames subsiding, and when I felt the water cut off, the flames were barely a foot high.

"Jump," I told Odion. There was no way to tell if they would go up again.

He hopped over the circle, and we were out the door and into my car.

For some reason—instinct again, I suppose—I headed to the Lemon Drop. I wasn't sure Lucien would approve of Odion seeing his lair so soon, and if Solomon Rise was still playing with fire, I wasn't sure home was the best place to be either. But I needed somewhere safe to gather myself, sort things out. Among friends seemed like the safest place we could be.

Lucien had been right. For a sliver of a moment, I felt guilty leaving him like I had in the warehouse. But had the tables been turned, he would have done the same to me.

I wound my way through the back streets that soon deposited me at the Lemon Drop. I was exhausted. I dragged myself out of the car, shouldered my purse, and gestured for Odi to follow.

Inside, the bar was empty; not even Chicken would be here this early in the day. No music played. Heart pounding, I searched Darryl's face from where he hunched over a table, cleaning. He looked up. "Uh-oh." His voice was soft.

I followed him into the office, noting that his limp had eased. Odion sank onto the love seat where I had napped more than once. He bowed his head, his arms wrapped around himself.

"I'll get y'all something to eat," Darryl said. With that, he turned and left, closing the door behind him. There was a glass of juice on the desk. I couldn't help myself—I was still depleted. I practically snatched the glass and drained it.

"How did you find me?" Odion asked. I cleared off Darryl's chair and pulled it around so that I could sit closer to the kid.

What could I tell him? I couldn't half explain it to myself. "The lwa demanded it, and we made it so."

Odion untangled himself and looked up at me. There was another question coming, probably several. But he just pressed his lips together and nodded. "I understand there is much you cannot say."

"And what happened after—after I lost you?"

"We went back," he said. "To the home where you found us that first time. There was a knock at the door. Edmund and I both found that strange—of all the men that had come to the house previously, they all had a key. I hoped it was you, but while we stood there debating whether or not to answer, they rammed the door open."

"ICE," I guessed.

Odion frowned.

"The authorities," I explained. "Did they flash badges?"

"Yes," he said. "I took off, hoping to get out back, and I . . . I thought Edmund was behind me."

I sat beside him and wrapped an arm around his narrow shoulders. "And then you got out."

Odion looked straight ahead. "Through a window," he said. "He called out to me, you know. But I ran. I left him."

There would be little we could do for the other kid. Chances were they already had him back on a plane home. This country could be ruthless about immigrants it didn't deem worthy of a seat at the American table.

"Where was Arthur?" I asked.

"Out," Odion said. "We hadn't seen him in a day."

I suspected that Arthur had figured the game was up. He had probably dropped a dime himself and bailed.

"And how on earth did Solomon find you?" I had so many questions. The lwa, my mother, but patience would be called for.

"That I cannot explain." He sat back, leaning his head against the wall. "After what happened at your home, I did not want to go back there, so I wandered all night. Caught a nap in an abandoned car. At some point this morning, as I was walking again, a car passed me a couple times, then doubled back. I was about to run when he jumped out and used your name. He said you sent him to help me."

"You're safe now," I said.

I'd have to ensure that, through Darryl, none of this would make its way back to Darby—and ultimately Roman. That was the trouble with lies: too many threads to keep in check. I just hoped that one day, it wouldn't all unravel.

I felt a familiar stirring. Odion was over six feet tall and had a bit of peach fuzz growing above his lip, but to me, when I looked at him, he was still a child. The bed in the spare room might be too small for him. I could rearrange all my appointments so that I could shuttle him to and from school. Where would I find shoes to fit him—

"Mambo Dumond?" Odion was watching me with that expression again, the eyes that weren't quite his.

"There is another vodouisant. One like me." I paused, considering. "And you—we can trust him." I nearly choked on that part. Trust? Lucien? Who was I kidding? He was the most self-serving human being I knew. But it was becoming clearer to me that Odion was a Beninite.

"I can't wait to meet him," Odion said.

I hated to admit it, but through his political contacts, Lucien would be able to smooth things over, get Odion a legitimate passport. Ensure he was taken care of. I wouldn't let him take over, though. We would train him together. Uncover his skill and his patron lwa. And then, *then*, I could probe him for what he knew about my mother.

But first things first.

⌁

It was a bright afternoon, warm and dense, absent any breeze, as if the air hung in a holding pattern. Like me. Odion and I stood outside the bar with loaded plates of food in hand. Indecision rendered me a statue.

Thus far, I had not lifted a finger to call Lucien. Even if he was still incapacitated, I could have left a message telling him that I had the teen safely in tow. I would, but I had to do something first.

"Is everything all right?" Odion asked, and in that moment, my decision was made.

"It will be," I said.

On the drive back to my house, Odion was quiet, and aside from a reassuring forearm squeeze, I let him be. No spell or ritual, rallying speech, or coddling would rid him of the guilt he felt at leaving his friend, Edmund. Time would dull it, but unless he found a way to help him, it would always be there, popping up unexpectedly and receding again like a cold sore.

Soon we were back at my house, our plates deposited in the kitchen. After getting us glasses of water, I asked Odion to join me at the table. "There's a ritual," I began. "It will tell us which of the lwa favors you. If you're comfortable, I would like to try it."

Chin to chest, he sighed, rolling his glass between long, slender fingers. "It is not what my parents want for me."

My heart sank. "But what do *you* want?" A part of me knew that I should back off, not push. But Odion knew (or maybe just sensed) something about my mother, and that part of me, the whole of my being that wanted her back more than anything, wasn't about to stop now.

His head jerked a little, as if surprised by the question. When his gaze rested on me again, I didn't put on the mask, the one that said I was cool no matter what. No, I implored him with every scrap of desperation I had.

"I want to try," he said, pushing the glass away and standing. "The place with the yellow bench in front. That is where you work, no?"

After practically dragging Odion outside, I settled him in a chair while I thought about what to do first. Mel had been my last customer here at my home. Unbeknownst to her, she had given me a clue with her talk of the NBA. Odion didn't need such directly connected negativity, so I would cleanse the space. The process was a simple one: smudging.

I always kept a fresh bundle of sage around for just this purpose. Back of the room, the drawer closest to the floor. I moved aside a partially used bundle and grabbed a fresh one, along with a match. Once lit, I let it burn until I had a nice smoking ember, then blew it out. The sharp aroma soon wafted into the air. I opened the window so that the negative energies would have a place to flow out.

From the front door back to the sink and cupboards, I fanned the smoke with my hand, asking the spirits to clear the peristil of all negativity. With a brief prayer of thanks, I was done.

I had just sat down, ready to explain the ritual I was about to perform, when I heard what was becoming a distinctive but all-too-familiar low growl flow in through the window I had forgotten to close. I got up and went to let Lucien in. It wasn't like I could hide.

He sniffed at the air. "I expected you to try to do this without me."

I wanted to slam the door in his face, to shut everyone out until I'd learned what I wanted. Instead I turned to Odion. "This is the houngan I told you about."

"It's dangerous being here," Lucien said. "You know that."

Whatever city or sports official had threatened my business knew of my involvement. I thought that with Solomon out of the picture, that would all go away, but it looked like he was still out there, pulling some strings. And he'd been inexplicably released on bond. Until I was sure he'd been put away permanently, there was no sense in taking any chances.

And because I knew Lucien was right, I let the fight drain from me like water from a tub.

"You'll be safer with Houngan Alexander for now," I explained.

"But you will visit with me?" There was an earnestness in Odion's voice that broke my heart.

"You can count on it."

I hugged Odion and assured him that I would see him soon. Then I let Lucien and his driver whisk him away.

"We'll do this the right way," Lucien said as they were leaving. "Once I get his visa situation taken care of."

I sat down at my table, knowing that I'd done the right thing but angry all the same. Answers about my mother, it seemed, had escaped me once again. Slipped from my grasp like a mist. I had waited a decade to find out if she was alive or dead. I would be waiting a little more.

CHAPTER THIRTY-NINE

Watching Odion drive off with Lucien felt akin to building a new home, plank by plank, and then, once the key to the lock was in your hand, turning and walking away instead. I wouldn't be getting answers anytime soon, and any training was on hold.

Solomon Rise was free for now, but I hoped not for long—the prosecutors had enough to build a solid case. I had done my part, and now I was as idle as a moored ship.

I had one last score to settle, however, so I picked myself up, tucked my hopes away again, and drove over to Bywater to see Mrs. Evangeline Stiles. After everything I had uncovered over the last couple of weeks, I doubted she would ever be "Ms. Vangie" to me again.

I didn't turn on the new stereo system Tyka had gifted (or boosted) me; instead I rolled down the window, letting in air cool and indulgent. Music was everywhere anyway: cars pulling up next to me at a stop, a school band practicing for competition, even the crickets and cicadas croaking in harmony.

I had been distracted over the last couple of weeks, preoccupied to such a degree that I had almost let fall pass by unnoticed. It was my favorite season. This time as I drove, I allowed myself the small pleasure of watching life unfold around me.

I navigated cratered roads and one-way streets that were mere suggestions. A swarm of police cars crowded in front of a tenement building. A crowd of spectators streamed in and gawked, ensnared like flies caught in a flytrap. At a stoplight, I witnessed the kindness of a younger woman offering her seat to an older person at a bus stop. Ours was a city of contrasts. Nowhere else did people love life and relish in its celebration more while also walking a fine line with danger, ready to pull them over to the other side without so much as a warning.

If my guess was right, my client had returned home. That's where I would look first.

The gun-toting neighbor I had faced down on my last visit was, thankfully, nowhere in sight. The blue, late-model Toyota *was* sitting in the driveway, so there was a good chance she was at home. I hadn't called. Didn't want to give her a chance to come up with a story to placate me, or disappear before I arrived. Some probably thought me rude—any other time I would have agreed. That didn't stop me from marching right up and ringing the doorbell.

Bluesy music played at a respectable volume that, after a few moments, was turned down lower.

I heard movement, then annoyed grumbling close on the other side of the door before I sensed someone watching me through the peephole. Locks turned, and I heard the sound of a chain clattering against the wall.

It was midday, but Evangeline still had her hair done up in neat pin curls. She was draped in a newish-looking silken robe, a long gown underneath. I raised an eyebrow. The prim, conservative clothes she always wore to our appointments had hidden her enviable figure.

My client's face went from annoyed, to shocked, to ashamed and back in the moments before she spoke. "I know your mama taught you better than to show up at somebody's door unannounced."

How dare she even mention my mother. "We doing this outside"—I peered over my shoulder at a kid ripping past us on a skateboard—"or inside?"

With a huff, she stepped aside. The smell of bacon permeated the air, nearly done. A black duffel bag sat open on the floor, clothes hastily spilling out, while another pile was dumped on a high-back chair. Men's clothing, from the looks of it. I pulled my gaze away and trailed Ms. Vangie into the kitchen.

Bacon sizzled and popped on the stove. A few jumbo brown eggs sat on the counter nearby, ready to go, but she turned off the burner, leaned against the counter, and crossed her arms. She cocked her head at me. "Tell me what you think you know."

Best to start at the beginning. "You lied."

"Everybody tells lies. Even you," she snapped. "You found Arthur and didn't even pick up the phone to tell me. And I know you figured out where he got the money."

"Arthur got paid twenty-five thousand dollars for his part in that mess. You told me it was five grand," I said, ignoring her.

She cinched her robe tighter as if protecting herself. "The amount was really none of your business, now, was it?"

It wasn't. None of this was my business. That hadn't stopped me. This time, I couldn't hide behind protecting my tradition, or saving a fellow vodouisant. No, I had walked into this, eyes wide open, because I wanted to. Because the lwa, Erzulie, had wanted me to find Odion.

I planted my hands on my hips. "You and Beau Winters. Want to tell me about that?"

For the first time, Ms. Vangie's stiff exterior cracked. She splintered and welded herself back together in the span of a few ragged breaths. If I'd had any doubts about the nature of their relationship, they were dashed. She had been romantically involved with her husband's friend, and she was aware that he was now dead. In that moment, I forgot that

Ms. Vangie had deceived me. She was my old client again, and I wanted nothing more than to go over and wrap an arm around her shoulders.

"You don't get to stand there and judge me," she said, and I let the feeling pass. She walked past me to the small kitchen dinette, ripped open her purse, and started digging around inside.

The stove was off, but the burner was still hot. Still sizzling on the stove, the bacon had begun to smoke.

I went over and grabbed the spatula sitting on the counter, scooped up the burned and blackened pieces, and dropped them onto a plate. The smell of comfort, of a Sunday-morning breakfast with family, gone, replaced by scorch and ruin. I moved the skillet off the burner.

When I turned, she was standing there with what looked like a check in her hand. "Just take the money and go." She thrust it at me.

I reached out, my fingertips brushing the check, and then I snatched my hand back as if I'd been bitten by a rabies-infected mutt. This money was tainted, part of a scheme where everybody won but those kids.

At least some of the time. Out of the three I knew of—the homeless kid, Edmund, and Odion—I was fairly sure Odion would be able to stay, and that he would excel at whatever he chose to do with his life here. And I was living in a fantasy world: Was there even such a thing as clean money? This time, when my benefactor waved the check at me, I took it.

As I was stuffing the check in my purse, a thought occurred. "Why did you let Beau hustle Solomon Rise for more money? You had to know he and Arthur were dealing with some potentially dangerous people."

"Who is Solomon?"

Oh.

Arthur had hidden that part from her. "Doesn't matter," I said.

"I went over to tell Beau I was breaking things off with him," Vangie said and then paused, clearly upset. "He didn't want it to end. Do you know he threatened to tell my Arthur about us? Yes," she said, indignant. "I took a swing at him. We had made a mistake, an ugly one, I admit it. But when he grabbed me, I pushed him, and Arthur chose that second to walk in. I . . . I ran."

Ms. Vangie's face crumpled again, and this time she couldn't blink back the tears. "Wait," I said, coming over to pat her shoulder. "You think—"

I stopped. She thought Arthur had committed the murder. I could have let her off the hook. Explained how Beau really died. But I hadn't. Arthur and Vangie had mended ways; he had forgiven her and she him. Had the couple been preparing to make an exit?

"You need to sit down," I told her.

She stood there watching me. I pulled out a chair, sat down, and crossed my legs. Soon enough, she joined me. "Arthur didn't kill Beau," I said. I had to give her this piece of the truth, at least. "The cops are still investigating, but trust me, he didn't do it."

She blinked and wiped her eyes with a corner of her robe. It was as if the display of emotion had embarrassed her. "Beau and Arthur were involved in this kind of Africa-to-NBA pipeline," I said. "That's where the money came from."

"Africa to NBA," Ms. Vangie said with a frown. "What are you talking about?"

It hit me then that she had been honest about the reason she'd come to me. She really had no idea what her husband had been involved in. Probably smart of him to keep her out. Not smart of him to drop money in a shared bank account with no explanation. While I explained everything about the scam her husband was involved in, and endured countless interruptions to answer questions, I moved on to my next point.

"The bags out front. You coming or going?"

She looked uncertain, fiddling with her hair. It confirmed for me that she hadn't known the full extent of her husband's involvement and was considering her next words carefully.

She pressed her lips together, then sighed. "Me and Arthur are still trying to figure out our next move."

I understood her reticence. I was in the same place with Roman. On this matter she was right—I couldn't judge her. What went on between couples was as complicated and irrational as a gecko on a snowy mountaintop. "I'll wish you both luck then."

I gathered up my things then and left, uncertain if I could still call Ms. Vangie a client but certain that, all along, she had never been a friend.

CHAPTER FORTY

I was at my dining room table, adding up all the receipts for what I had paid toward owning my home, when from the other room, I heard the WDSU newscaster mention Roman's name.

I rarely turned on the news, but I hadn't heard anything about the fallout from the murder, and I dared not broach the subject with him. To do so would give him the hint he needed that I cared and was perhaps involved. A quick search on the internet had only revealed snippets.

So I rushed into the parlor as a mug shot of Solomon Rise filled the screen. I turned up the volume.

Local athletic director Solomon Rise was caught in a hidden room in a Broad Street men's club, a suspected front for drug distribution. Already out on bond, he was found in possession of human growth hormone, or HGH, which has been known to provide a boost to workouts and help with quicker healing, but also for its dangerous side effects, including delusion, aggression, and heart and liver damage. Detective Roman Frost responded to an anonymous tip—

"HGH," I mouthed to myself. That must have been what he was shooting up with. And along with having very little idea of what he was doing, that's what had twisted his magic and resulted in Beau's death, and almost my own. "Get to the good part." I wound my hand, willing them to skip over the unnecessary details.

Drug use among college and professional athletes continues to plague the country. It has also been revealed that other college and high school officials, along with members of local government and immigration, have been implicated in a scheme involving foreign student athletes. Mayor Richard will be facing a public inquiry. Mr. Rise has been relieved of his duties as president of the NCAA Board of Governors and is also stepping down from his role as athletic director, ostensibly to spend more time with his family.

Then a pan to a video clip where, under the glittering lights of a press conference, he wept his way through, droning on about how he had been working too hard and turned to drugs to help him keep up with the pace of his demanding job.

Finally, the news anchor explained how Solomon Rise would be sent to what amounted to a country club rehab center for six measly weeks.

The story ended shortly after that. I threw a sock at the TV, then grabbed the remote and turned it off.

No mention of Gwendolyn Guillory or her school. Not a peep about the connection to Beau Winters or Arthur Stiles. The whole thing smelled of a brewing cover-up. Anger boiled in me at the thought that Solomon would get off.

I suspected that without his drug, he would not have been able to do what he did. Something told me, something more than hope, that he was done with his attempt at messing with our practice, but if he ever crept back out of whichever prison cell he would soon be calling home, I would be ready.

CHAPTER

FORTY-ONE

A week later, Darryl, Tyka, and I finally had the dinner that we had attempted following the events of the French Quarter murder—the one where Tyka never showed. This time, Darryl took the lead, relegating me to sous chef, chopping, prepping, and generally staying out of his way.

Not too gently, they had each separately suggested that I not invite Roman. I was more than a little offended. I countered, explaining how selfish they were, not considering whether this would hurt my feelings, let alone Roman's. The latter mention only earned me rolled eyes and rude, loud exhales. I asked how they were ever supposed to get to know each other better if I kept excluding him. In the end, I gave in, but I would try again another time.

No surprise who arrived first.

"Here, take this." Darryl shoved two shopping bags at me as he pushed through the door and kicked off his shoes. He rummaged around in the smaller cloth bag, produced his slippers, then shuffled over to the sofa. He sat down with a slight wince to put them on. "Go on," he said, waving his hand at me. "No need to stand there gaping at me. I can find my way to the kitchen."

I gave him a side-eye but did as told. I was setting out ingredients on the table when he came up behind me.

"I can finish that." Darryl tried to elbow me aside.

"I'm almost—" Then I saw it. At the bottom of the bag, wrapped in a sock, an amber-colored glass vial. Only one houngan I knew used them. My mind groped back to my last visit to Manchac, the candy wrappers . . .

"You went to see my father," I said, rounding on him.

Darryl's eyebrows shot up to his receding hairline. "Ain't there some such thing as an oath or something y'all take that says you ain't supposed to discuss your client business?"

"There is," I said. "And Papa kept it. He didn't tell me anything. *You* did." I held up the vial.

"Solve a case or two"—Darryl snatched the bottle, set it down on the table, and busied himself fumbling around with the stuff on the table—"and you turn into some kind of detective."

"You're avoiding the point."

"I ain't avoiding nothin'. I'm clearly not talking about it."

I took the shrimp out of his hand. "But you can talk to my father?"

"Put that in the refrigerator while I get everything else ready."

"You're really not going to talk about this?" I set the shrimp back down.

"Guess you need another clue to figure that out?" Darryl snatched up the shrimp and tossed it in the refrigerator himself.

"Fine," I mumbled while we went about unpacking and getting everything ready. If only I could have gotten a look or sniff at what was in the bottle, that might have told me what was wrong. His coloring was fine. Eyes clear. *Eyes.* How was his vision?

"How much sodium does that tomato sauce have?" I asked him.

He picked up the can and read off the small print. "If you watching your salt intake, you better start tomorrow."

The man consumed enough candy to start his own store, so I had guessed diabetes. But he had spent the night here before, and I hadn't noticed any frequent urination, and his weight was steady; the blurry-vision check was just me groping. I had little else to go on.

He had a limp, some pain when he sat or stood, and he seemed to get tired easily—all symptoms of about two, maybe three, hundred ailments. I could only pray that Papa was helping him. He did seem better than he had been a few months earlier.

My friend must have felt bad, because he broke the tense, angry silence that had settled. "You placing bets on whether or not that lil' old gal is going to show up?"

I nodded and with certainty that I didn't feel said, "She'll be here this time."

I could tell by the look in his eye that Darryl was hopeful that our little makeshift family could actually sit down and have a nice dinner together. He had asked her to come early to help with the preparations. That, however, was a long shot. In our little crew, we had our roles, however unclear they were. Surrogate parents? Best friends? Youngish aunt? Old, surly uncle?

Perhaps one day, if I were blessed, I could add to our family.

"Okay," Darryl said, snapping me out of my thoughts. "Get out your best skillet."

Best? I only had one, so I whipped it out of the cabinet beside the stove and held it up. "My best skillet," I said with a smile. "Ready for action."

"Yeah," Darryl said, taking it from me and setting it on a burner. "Now get your cutting board."

I reached into my junk drawer and produced it. Darryl looked from me to it, and frowned.

"What is that?" he asked, incredulous.

I shrugged. "What's wrong with it?"

"It's the size of a washcloth," Darryl said. "That's what."

"It gets the job done." I set it on the counter.

"Work at the table," Darryl commanded. "Don't want you tripping all over me."

"Whatever," I huffed.

"Now take that onion, the green pepper, celery, and garlic and chop those up. Not big chunks but not too fine either."

I took my bite-size cutting board and retreated to lick my wounds and chop at the dinette table. Every few seconds, Darryl peeked over his shoulder to make sure I was doing it right.

A banging at the door sounded. "You don't think . . . ," Darryl said.

"No way," I said. Despite what I'd said, I thought the chances of Tyka showing up today were slim. I trotted to the door, half expecting to open it and find Ms. Lucy there to chastise me about upsetting her friend Vangie.

"You know better than to whip the door open without asking who it is. Check the peephole or something," Tyka said.

She had a jacket draped over her shoulders, and it wasn't until she came in and shrugged out of it that I noticed her arm was in a sling. "What happened to your arm?"

"Wrestling accident. Dude is in worse shape than me, though." She diverted to the bathroom and slammed the door.

"What's wrong with her?" Darryl asked as I took my place back at the table.

"The sun came up? The moon is shining too brightly? There isn't world peace?"

Darryl swiped a forearm across his forehead. "Or it's something to do with that father of hers."

The knocking in the wall behind me told me that she'd flushed the toilet. A moment later, Tyka stood in the doorway, looking from Darryl to me with a scowl. "Food ain't ready yet?"

To this, Darryl tossed a towel at her. She snatched it out of the air with her right hand.

"What happened to your arm?"

"What happened to that little limp you tried so hard to hide?"

The two glared at each other and only stopped when I failed to stifle a chuckle. That broke the tension.

"All right," Darryl said. "I've got to make the rice. I guess this here lil' gal can't even peel the shrimp."

"That's right," Tyka said, sitting and propping her feet up on my other chair. "I need to rest my arm."

"I'll do it." I got up and, after a bit of shoving back and forth, managed to pry the package of shrimp from Darryl's grip.

"So what happened to those boys?" Tyka asked behind a yawn.

I went on to explain what I could about the whole matter—minus the part where I'd left her out.

"He's like you, ain't he?" Tyka asked. "That one that walks around like Jesus risen."

"She does get a little full of herself," Darryl added, pouring rice into a pot before setting the burner on low.

I snorted. "He is special. Lucien and I will help him." They were my friends, like family, but they weren't of the tradition, and there were simply some bridges that you didn't cross. What I loved about them most was that they respected that difference and never pushed the issue. Never questioned.

"What happened to that lady judge then?" Tyka popped a green pepper in her mouth, scrunched up her face, then spit it out into a napkin.

I realized I didn't know, but Darryl, the neighborhood newscaster, did. "Word is she's going to be charged with conspiracy to harbor aliens. And your boy Arthur?" Darryl pointed a spoon at us. "When they find him, he's going down for obstruction. Something small enough to bounce him back inside for a bit."

"You know you sent me to Juju, and he gave me bad information. He thought it was all about flipping houses," I said.

"I gave you a source—up to you to check it out," Darryl said over his shoulder. "You being some vodouisant turned big-time detective and all."

"I'm still a vodouisant. Want me to invite Erzulie to our little party?"

Darryl turned, eyes wide and subdued. I pulled the shell off the shrimp, ripping away half the meat in the process. I tried to hide it, but Chef Eagle-Eye had already spotted my snafu and came over to demonstrate how to do it properly.

"Tyka could do a better job with one arm," he admonished. "Pay attention to what you're doing. I want shrimp, not Kibbles 'N Bits."

With that, we dropped the matter of Ms. Vangie, Arthur, and the Africa-to-NBA pipeline.

The rice simmering on the stove, Darryl returned to the table, pulled the remainder of the shrimp away from me, and took over the task himself.

"And school," he said, cutting his eye at Tyka. "Guessing you didn't go?"

I put down the shrimp I had picked up. "School? What are you talking about?"

"Oops." Darryl threw his hands up.

Tyka frowned. "You keep your secrets just fine. Why you so free with everybody else's, I'll never understand."

"Is somebody going to tell me what's going on?" I was so tired of the secrets.

Tyka picked at her nails, painted a shiny black. "I signed up. Something else came up. I didn't go. That's all there is to say about it."

"But—"

Darryl held up a hand, willing me to drop it there.

"There's always next semester." I got it in anyway. He shot me a glance that I waved off.

Tyka didn't respond. She got up, grabbed a spoon, and stirred the rice. We went on to rib each other in the way that only good friends, family, can.

Darryl banished us to the dining room while he finished up, adding his special secret ingredients to the shrimp Creole.

When Darryl called out that everything was done, we set the table. I poured sweet tea for each of us, then set a shot glass beside Darryl's plate for his whiskey.

We sat down to eat. Laughed, ate too much, and in the end, Darryl fell asleep on the sofa, while Tyka slunk back into the night. Along with the plate I'd convinced her to take with her—for Eddie, of course—she left with the general wellness tincture I'd slipped into her pocket when I handed her jacket to her.

This evening had left me renewed. I knew its memory would sit in a corner of my mind to be revisited often, glanced upon fondly. But as hard as I tried, and I did put in the effort, I couldn't see how Roman would have fit into this perfect picture.

CHAPTER
FORTY-TWO

The morning after the dinner with my friends, I'd just woken Darryl, whom I hadn't had the heart to send home so late. He was sitting up, groggy, clutching the blanket I'd draped over him, when I heard a key in the door.

"If it ain't Detective Frosty," Darryl said as soon as Roman stepped through the door.

I glared at Darryl. The nickname was courtesy of Tyka. Roman hated it.

Though I had spoken to him by phone and had exchanged a few text messages, I hadn't seen Roman in a couple of days. His tie hung loosely around his neck. His clothes were a bit rumpled. Shadows had resumed their place beneath his eyes. In a word, he looked haggard. I'd warned him that his job would take a toll, and he had flung back the same warning about my impromptu detective work.

"Guess I didn't get an invitation to the party," Roman said to Darryl, but his eyes and all their venom were on me. I'd had to harangue Roman to apologize to Darryl over the food-permit hassle at the Lemon

Drop, back when Roman and I weren't on great terms. He'd done so, and they'd been civil, if not friendly, since then. But now?

"Last I heard, you worked late nights. An invite would have been downright mean. What we did do was leave you a plate of leftovers," Darryl said, coming to his feet. "Shrimp Creole. Nice and spicy."

"It got really late," I added, a little surprised and impressed that Darryl had tried to cover for me. "After we cooked. I didn't want him driving home tired."

Roman actually took a moment to consider, then nodded. "Makes sense. If you two buddies will excuse me, it's been a long night."

With that, he strode off toward the bedroom. The door closed with a soft click instead of a slam.

"You think he's going to the can?" Darryl asked, folding the blanket. He handed it to me and did a few stretches.

"Go ahead," I urged, motioning toward the bathroom.

While I waited for Darryl to finish cleaning up, I packed all his things and put them back in his shopping bags.

"Gonna head on home and change before I head to the bar."

I bade him goodbye with a peck on his cheek that he feigned wiping off. With a backward wave, he was gone.

"So you doing sleepovers now?" Roman had somehow snuck up behind me. He was in his boxers and a T-shirt, but he still wore his black socks. Any other time, the sight would have been funny. "I half expected to find Tyka in the spare room."

"Why can't you just try to get along with my friends? Why don't you like them?" I headed to the kitchen and set the kettle on the stove. If we were going to fight about this, I would at least do so over a steaming cup of jasmine tea.

Roman filled the doorway, a curious expression on his face. If I didn't know better, I would've said he was disappointed. "Did they say they didn't want me here?"

They most certainly did. "No," I said. "What Darryl said was right. Why invite you when I know you'll be working?"

My answer must have satisfied him because instead of an explosion of harmful words, he marched to the cabinet and took out two mugs and his instant coffee. As relief settled the knot in my shoulders and dissipated with a strong exhale, he left the room.

As a gesture of peace, I'd make us a small breakfast. Eggs, toast, sausage. I didn't have the heart, or as Darryl suggested, the skill, for grits.

I had popped sausage in the skillet Darryl had so meticulously scrubbed and turned on the burner when Roman came back.

"This rent-to-own agreement of yours. It's shit," he said. I turned to find him holding up a sheaf of papers. I'd forgotten he had asked to look them over. Ever the showman, he slammed the small stack on the kitchen table and tapped it. "Don't get me wrong," he corrected. "It's legal, but it's a sham. You'll own this home when you're two hundred and seventy-five years old."

"What are you talking about?" I stomped over and snatched up the papers, as if looking at them again would change what he'd just said.

"It's right there, the places where I put a highlight." Roman flipped through the pages, pointing to highlighted sections. "Did you have an attorney look it over beforehand?"

He knew that I hadn't, and it pissed me off that he asked. "I read it myself."

He raised an eyebrow. "I scanned," I corrected, head slumped. "And I trusted."

I was livid. At the landlord, at Roman. But Roman, strip club frequenter, was the one right in front of me.

"Seems like you have it all figured out," I said curtly.

"Don't get mad at me. I didn't do anything."

"Do you still go to that strip club over in the Quarter?"

Roman faltered. He averted his gaze. That was a yes, as plain as day. "Where is this coming from?"

"Can you answer the question?"

"Can you focus on what we're talking about here?"

I was mute, arms crossed.

"No," he said, pushing away from the table. "I don't go there. But most of the force does. I might pick up and drop off, but I don't go in."

I leveled my gaze on him. Considered using a certain spell to ascertain the truth, but I stood down.

Roman whipped out another piece of paper from the stack. "Take a look." He shoved the paper in front of me where I'd sunk into a seat at the table. "Shit," he said and then raced over to the stove to attend to the sausage I'd already forgotten about.

"Look at it, Reina," he commanded, gesturing with the spatula.

On the paper was a picture of a small storefront. From the looks of it, it was in a neighborhood more than a commercial center. A decorative door, a series of small windows that would provide light and privacy. It didn't appear to be much larger than my . . . peristil.

"You need to get out of here and move in with me." Roman dumped the sausage on a plate and cracked the eggs directly into the pan, haphazardly scrambling them with the spatula. And some people talked about my cooking. When the kettle whistled, I got up and poured the water into our cups. I needed something to do with my hands.

"I found you a new place to conduct your business." His hesitation before the word "business" was slight, the breadth of a human eyelash perhaps, but it was there. That struggle to accept my practice. "It's about a mile from the house. It's safe. It's cheap. I can buy it for you outright. I know the owner."

My mind was the picture of chaos. In the span of a few minutes, I'd learned that I, a duly initiated mambo, had been swindled. That the dream of homeownership was nothing more than a lie for me. All the years of work I'd done on this house and the peristil . . . I just couldn't fathom all that going down the drain. But what could I do?

"Are you going to say something?" Roman said with his back turned while scrambling eggs probably filled with burned pieces of sausage. "Never known you to have a lack of words."

"Can I think for a minute?" I asked. "It's a lot to take in."

"Grab some plates," Roman said, pulling the skillet off the stove.

I trudged over, got the plates, and set them on the table while Roman shoveled out the brownish eggs. We ate and sipped in silence for a while. Thankfully. Waiting was not one of Roman's strong suits.

"I get it," he said between bites. "I know you're mad. But I see this as a sign." He paused, then continued: "About us. You need to be with me."

There it was. The note to a song my heart so desperately wanted him to pluck. I swallowed my food and tea without tasting. Images of the family I wanted. A life with Roman that wouldn't have gaps of days or weeks at a time. Everything I wanted.

But.

"When can I take a look at the space?" I sipped some tea to chase down the bile that was churning in my stomach.

Roman's face blossomed in a way that melted my heart and squashed some of the queasiness. "I'll talk to the owner, but I bet we could look at it this weekend."

I steeled my shoulders and met his eyes. "It doesn't have to be fancy. It most certainly shouldn't be expensive. I won't even entertain thoughts of a blood diamond." I lifted my eyes and took in his. "But I do want a ring."

He didn't speak immediately. And it infuriated me that he fixed that blank detective expression on his features. He licked his lips, reached across the table, and took my hand.

He smiled.

I held my breath.

He brought my fingertips to his moist lips. "We will most definitely talk about that after you move in."

My heart deflated like a spent Mardi Gras float. But I didn't let on. There was no reason to scream and fight. I'd played my card, and Roman had countered with his own. The ball, as they say, was in my court. I needed to make a decision. Was I being stubborn about a ring that didn't matter? Or should I stick to my archaic principles?

We finished up breakfast, and I let Roman get what rest he could while I cleaned up the kitchen. I hadn't made a decision about the ring, but I did decide something. There was no way I'd been paying into a black hole for the last three years. Even if I ended up with Roman, I was not going to let my landlord get away with this. I was a woman, and in that, all he saw was someone to take advantage of.

For true? I had to own my pride. So determined was I to do this on my own, I'd let my good sense go hide in a corner.

No, I thought to myself. My landlord would learn to think twice about swindling a woman, or a mambo, ever again. I would win ownership of this home one way or another, even if that cost me with Roman.

CHAPTER FORTY-THREE

Halloween was always a special time in the Vodou tradition. It was during this time that the barrier between the worlds of the living and those departed was, for lack of a better term, thinnest. If what Odion had said was correct, that he'd sensed something about my mother, then there would be no better time to act.

Lucien remained tight lipped about his political contacts, and with Kiah always lurking around, it was possible that somebody had been strong-armed as well, but I didn't concern myself with how. All that mattered was that he had secured the kid a proper visa and settled him in with a family in Gentilly, empty nesters who were proud to foster a teenager from the African continent.

Married for thirty years, together they had raised a family, three children, one more perfect than the next. Their extra bedroom held a king-size bed, not the full that I had. An extra bathroom Odion could have to himself. Through work with her sorority, the mother had traveled to every corner of the motherland twice over. They had the disposable income and savings to purchase Odion a ticket home to see his parents at Christmas.

They had everything that I didn't. So I did what I had to. I gritted my teeth and smiled my way through convincing Odion that their home was the best place for him.

But I could teach him once he was settled. Lessons would alternate between Lucien and me. He was still getting acclimated in school, having started the semester weeks behind. He was sharp, though, and we learned that he was light-years ahead of the kids in his class. Odion, it seemed, would be graduating early and heading to college. The only question was Tulane or LSU. I petitioned for Southern, but the basketball program didn't hold the same allure as the bigger schools'.

Even with the leadership shake-up at the NCAA effectively voiding whatever deal Solomon Rise had trapped him in, I wasn't comforted by the thought of Odion getting involved with any of those sharks. No matter where he went, he would be free of any financial commitment to anyone but himself.

Of my mother, we'd come up empty. Several rituals and promptings, but he couldn't see anything more than what he'd sensed on that first day. I steeled myself for what I'd been denying for years. My mother was likely with the ancestors. Swept away with the water and never recovered, like so many others during the storm.

I wasn't surprised when I received the hand-delivered note from Lucien a week ago. The first meeting of the New Orleans Voodoo Council was set for three o'clock this afternoon at Lucien's warehouse in New Orleans East, the American spelling the result of weeks of haggling and hurt feelings. There was no question that Papa would not make the trip, though he'd be waiting for a full debrief after it was over.

I dressed in a simple tie-dyed skirt and white long-sleeved blouse. I pulled on my knee boots and headed outside.

A baby-blue sky was littered with clouds, but soon, the wind pushed them onward and my mind cleared like the spaces they had left behind. The air tasted of smoked meats and exhaust. The sun was warm on my face as I held it up to drink in the rays. I drew in a bit of moisture from deep within the soil, just for a quick replenish.

I hopped in my car just as Ms. Lucy was coming outside. She scowled at me; probably Ms. Vangie had told her of my visit. I blew the horn and waved, just to annoy her more. She returned the wave, and I was off down the street.

Preparations for a holiday parade were visible in the streets. Pumpkins, black-cat cutouts, and skeletons. I wondered again at the strange American imagery associated with this holiday. In Haiti, we celebrated Fèt Gede, our version of the Day of the Dead. Faces powdered white, we dressed in shades of black or purple, sometimes white. It was a day to pay homage to Baron Samedi, the god of life and death, and to celebrate our ancestors with food and drink. Candy and costumes didn't factor in.

I got to the warehouse in record time, only thwarted by one pothole the size of a moon crater. I winced thinking about what repair might be necessary.

The parking lot was already filling up, vodouisants spilling forth from their cars. Like me, they were dressed simply. I joined the throng and exchanged a few greetings as we filed inside.

The thump of drums flooded the space, Petwo rhythms. Since my last visit, the warehouse interior had been transformed to include soothing recessed overhead lighting, which bounced off every surface and painted the room in a subtle but diffused glow. Candles burned in the candelabras placed along both sides of the walls and surrounding the dais at the center of the stage. Folding chairs laid out in rows were already nearly full.

With this many vodouisants gathered, there was a strong sense of the spirits around us. A calm and ancient force. A flutter in the belly and a whisper against the skin.

Refreshments were set up along tables behind the last row of seats. I grabbed a cup of water, downed it, and made my way to the front of the room. Lucien was talking to a houngan with a small practice in trendy Uptown. Three others waited in line behind him.

We locked gazes, and he greeted me with a slight lift of his chin, which I returned. He motioned to a chair in the front row. I couldn't believe he'd reserved one for me. And there, two seats down, sat Salimah. She had done herself up for the occasion. A simple but stylish dress, a colorful scarf skillfully tied around her head with an off-center knot. She'd even put on makeup. Her entire visage said she was going through with her intent to challenge Lucien.

"Mambo Grenade," I said. "Good to see you."

She stood and took my hand, bending close to my ear. "You don't like him any more than I do," she said with a squeeze. "Support me."

I pulled away, annoyed at the forceful nature of her request. If she thought she could hold guilt about Rashad over my head, she was mistaken. I'd made my peace with the lwa and couldn't care less about what she thought. "I'll consider it," I said and then went to take my seat.

Just as I sat, Odion emerged, with none other than Kiah in tow. I shouldn't have expected Kiah would be absent for this little event, but I'd held out hope. Odion's face split into a grin as he made his way over to me. Just then, his steps faltered. Kiah caught him. Lucien raced over as I closed the distance between us.

The few vodouisants who'd noticed stopped talking and turned their attention to us. Lucien waved them away, and we moved off to the corner of the dais.

"What is it?" I asked Odion, lifting his chin with my finger. "What's wrong?"

He jerked once more and shivered, and a film came over him. It was as if, before our eyes, he'd zipped an invisible suit over himself. His features were his, with a shadowy overlay. Then it was gone.

"She doesn't belong," he said, his voice hoarse.

"Who?" Lucien and I asked at the same time. Even Kiah looked confused.

For reasons I didn't understand, the small hairs on my arms, the fine fuzz at the back of my neck, all stood on end. "What? Who doesn't belong where?" I urged again.

Odion turned his gaze on me. Something unreadable in his eyes. "Merline Dumond. Souls must pick a side. They cannot sit in the middle."

Before I fainted, the sight of the great houngan Lucien Alexander, afraid, shot a pang of terror through me that sped my way to the darkness.

$$\backsim$$

I came to on a leather love seat in the warehouse's back room. I sat up. The tension in the room was as thick as the carpet beneath my bare feet. I blinked a few times to orient myself. My mind had gone blank. In a few moments, I had at least calmed my breathing.

Odion sat on a carved African stool, right in front of me. The visage that I now knew was his patron lwa was gone. But I had my suspicions of who it was. The teen handed me a bottle of water. I gulped down half of it. Lucien sat in the wingback, his forearms on his knees, his head bent. Kiah leaned against the wall across from him; even he looked worried. Then it all came back to me.

Manman!

"My mother." I looked between them both. I was afraid to ask, to confirm what I thought I'd heard. "What did you mean when you said she doesn't belong?"

Odion looked to Lucien, who just shook his head.

"Odion's message came through Baron Samedi," he said.

My hairs stood on end. This teenager from Benin was actually connected to the lord of life and death. Giver of life, the rising sun. The guardian of the old bones who sits at the gates where life and death intersect.

Odion nudged me over and sat beside me. He took my hand, a patience in his eyes that belied his years. I snatched it away. If he was going to tell me my mother was gone, I just wanted to hear it. He sighed, inhaled, and let it all out in a jumble. "She is in the place between the living and the afterlife."

The place between the living and the dead. It was supposed to be a temporary place. A place where souls crossing to the other side either made the final trip or healed and came back to the land of the living. How had she gotten there? Had she been injured during the storm? All those years that the water-gazing bowl only showed a cloud when I tried to find her. I could have slapped myself: it had been showing me exactly where she was. My heart constricted. When Papa heard this, he would be heartbroken.

My heart thrummed like a million guitar strings. Sweat erupted from my pores. Erzulie fought to control everything in my body that was suddenly out of whack. I didn't know whether to mourn her loss or rejoice that she wasn't quite gone. My mouth opened, but when I tried to speak, no words came out.

"She is there," he continued. "Surrounded in some kind of cloud."

"Is she"—I struggled with the next word—"dead?"

"Not exactly." It was Lucien who spoke, though he hadn't looked up. "She's asleep. She isn't suffering."

"She wouldn't even be aware of the passage of time," Odion said.

"Ten years." I shot to my feet. "Ten years, my mother has been asleep between here and Ginen? How?"

Odion looked to Lucien, who blew out a tired breath and finally looked at me. "It was after the storm," Lucien began and then put up a hand to pause. His voice cracked with emotion. When he looked up again, tears had welled in his eyes.

I couldn't stand this anymore. Just what was going on? "Tell me," I said in as even a voice as I could muster.

"She couldn't get to you. Josué was out there holed up in Manchac. She called me. She'd witnessed something—" Lucien cleared his throat. "Something awful. She saw it, Reina, saw all the horror that took place after those waters flooded our city."

My mother had called Lucien, and he never thought to mention it? After I'd begged and pleaded with her, it had been too late. The phone lines were down. I was stuck out there and couldn't find her. I squeezed my eyes shut at the sudden, sharp pain in my chest. All this time, Lucien had kept this from me. Everything in me wanted to erase this man, but I needed to hear this. "What did she see?"

"She didn't see the murder. She saw the cover-up." Lucien stood, pacing. "Two bodies, a couple, she thought. Shoved into an abandoned car. They set it on fire. The bodies, the car. She thought one person was still alive."

I sank back to the love seat. Horrified at what my mother had witnessed and sickened that neither of the people she loved had been there to help her. Then it hit me. "Who? Who did she see doing this, and what does that have to do with her being in the in-between?"

"NOP—"

"D." I filled in the last letter, remembering the last text message my mother had sent me. Somehow, those first three initials had shown up on my phone days later than she'd sent it. And I hadn't connected the dots at the time. "She witnessed a police crime." It all made sense now. She thought they'd come for her next.

"She was terrified," Lucien continued, rubbing his pant legs as he spoke. "Scared out of her mind. They'd seen her, and she was sure they'd find her and get rid of the only witness to their crime."

Some part of me felt as if I should thank Lucien, but there was something he was leaving out; I could feel it. I waited.

"It was a spell," he said, and I gasped. "It was only supposed to hide her. But I lost her." He dissolved then. "I couldn't bring her back.

I tried everything I knew. I consulted with every top priest I could find. She was gone."

"Except me!" I screamed, drawing on my power. "You didn't tell me or . . . or—wait. Does my father know about this?"

There was a plea, real pain, in Lucien's eyes. Odion laid a hand on my shoulder, and it stilled my magic.

"He doesn't." Lucien's shoulders slumped. "I thought I'd killed her."

"And you let us assume the storm took her to protect your bruised ego?"

"Ego had nothing to do with it," Lucien countered.

"Ten years!" I said on the verge of angry, hot tears. "Ten long years. You let us suffer."

"Can't you see I was trying to protect you?"

I stood then, pulled away from Odion's grasp, and stalked over to Lucien. My chest was heaving so hard it hurt. "Do I look like I need your protection?"

Lucien stood to face me. "You were a kid. Barely out of college. Think what you want, but I tried. Still try every day. Why do you think that despite how ridiculously rude you are to me, I keep inserting myself in your life? I'm doing what I can. Helping you. Being there."

"Because you feel guilty as hell."

Lucien lowered his head. "Because . . ."

Suddenly, Kiah was there, holding me—*me*—back.

Odion's shouts rose above us. "Enough fighting! I can help." His voice became tentative. "I mean, I think I can wake her."

That stopped me in my tracks. I shoved Kiah away and rushed over to Odion. "Let's do it. Now."

Lucien came and stood beside me. "Hold on a minute. You've barely had any training. We need to talk this out first."

And then a commotion on the other side of the door drew our attention. There was a banging. Kiah popped his head out.

"You better come out here," an anxious voice said.

I wanted to slam the door. To shut everyone out. But I followed them into the warehouse. Anger and confusion laced the hushed conversations. Worry dented the brows of everyone there. Even Salimah sat nervously rocking back and forth.

The focus of everyone's attention was a few rows from the front. A small figure, hunched over, grief etched across her face. Sitting in a chair, a handkerchief to her eyes, was a mambo from Algiers. I'd forgotten her name.

"It's Houngan Walters!" she said between wails. "He's dead."

ACKNOWLEDGMENTS

Three novels in three years. I get chill bumps just saying that aloud. I cannot express the gratitude I feel for you, reader, reviewer, book club member, librarian, bookseller—all who champion my work. Because of you, I got to do this again. You've made Mambo Reina, Tyka, and Sweet Belly quite happy.

A repeated but very necessary thank-you goes out to the experts who helped with the first novel in the series: Brianne Joseph, LPI, of Sly Fox Investigations in New Orleans; Manbo Hathor Erzulie Akunaten; Dr. Jeffrey Anderson, professor of history at the University of Louisiana Monroe; and Dr. Leslie Desmangles, professor emeritus at Trinity College in Hartford, Connecticut.

I'm humbled to add journalist and *60 Minutes* reporter Jon Wertheim to this list. It was his story about the Africa-to-NBA pipeline that became the seed for this novel. Thank you for that fine piece of investigative work and for taking the time to talk to me from an airport far, far away. Journalists are the true superheroes.

Deepest gratitude and thanks to my agent and tireless champion, Mary C. Moore, and the team at Kimberley Cameron & Associates. I also have to thank editor Adrienne Procaccini for being the most brilliant and understanding editor on the planet. Shout-out and major thanks to editor Camille Rankine for her insight, honesty, and relentless use of strike-through. She never lets me off the hook easily, and I'm lucky to have her in my corner.

To the team at 47North, thank you for setting the bar so high. We did it again.

ABOUT THE AUTHOR

Veronica G. Henry is the author of *Bacchanal* and, in the Mambo Reina series, *The Quarter Storm* and *The Foreign Exchange*. Her work has debuted at #1 on multiple Amazon bestseller charts and was chosen as an editors' pick for Best African American Fantasy. She is a Viable Paradise alum and a member of SFWA and the MWA. Her stories have appeared, or are forthcoming, in the *Magazine of Fantasy & Science Fiction* and *FIYAH* literary magazine. For more information, visit www.veronicahenry.net.